THE PROJECT

ALSO BY
COURTNEY SUMMERS

THE
PROJECT

COURTNEY
SUMMERS

WEDNESDAY BOOKS
NEW YORK

First published in the United States by Wednesday Books, a division of St. Martin's Publishing Group

THE PROJECT. Copyright © 2021 by Courtney Summers. All rights reserved. Printed in the United States of America. For information, address St. Martin's Publishing Group, 120 Broadway, New York, NY 10271.

www.wednesdaybooks.com

Designed by Anna Gorovoy

Endpapers designed by Kerri Resnick

Library of Congress Cataloging-in-Publication Data

Names: Summers, Courtney, author.
Title: The project : a novel / Courtney Summers.
Description: First edition. | New York : Wednesday Books, 2021. |
    Identifiers: LCCN 2020037484 | ISBN 9781250105738 (hardcover) |
    ISBN 9781250807397 (signed) | ISBN 9781250798800
    (international, sold outside the U.S., subject to rights availability) |
    ISBN 9781250105745 (ebook)
Subjects: CYAC: Cults—Fiction. | Sisters—Fiction. | Journalism—Fiction.
Classification: LCC PZ7.S95397 Pr 2021 | DDC [Fic]—dc23
LC record available at https://lccn.loc.gov/2020037484

Our books may be purchased in bulk for promotional, educational, or business use. Please contact your local bookseller or the Macmillan Corporate and Premium Sales Department at 1-800-221-7945, extension 5442, or by email at MacmillanSpecialMarkets@macmillan.com.

First U.S. Edition: 2021
First Signed Edition: 2021
First International Edition: 2021

10 9 8 7 6 5 4 3 2 1

This one's for me.

PROLOGUE

1998

She's at Mrs. Ruthie's house, eating one of Mrs. Ruthie's peanut butter cookies, staring out Mrs. Ruthie's living room window and waiting for her parents to come home.

From here, Bea can see her house with all its lights off and the front door locked. The wooden swing hanging from the tree in the front yard rocks idly in the summer breeze. The driveway is empty. All of this makes her stomach hurt, but not enough to abandon the cookie, so yummy and so soft. She wants to be where the action is—at least that's what she heard her father say when he left her with Mrs. Ruthie. Bea made it no easy feat, screaming and clutching at his legs, a wild thing, while Mrs. Ruthie watched, aghast. (She was very relieved when the tantrum deescalated into woeful sniffles and that was when the peanut butter cookies appeared.)

Her father kneeled in front of Bea and gave her a kiss.

I'd take you if I could, Buzz. One of his many nicknames for her. Bea, Bee, Busy-Bea, Buzz. She awaited a promise—*Mom and I will tuck you in tonight*—but he made none. He was going to the hospital. A little sister was waiting there, much earlier than expected. There was supposed to be one more calendar picture to go.

Bea is six years old, old enough to know what a big sister is. Her best friend, Ellen, is a big sister and she's seen plenty of them on TV. She understands it means that she came first, and if being a big sister were only that, it would be easy enough. But there's something else about it that feels harder to accept; she sees Ellen, and those girls on TV, as slightly outside the spotlight, little more than an afterthought. Bea doesn't want to be a big sister. She's been the one most loved by her parents and always wants to be the one her parents love the most.

She spends an uncomfortable night in Mrs. Ruthie's guest room. Mrs. Ruthie doesn't know how to say good night to her like her parents do, and the next morning when her father comes to pick her up, tired and strained, Bea hits him in the side like she did when she was three and he was saying something she didn't want to hear. He holds her wrists gently in his hands and says, *We don't hit people, Bea, you know that.* She starts to cry. He lets go of her wrists and just holds her, asks her what the matter is. *You left me with Mrs. Ruthie and you forgot my bear and I don't want a sister,* is what she wants to say but doesn't. He thanks Mrs. Ruthie and carries Bea back to the house. When he lets her down at the threshold, she runs to the baby's room and there's no baby there and she's very relieved. She calls for her mother, but her mother isn't there either.

They're at the hospital, Dad tells her, where the action is.

They meet Mom in the waiting room and Bea is confused because she still looks like she has a baby in her. Mom gives Busy-Bea a hug and waits for Bea to say something honey-sweet but Bea can't. *Let's go see your new sister,* her mother finally says, and Bea yells, *I don't want a sister!* and sits on the floor with her arms crossed and her lip jutted out. Her parents exchange helpless looks over her head. Dad finally picks her up, but Bea wants to be carried by Mom. Mom can't carry her because she's sore and stitched-up from the birth.

Just one more reason to hate the new baby.

They keep her sister in a special place. At least that's how her parents describe it to her. *It's because she couldn't wait to get here and see you,* they say. Sure. When Bea thinks "special," she thinks of things that are pretty pastel and glitter-adorned, but the room her parents lead her into—after she washes her hands—is cold and scary. They take her to a see-through box and inside it is a little baby, tubes sticking all in and out of her, up her nose, kept in place by tape that barely seems able to hug newborn skin.

It's so upsetting, Bea starts to cry.

It'll be hard, having a new baby, Mom tells her when they're in the family area, which cannot disguise the hospital of itself. They sit on a threadbare couch, Bea tucked against her mother's side, her head rested against her mother's swollen breasts. *It'll be hard, you having a sister.* Bea doesn't want to hear this. She wants to hear that it will be easy and nothing will change.

I hope, Mom continues, *you'll still have room to love your father and me.*

A question forms in Bea's eyes and her mother explains how different it is, the connection between siblings. It's not like what Bea has with Mom and Dad. Having a sister, Mom says, is a place only the two of them will share, made of secrets they never have to say aloud—but if they did, it would be in a language only the two of them could speak.

Having a sister is a promise no one but the two of you can make—and no one but the two of you can break.

When they go back to the cold and scary room, Bea studies the baby. She's so tiny and new. The baby seems to sense family near, her impossibly small limbs twitching a little in their direction. Mom and Dad each have a hand on either of Bea's shoulders. Her father asks if Bea would like to name the baby. Bea wonders for a long time if she wants to when suddenly, a name finds her like lightning, in a voice that isn't her own—as if it came from that place her mother just told her about, spun of secrets yet to be shared. The beginning of a language only the two of them can speak. A promise.

2011

Bea stands over the body of her little sister. Tubes run everywhere in and out of her, kept in place by flimsy hospital tape and tethered to machines whose rhythmic, persistent noises offer the only proof of life. A ventilator helps her to breathe.

Breathes for her, Bea corrects herself.

Because Lo is not breathing on her own.

The parts of Lo that are visible beneath all the hospital's trappings look like bruised fruit—but the kind you throw away, the kind you can't even cut open to find pieces to save. Bea reaches out, letting her palm hover over the top of Lo's hand. She's afraid to touch her, afraid any contact she makes will disturb Lo's tenuous connection to life.

And you are not allowed to die.

She was at the movies with Grayson Keller when it happened. *The Thing.* A doomed team at an Antarctic outpost who didn't know better than to leave well enough alone splashed across the screen while Grayson's hand was up her shirt and then, despite her best efforts, down her pants. She's not sure what part of the movie was on when the semi crashed into her parents' SUV, killing them both on impact, and she doesn't know if the credits were rolling by the time they got the Jaws of Life to pull Lo from the wreckage. She'd turned her phone off, as the theater so kindly asked everyone to do, and forgot to turn it back on again. Then Grayson took her to a party where she made sure he saw her up against a wall with another boy, one who let her guide his hands where they felt best and trespassed nowhere further.

On the walk home, close to midnight, she thought it was strange her parents hadn't texted her. Sure, she was older than having a curfew so it was nothing they *had* to do, but Bea likes to be where the action is and now, more than it ever used to, that makes Mom and Dad worry.

When she reached the house, the driveway was empty.

The front door was locked and the lights were off.

She buried her parents alone because it couldn't wait. She hopes she did it well enough. Mrs. Ruthie was a big help and now she's spending her days trying to track down their great-aunt Patty, the only living relative Bea and Lo have on their (dead) mother's side. They've never met but Patty should probably know this happened.

There's so much wrong with Lo now that what the accident did isn't going to be what kills her. It's the infection she's gotten since. The doctors have met it with every antibiotic they have and Lo is full of so much fluids, her fingers and arms and feet and face swell. Today, when Bea steps into the hospital, a nurse tells her to stay the night if she can stand it. Bea can't stand it.

Stay anyway, the nurse tells her.

Lo was a strange kid; her whole childhood foreign to Bea, lacking all the magical impulses of her own. Bea ran toward the world without looking back and Lo couldn't seem to head in any direction without the assurance of a point of return. When she was six, Lo would wake up in the night crying with her sheets soaked through and go to Bea about it, never Mom or Dad. She always looked so pitiful, Bea couldn't be mad.

I had a nightmare, Lo would say in one breath while begging Bea not to tell anyone she'd wet the bed in the next. Bea didn't have the heart to tell Lo that Mom and Dad knew— who else was doing the laundry? Still, they'd change the sheets together and clean Lo up, and Bea would tuck her back into bed, trying, unsuccessfully, to get to the root of whatever terrified her sister awake so she could make it stop. One night after Bea put her to bed, Lo looked at Bea with wide eyes and asked her if she was ever afraid of all the things she didn't know could happen to her. Bea told Lo no. She only believed in things she could see.

Lo wants to be a writer.

Bea is tormented by all the stories her sister will never get the chance to tell.

Bea goes to the hospital chapel where no one is, the journey comprised of one halting step in front of the other until it comes to an end. She collapses in front of the altar and the cross, pulled down by the weight of her grief, and she weeps.

I'll do anything, she says to the ground because she doesn't know where else to look.

I'll do anything.

She lies down right there, her eyes bloodshot, her cheeks slick with tears, the skin around her lips and nose breaking away from her, rubbed raw and sore.

God, she whispers and it's all she whispers, over and over and over again. *God, I'll do anything. Please, God . . .*

And then He appears.

PART ONE

SEPTEMBER 2017

I woke to the promise of a storm. It wasn't in the air but I felt it in my bones. Sunlight edged the corners of my covered window and if I'd told anyone to pack an umbrella, they would have told me I was crazy because when I threw the curtains wide, there wasn't a cloud in the sky. But my body never lies and by the time I get to the train station, it's raining.

"Damn."

I slowly raise my eyes from my lap, unclenching my fingers from fists. My cab driver is leaned forward, staring through the windshield at the dark gray shroud overhead. I dig my wallet out of my pocket and fumble for some bills, passing them over the seat before getting out. The first few drops of rain land cold against my skin and the downpour starts in earnest the moment I'm safely through the automatic doors. I turn to watch the people who didn't get so lucky as they scramble for cover.

"Fuck's sake," a woman mutters as she fumbles in, drenched, dragging two miserable toddlers alongside her, a boy and girl. The boy starts to cry.

I face the station and check the noticeboard against the wall. I'm ten minutes early; no delays. A relief, though not in terms of arrival. When I close my eyes, I see the mess of blankets atop the bed I forced my aching body from, awaiting me.

I turn and stumble into a human wall, a man. Or a boy. I'm not so sure. He might be a little older than me, maybe a little younger. Time has yet to stake a claim on him in any definable way. His eyes widen just slightly at the sight of my face.

"Do I know you?" he asks.

The apples of his cheeks are a fevered red against his pale white skin, and there are dark circles under his brown eyes, like he hasn't known sleep in any recent sense of the word. He has a greasy mop of curly black hair and he's very thin. I've never seen him before and I like the way he's looking at me less and less, so I sidestep him, leaving him to his mistake.

"I know you," he says at my back.

I join the crowd gathering at my platform. I hate the pre-boarding jostle, of finding myself amid an impatient collective that has lost all sense of assigned seating. Soon, I'm surrounded by twitchy passengers, their shoulders touching my shoulders, elbows touching my elbows. I press my lips together and close my eyes, rubbing my hands together. I love wasting a day off at the doctor's office for my annual diagnosis of *still kicking,* whatever that means.

"Whoever will lose his life for my sake will find it."

I still at the strangeness of the words, at the newly unwelcome familiarity of the voice they belong to. I open my eyes and glance beside me to see if anyone else heard, but if they have, they do what I don't, keeping their faces pointed down the tracks, awaiting the train. I decide to do the same, ignoring the heavy presence behind me until there's a push against my back, and those words again—but closer.

"Whoever will lose his life for my sake will—"

I face him. "Look, would you back the fuck *off*—"

"You're Lo," he says.

It stuns me into silence. His eyes broker no argument, more certain of me than I've ever been of myself. Before I can ask him how he knows my name, where he ever could have heard it, he opens his mouth once more. The rumble of the oncoming train drowns him out, but I read his lips: *Find it.* He grasps my arm and moves me aside to push through the disgruntled travelers standing between him and the edge of the platform. The edge of the platform and the . . .

"Hey," I say at his back. *"Hey!"*

No one sees him until he's made a clean jump onto the tracks and then everyone sees him and they all watch, waiting for what he'll do next.

"There's still time," someone yells.

There's still time. Maybe he just had to get this close to the other side to realize it was there all along because sometimes that's the moment life brings you to. But more often than not, it feels like it's this one: you lie down on the tracks and the train is coming.

The boy, trembling, lifts his head to be sure.

I turn away, my heart pounding, and force myself back through all the bodies until I'm free of the immediate crowd, only to be trapped by another greater swell of onlookers.

One of them screams, *"Don't do it!"* But it's already done.

OCTOBER 2017

I've been answering Paul Tindale's phone, replying to Paul Tindale's emails, scheduling Paul Tindale's appointments and getting Paul Tindale's coffee for exactly one year. Lauren brings this to my attention—as if I wasn't already acutely aware—when I arrive at the *SVO* office, eight a.m. as usual, balancing breakfast in my arms. I artfully arrange the assortment of bagels, croissants and donuts on the kitchen island and watch as she plucks a pastry from the center of my masterpiece, fucking with the whole aesthetic. She's flawless as always: black hair knotted into a messy top bun; large, black-rimmed glasses a stylish interruption across her face; her signature merlot lipstick perfectly complementing her golden-brown skin. She says, "Happy anniversary, newbie," ahead of her first delicate bite before wandering away.

Low-rolling thunder sounds over the building, a precursor to a greater storm. I grab a chocolate croissant and make my way to my desk tucked in the corner directly outside Paul's office. I pass a row of cubes to get there, empty for now, but in another hour, the dissonant sounds of keyboard clatter and office banter will float over dividing walls. It's a small space but *SVO* makes good use of it on account of having such a small staff. Two years ago, Paul founded the magazine out of pocket, envisioning a place for "radical perspectives and bold new voices." He's been paying for it ever since. He's hoping a few out-of-the-box choices on his part—establishing outside of NYC, pushing premium content—will eventually pay off and get him acquired by a publisher that can pull him back into the city while retaining total control over his vision. For now, it's respectably fledgling and it's exciting waiting for the moment we take off and fly, knowing that when it happens, I'll get to say I was part of it.

I log in to my desktop and check his Google calendar. He's got something at lunch, but it doesn't say what. After that, two conference calls with potential sponsors.

The phone on my desk rings. I pick it up.

"*SVO*. Paul Tindale's office."

After twenty seconds, there's no response—just the faint sound of someone breathing. I look to Lauren, rolling my eyes.

"Breather?" she asks.

I hang up. "I'm so sick of this shit. Who did he piss off this month?"

"Who *doesn't* he piss off?"

I close his calendar and open up the feedback inbox next, sorting hate mail from constructive criticism, and, every so often, a compliment or two. I've just deleted a message that says *Paul Tindale is a real asshole* when he makes his entrance, clapping his hands together. "Hustle harder, folks." His rallying cry. I still remember the heady thrill I got the first time I witnessed the morning ritual I'd read about—and memorized—from his *New York Times* profile.

Paul Tindale: Any Truth, Any Cost.

He winks at Lauren and raps his knuckles against my desk as he passes, says, "Straight up, Denham," which means coffee. I make my way to the kitchen and put the percolator on, trying to ignore the flush of embarrassment his lack of anniversary-acknowledgment inspires. I couldn't believe it when *the* Paul Tindale caught me at the end of his public lecture at Columbia University. I'd braved NYC for the first time on my own just to see it, and I was—for once in my life—immediately rewarded: he asked me to work for him. Paul made a name for himself in his early twenties by connecting the dots on a series of cold cases, ultimately uncovering a still-active serial rapist who just so happened to be a rising star in the NYC political scene—then made an even bigger name for himself by exposing every bigwig who knew and helped cover it up. I said yes on the spot, thinking it was as close to a movie as my life was ever going to get. Now I've been answering his phone, replying to his emails, scheduling his appointments and making his coffee for exactly one year.

Arthur Lewis is Paul's twelve o'clock. He arrives wearing the storm, his clothes soaked through. I immediately understand it as something he's subjected himself to on purpose; a way for the world to bear witness to his pain. His suit hangs heavily off his frame, reminding me of a boy playing dress-up in his dad's clothes, though this man is long past his boyhood. Rain collects in the harsh lines of his ruddy face and plasters his thinning black hair to his forehead. His red-eyed gaze travels over the room with a certainty belied by his pitiful demeanor. It's an odd juxtaposition, his being so out of place and still somehow looking like there's no place else he's supposed to be. This is the first time I've seen Arthur in over a month. A series of condolences float through my mind, all of them offensively lacking. It doesn't matter anyway, because when Arthur shuffles over to my desk, the black hole of his grief steals my voice away.

I didn't tell Paul I was at the station the day Jeremy died.

Didn't tell him even after he told me Arthur was Jeremy's dad. Arthur, who shows up at the office every now and then to grab lunch with Paul. He's always been nice to me.

After it happened, I was haunted. I lay in my bed at night and replayed the moment over and over: the rain and the train, Jeremy saying my name, the slow forming of words on his lips—*"Find it."*—and the feel of his hand on my shoulder as he gently moved me aside for his own ending. It was a relief when his connection to Arthur revealed itself because I knew, then, I must've been a story his father told him that Jeremy couldn't quite shake. Girl with a face like mine. The only remaining question was what to do with the story Jeremy gave me. Tell it to Paul? Let Paul tell it to Arthur?

There's black-painted lettering on the stark white wall of *SVO*'s office:

ALL GOOD STORIES SERVE A PURPOSE.

I realized mine served none.

So I didn't tell Paul.

Arthur blinks, dazed as the wounded, but before either of us can say a word, Paul emerges from his office. The contrast between the two of them is almost obscene. Paul's face hasn't hurt his career any, which is something I'd never say to him. Even in his forties, he has a rugged handsomeness that, when he was younger, they called beautiful. He's white with thick, dark blond hair gelled back from his face and a neatly kept beard taking up its lower half. There are hints of middle age at the corners of his eyes and mouth suggesting a life well lived outside. His body is in the kind of shape that suggests it too. He might as well be the sunrise to Arthur's gloaming and it makes it painfully uncomfortable to look at them both.

"Art," Paul says, his forehead creasing. "Hey."

Arthur loses himself in Paul's tenderness, reaching his hands out to his old friend. It becomes a scene: Paul folds Arthur into his arms, acting as a shield between him and everyone else in the office who can't seem to turn away. Arthur sobs, and the spectacle of him makes my stomach turn. Paul is easy about it, though, because Paul is easy about everything. He begins guiding Arthur into his office and then his eyes meet mine over the top of Arthur's head. He asks me to pick them up lunch.

SVO shares the building with a bar and it's possible Paul meant something liquid when he said lunch, but I head across the street to this trashy diner, Betty's Kitchen, and pay for two to-go bowls of bacon mac because it's the most comforting sounding thing on the menu and maybe Arthur needs something like that, if he can eat at all. The place is busier than it usually is; people seeking refuge from the weather for the cost of a dollar pop. I wait for my order by the door, leaning against the noticeboard on the wall with my eyes shut, flyers fluttering against my shoulder with the arrival of each new customer. Forks and knives against plates. Murmured conversations happening over them. The television in the corner plays *Days of Our Lives,* which makes me think of Patty, who missed more church than episodes even though there was no one she loved more than Jesus.

"Mommy, her face."

I open my eyes.

"Mommy, what's on her face?"

The tiny, inquisitive voice comes from my left, and I turn to it and find a young girl—maybe four or so—staring up at me from the table she's seated at with her mother. She has wild, curly hair pulled into tight pigtails that look like pom-poms on either side of her head.

"Mommy," she says again, while looking right at me. "What's on her face?"

Her mother finally looks up from her phone. "What, baby?" Then she follows her daughter's gaze to mine, her expression immediately desperate, begging me for an out. She wants me to pretend I didn't hear it or, barring that, explain it kindly to her daughter for both their sakes. I look to the little girl and her eyes widen. My undivided attention and its absence of warmth unsettles her to the point her lower lip trembles and she starts to cry.

"Thirteen," the woman at the counter calls. My order. "Lucky thirteen."

When I get back to the office, Jeff stops me at the door. Jeff is cool. It's Jeff's job to be cool. He's tall and striking, with deep black skin and medium-length dreads tied into a ponytail. His job at *SVO* is social media manager—which sounds like a nightmare to me—but he looks every part an influencer with his phone permanently attached to his hand.

"Wouldn't go over there if I were you," he tells me.

I look toward Paul's office and before I can ask, I hear it: Paul and Arthur shouting over each other through the closed door. It's a shocking sound and despite Jeff's warning, I follow it until I'm standing at my desk watching Paul's and Arthur's silhouettes through frosted glass. Arthur's moves back and forth, agitated.

"You're not fucking listening—you *haven't* been listening—"

"Art, I've done what I can—"

"Bullshit! They murdered my son!"

There's a brief hush through the entire office.

Conversations stop, fingers hover over keyboards, still.

Paul's door flies open and Arthur stands in the center of it and something about his anger makes him look whole. He storms out of the office. Paul's door swings slowly back and forth in the aftermath and if it's anyone's job to close it, it's mine, so I move to do just that. His office has a good view, probably the best on our floor. This side of *SVO* is turned away from Morel's downtown core, a series of ugly old buildings, and faces the Hudson River, which looks gorgeous in the summertime, sunlight shimmering over its reflected blue sky. Morel is a small town of about ten thousand—just beyond Peekskill, about an hour from NYC by train. Sometimes it feels like a place at the end of the world and sometimes it feels like it's not far enough from it. Today, the Hudson River is a moody, frothy black, the raging current accepting the downpour into itself. Rain or shine, Paul keeps his back to it and when I asked him why, he told me, "I'm not here for the view." His back is to it now. He's leaning against the front of his desk, looking as upset as I ever see Paul.

"Don't ask," he says, before I can ask.

All I want to do is ask.

"Got your lunch."

"Leave it." I set it on his desk and he holds up his hand. "Wait. Join me. Happy one year at *SVO*." At the look on my face, he smiles. "You think I'd forget a thing like that?"

"Didn't put it on your calendar." Lauren probably told him.

"We should do something to mark the occasion. Seems wrong not to."

"I can think of better things than a cast-off lunch." I stare at the brown paper bags, cheese congealing inside them. "And I wouldn't have picked the bacon mac and cheese."

He pretends to perk up at the bacon mac and cheese but it's clear his confrontation with Arthur has left him with wounds to lick and he's the kind of guy who likes to do that kind of thing in private. I've just turned to the door when he asks, "What things?"

"What do you think, Paul?"

I face him and he's looking at me in a way I hate. *We've had this talk,* I think in his voice just before he says it out loud: "Denham, we talked about this."

"Right. I'll just answer your phone forever."

He rubs his hand over his face. "Look, I never said that. Your ideas are undercooked. Your pitches are weak. Your writing isn't there." He grabs the take-out bag and begins to unpack it. "And newsflash: there are a lot worse things than being Paul Tindale's assistant—and remind me again how qualified you were for *that* job?"

I stare past him to the river outside, biting the inside of my cheek to keep what he's said from showing on my face. I know I'm lucky in at least this small sense of the word: Paul Tindale, charmed by the fact I was the only "kid" in a room full of adults who paid to hear him talk—and asked better questions than any of them—plucked me from obscurity and invited me to work for him despite my total lack of qualifications and higher education. But I've been here a year and I know things now. I don't want to be his desk jockey forever. I want to *write.* Last month, it got the better of me and a recklessness overtook: I set a file folder of my best work on Paul's desk and then sat back and waited for him to call me a genius.

I'm still waiting.

"You're not getting nothing out of this, just because you're not getting exactly what you want," he points out. "You could take your year here working for me and parlay it into any other job at a lesser publication."

"I'd probably get my byline."

He holds my gaze for a long, uncomfortable moment that makes me feel raw and exposed. There's something about Paul that's like he can almost read my mind, and if he's doing that right now he knows I'm imagining a future where the most notable thing on his Wikipedia page is a paragraph where it says he discovered *me*.

"Look, Denham—" He pauses. "I'm done. It's been A Day, so why don't you take the rest of it? Get an early weekend going on *SVO*. Come back Monday. Fresh start."

Is it? I want to ask, but I don't. I just nod and leave his office, using all of my restraint to shut, not slam, his door behind me. I log out of my desktop, sensing Lauren's presence before she enters my line of vision.

"Where ya headed, Lo?" she asks.

"Home."

Lauren and I aren't friends, but Paul talks to her about me as though he needs a female perspective to help shape his approach. It's vaguely insulting. There's a dearth of women at *SVO*, one of the most difficult of Paul's weaknesses to reconcile, and there's also a sick little part of me that likes being one of the chosen few. I think Lauren's the same and I think that's probably exactly why we aren't friends—that and the fifteen-year age gap. Also the fact that she started out as Paul's assistant and now she's exactly where I want to be. It's hard not to hate her a little for it, especially since she knows I do. She enjoys knowing it.

She perches on the edge of my desk.

"Advice from a former assistant?"

"Go nuts."

"You can't tell Paul anything. You have to show him because the thing about Paul is he's going to meet you exactly where you meet him."

"And?"

"And you're always sitting at this desk."

As if on cue, its phone rings. Lauren smirks. I let it go to voice mail and leave for home, stepping into the rain, passing the front of the bar, McCray's, on my way. Sometimes Paul and the rest of the staff end up there after a long workday but I rarely join them. A sorry-looking figure in one of the booths catches my eye. Arthur. Didn't get very far. I stop and watch him, letting myself get steadily more soaked. There's something so awful and sad about it, this man at a bar, profoundly alone in his grief . . .

And what kind of friend is Paul, if he's just letting Arthur sit there, alone in it?

They murdered my son.

I step inside. It's all dim lighting, the lull of old country music floating from weak speakers. It has the hum of a place that's seen some shit and with a bunch of journalists working directly above it, I've no doubt it has. I head to Arthur's booth, where he's slumped forward, head down. Once I'm in front of him, I regret whatever it is I think I'm doing. I don't really know Arthur that well, all things considered. He knows my name and takes a slightly-more-than-perfunctory interest in my life by asking how I am when he sees me, or asking after things he might have remembered from the last time we talked. Likes to give Paul shit on my behalf on their way out of the office. (*"When you gonna promote that one, huh?"*) They went to college together and he's always promising me some devastatingly embarrassing stories about my boss "for leverage" but they never come. He looks up at me at the same time I'm wondering if I shouldn't just walk back out, no one the wiser.

He squints.

"Lo?"

I clear my throat. "I just wanted to say I'm really sorry about Jeremy."

"Oh. Thank you. I . . . ." He pushes his pint aside, grabbing a crumpled napkin to wipe away the ring of condensation left behind. I don't know why he does it; maybe for something to do with his hands. He doesn't seem drunk. Just defeated. "I appreciate that. I'm sorry you had to witness . . ." He gestures feebly above us. "But thank you."

I hesitate. Arthur's sadness is confronting, brings the gravity of carrying his son's last moments to the fore. It makes me feel like I owe him something less than what I know—but more than leaving him like this.

"What was he like?" I ask.

"Jeremy?"

I nod and it seems to rouse Arthur as much as it undoes him. He straightens, but his eyes get bright. An impossibly important question, now that he's keeper of his son's memory. He looks pointedly at the seat across from him. I slip into the booth.

"He was a good kid. And a . . . a hard kid. My girlfriend and I, we were twenty-two when we had him. Didn't plan for it. But we were going to make it work. Well." He laughs. "She walked out about a month after having him and then it was just me and Jeremy. But we did it, we made it work." He pauses. "Would you like to see a picture?"

He digs into his pocket for his wallet. It's worn, held together by mere threads. Arthur notices me notice this and says, "This was . . . it's Jeremy's wallet. It's all he had on him when he died." My stomach turns as he opens it up and points to one side with a few IDs. "That's his side." It's so fucking sad.

A small card, a little bigger than a business card, catches my eye.

"What's that?" I ask, pointing.

Arthur blinks, confused, then pulls it out and shows it to me.

"A Bible Tract," he says.

There's a blue sky on it. A verse in the center. *But the Lord is faithful, He will lend you strength and guard you from the evil one.—2 Thessalonians 3:3.*

Jeremy was using it as scrap paper, it looks like. There are scribbles across the front, shaky-looking handwriting with a time scrawled on it: 3:30.

Arthur swallows, offers a guess without my asking: "I think he had an appointment . . . somewhere. And why would he have that in his pocket, reminding him, if he was gonna end it?"

I don't point out that the card lacks a date—that maybe the appointment had passed. He's turned his attention to the main event: a photo tucked into the billfold. It's a high school graduation photo, the Jeremy in it younger than the one I encountered. He has the kind of face that wouldn't be worth another look if I hadn't already seen him before, but because I have, there's something about it. Jeremy doesn't look happy, but he doesn't look sad. There's an absence of intensity. I could believe a smile on his mouth goes all the way up to his eyes. My throat tightens as I hand the photo back to Arthur.

"You never mentioned him," I say.

Arthur purses his lips.

"We've been estranged a few years. We rarely spoke."

A cold feeling settles over me.

Do I know you?

Arthur shifts, misinterpreting my sudden tension.

"Because—he was complicated. Jeremy. He suffered from major depression. He attempted to take his life a few times and sometimes I had to intervene against his will. He never quite forgave me for that, so . . . so as soon as he could get away, that's what he did. And that was just fine with me as long as he was—as long as he was here."

"I'm so sorry, Arthur."

"He got in with this real bad crowd." He closes his eyes and then, just as quickly, opens them. He takes his phone from his pocket. "Look at this." He angles the screen so I can see. "They kept him from me. They wouldn't let me see my son."

He opens the gallery and starts swiping through pictures of Jeremy. All of them have been taken in public, and in all of them Jeremy is surrounded by a small group of people of varying ages, races. *Real bad crowd* wouldn't be the first words they called to mind. Jeremy wears the smile I bet on before, the one that goes all the way up to his eyes—but this is a much more recent Jeremy than the one Arthur keeps tucked in his wallet. There's an unsettling, watchful distance to the photos themselves.

"Did you take these?"

"I hired someone."

He keeps moving through the gallery, going further and further back, the change of seasons evident by each shot's surroundings. Jeremy is the constant, unaware and seemingly happy in these small, captured moments. I can't even glimpse his future in this past.

"See?" Arthur asks. "Do you see?"

No, I think—but then a woman appears on Jeremy's right, her arm around his shoulder, her face close to his. My heart stops completely and everything around me seems to fall slowly away, the sounds of the bar buried by the buzzing in my head . . .

I know you.

I grab the phone from Arthur and as soon as it's in my hands, my heart starts up again, beating wildly. The sounds in the bar come rushing back louder than before. I stare at the picture for a long moment and then I swipe back through time, and there she is again . . . and again . . .

"He was in The Unity Project?"

"How did you know?"

I shake my head, the answer to Arthur's question residing in a place beyond my voice while my eyes stay stuck on the screen, on a face I haven't seen in . . .

"Lo?"

Years.

"Sorry," I finally manage. "It's just so . . ."

"I know," he says, but he doesn't. Arthur takes his phone back and I have to let him do it, even though everything inside me wants to look a little longer. Forever. I raise my eyes to meet his and he stares at me intently. He reminds me so much of his son, I have to look away.

"I just don't understand," he says. "Why would he jump? *Why?*"

The edges of the storm have found their way inside and the air thickens with the musty, almost metal-tinged scent of rain and pavement. That musty, metal-tinged scent of rain and station. I close my eyes and I see Jeremy, but it's different now.

"They murdered my son."

I open my eyes.

Arthur wraps his arms around his head and he starts to cry.

"Project's clean," Paul tells me.

I stand in the corner of his office with my arms crossed while he stands at his window staring at the dismal scene outside. Figures one of the rare times he'd allow himself the pleasure, there's nothing there worth looking at. He turns from the window and settles at his desk, his eyes fixed on his computer screen, hands over the keyboard. Usually, I take the hint—*conversation over, get back to work*—but I'm off the clock and I'm not leaving this building again until I know everything there is to know about Jeremy Lewis's involvement with The Unity Project.

"It's a fucking cult, Paul."

"So is the Catholic Church," he replies without looking at me. "And you're not the first person to say that about The Project. I took this as far as I could take it, Denham. I spent the last month digging in, connecting with their reps and talking to anyone and everyone tied to them—"

"You talked to Lev Warren?"

Paul frowns, but keeps his eyes on his monitor. Lev Warren hasn't spoken to the press since a 2011 interview with *Vice*. The magazine (allegedly) failed to disclose their feature would be part of a larger series on cults: *Rising social movement or emerging cult? Everything you need to know about seminary dropout Lev Warren, The Unity Project, and its divine mission to save us from ourselves. Vice*'s verdict: the potential was there.

When the story ran, The Project immediately released a statement that they'd been interviewed under false pretenses and Lev would no longer grant any media requests. Two weeks later, he was back in the news for a different reason:

Talking down a jumper from the Mills Bridge.

It was a three-hour ordeal, shaky phone footage uploaded to YouTube as it happened alongside live coverage on TV. Lev was identified about twenty-four hours in. The Unity Project's website and the *Vice* piece competed for top result on all related searches of Lev's name, exposing an untold amount of people to Warren's New Theory of Atonement and Redemption, which posits the sins of humanity have cut us off from God's grace, and the collective good works of The Project will atone for our sins *and bring salvation to the ends of the earth.*

The SEO keyword showdown was practically an invitation to the public to decide what they wanted to believe, but ultimately the viral clip of Lev's retreating figure as he eschewed all recognition and walked off the bridge into a crowd of people like he, himself, was anyone, made the more compelling case.

Since then, Lev's kept to his mystery while The Project's work does all the talking. Anyone who wants to hear him speak can go to his annual public sermon or become a member. Needless to say, if Paul landed an interview with Lev now, *SVO* could feast on it for a while.

"I'm telling you what I told Arthur: there's nothing to even remotely suggest they had any involvement with Jeremy's death."

"I don't believe it."

"I told you to go home, Denham."

I pull a chair away from the wall, placing it directly across from his desk, and sit. He sighs and finally relents, swiveling from his screen to give me his full attention.

"Fine. Let's take a look at The Unity Project." His tone suggests he's doing me a favor. He turns back to his computer, opens up a document and starts reading his notes. "Active in Morel, Bellwood and Chapman. They have twenty-four/seven drop-in shelters in each city. These shelters also run The Unity Connection, pairing people in need with Project-affiliated services, programs or professional advocates best suited to help them navigate their particular situation—various fresh start programs, youth and adult mentorships, support programs for at-risk youth, domestic violence survivors, addicts, counseling and legal aid, it goes on . . . not to mention the regular food drives, clothing drives and various fundraising efforts for non-Project charities . . . people go to that annual sermon at the Garrett Farm and they come out and they want to make the world a better place. What bad can you say about something like that?"

"They think Lev Warren has the spiritual authority to redeem mankind—"

"Through acts of service and community outreach. Wanna know what they're up to right now? At this very second? They're mobilizing aid for Puerto Rico."

"You a fan or a member, Paul?"

"Neither, but you think I'm gonna throw a murder accusation at one of the most beloved groups this side of New York without a single ounce of proof to back it up?" Paul asks. "More to the point: nobody pushed Jeremy. Lev Warren's known for talking people down, not off."

"There are a lot of ways you can push somebody."

"Then you're saying I missed something, which means you think I don't know how to do my job," he returns and my face burns. "Okay, I'll bite. Arthur, I understand. His son's dead. He wants justice and he's got one place he can point a finger. What's your stake, Denham?"

I stare at my hands and curl my fingers, stopping just shy of making a fist. I think of the boy from The Unity Project crushed under the weight of a train.

The dead boy from The Unity Project who knew Bea—

"Denham."

And me.

"I was there."

"What?"

I make myself look at him.

"I was at the train station when it happened."

He frowns. "When Jeremy—"

"I saw him die, Paul."

He processes it slowly. The longer he takes, the more I feel it.

"Christ, Denham . . ."

"Yeah," I say stupidly. "It was horrible."

Tears prickle at the corners of my eyes. I swipe at my face, but I can't seem to get ahead of them. Paul gets to his feet and crosses the room. The gentle trickle of water sounds from the cooler he keeps in the corner of his office and a second later, he nudges me. I take the paper cup he's offering without looking him in the eyes.

He sits back down. "Why didn't you tell me this?"

"Because it wouldn't have changed anything."

"So what changes it now?"

I set the water on his desk, my throat too tight to drink it.

"There was something he said before he died."

"To you?"

"Sort of . . . at anyone. I was close."

Paul hesitates. "What did he say?"

"Whoever will lose his life for my sake will find it." It's eerie, hearing the words in my voice. Even with the absence of any conviction behind them, they're intensely unsettling. Paul closes his eyes briefly, overwhelmed by them too. "It's a Bible verse. Where do you think Jeremy would've heard that?"

"Denham—"

I lean forward. "You should've told me you were digging into this because I could've told you what I knew sooner."

"First of all, I was doing a favor for a friend. One that required me to tread very, very carefully," he says sharply. "And second of all, Denham, I'm working a lot of beats I'm not telling you about. Some stories require more discretion than others. You know what you need to know when you need to know it."

"Well, you need to take another look at this."

"There's nothing here."

"But I just *told* you—"

"Let me walk you through it," Paul interrupts. "Jeremy was sick. I watched that kid grow up and if he wasn't fighting himself, he was fighting his father. Arthur stopped at nothing to keep him alive—and I get it—but it ruined their relationship. Soon as Jeremy turned eighteen, he was gone unless he needed money. I went through the whole thing in real time. After Jeremy's grandma died, he got a 25K inheritance. It was the last Art heard from him until he joined The Unity Project."

"And then what?"

"By all accounts, he was thriving. Worked in youth mentorship. Loved Lev Warren, like they all do. Arthur resented it. Jeremy wanted to reconnect with him through The Project, and his father's pride got in the way. That was the nail in the coffin between them."

"But what Jeremy said before he jumped—"

"He'd say a lot of things when he was going through an episode."

"Arthur said he had nothing in his savings when he died—"

"He gave willingly to The Project. His inheritance is probably doing more good than it would have otherwise." Paul scrubs a tired hand over his eyes and for the briefest second, I see pain on his face and suddenly realize how much Jeremy might have mattered to him too. "Look, you saw something pretty traumatic, Denham. When an event this senseless happens it's natural, it's very human, to want to assign meaning and reason—and in Arthur's case—blame, even at the expense of the truth, just so we can sit with it a little easier at the end of the day. But that's not what I'm here to do and that's not why you want to work for me." He sighs. "And I hope, eventually, Art can forgive me for it. But The Project's clean and that's that."

But what about the girl in the photographs?

What about the girl in the photographs with my last name, whispering in Jeremy's ear?

If Paul's not asking me about her, he didn't dig deep enough.

"Anything else?" he asks. I shake my head. He clears his throat and turns back to his screen in earnest this time. "Good, because I have a lot of work to get through on account of sending my assistant home for the day. Got it?"

"Yeah," I say, standing. "I got it."

———

By the time I make the walk to my apartment above Fraites' Funeral Home, every thought I've had since leaving *SVO* has taken root inside my head. More thoughts than space to contain them.

I trudge the two flights up and let myself inside. There's not a lot to the place I live. A kitchen that stretches into some kind of living area, two doors next to each other to the right, one leading to my bedroom, the other, the bathroom. It's fine; functional. Patty helped me pick it out.

They sent a card when she died last fall. It was like they could sense the question of whether or not I needed to reach out and let Bea know and then suddenly, in the mail: *Deepest Sympathies, The Unity Project*. Message received. Bea was all of them, they were all of her, and I was not a part of any of it.

I take my shoes and jacket off, leaving them at the door, fingers flicking the light switch, washing the room in a cold LED glow. I toss a frozen meal into the microwave and head into the bathroom, where I study my face in the mirrored cabinet above the sink. It's been a long day and I look it; my dark brown hair a mess from the rain and my eyes as bloodshot as my white face is bloodless. No one would notice these things if they were looking directly at me, though. What they'd notice is the thick puckered scar on the left side of my face, running from the top of my eyebrow and following the path of my cheek down, missing my mouth by a few lucky inches before finally coming to an abrupt halt. It's what I see every single day.

Some days, it's the only thing I see.

I reach out, pressing my palm flat against that side of my reflection.

"You're Lo," I say softly to it.

2011

Gloria.

Gloria. Latin. Glory.

When Lo began to babble, Bea so badly wanted her name to be the first real word to come out of Lo's mouth. *Mama* and *Dada,* she insisted, didn't count. She'd taken to hovering over Lo's crib during her nap, hoping to inspire the greeting as soon as Lo opened her eyes. Bea tried every other thing she could think of: the dull, arduous process of repeating her name over and over again—*Bea, Bea, Bea, Bea*—followed by an equally repetitive line of questioning: *Who am I? What's my name? Can you say my name, Lo?*

The first time Lo said Bea's name was the same day Bea had given up on the possibility. A beautiful afternoon outside. Dad was stretched out on the grass with Lo in his arms, dozing in the sun, and Bea was on the swing and she had a mission: she was going to pump her legs until her feet touched the sky. She'd always wanted to try for it but Mom and Dad told her she had to take it easy on the swing because the tree was so old. The tree might have been old, but Bea knew in her heart it was strong.

She started out careful, a gentle pace, determined not to call too much attention to her secret ambition, then she picked up speed, fast and faster still, which made her go high, higher and even higher than that—higher than she'd ever been.

Settle down, Buzz, Dad called, before she could kiss the clouds, and that caught Lo's attention. Her baby head swiveled in Bea's direction, eyes widening, and then—

Bea!

Beatrice. Italian; Latin. Bringer of Joy.

Bea never forgot how Lo said it. Not greeting nor exclamation—but a plea, as though Lo somehow understood Bea's intention was to take off and she was desperate not to be left behind.

They weren't raised to believe in God. As Bea grew, her lack of faith grew comfortably alongside her; it was simply a fact of herself and her world as she knew it. Belief required proof, proof of God was absent and religion struck her as a sort of magic show, the success of which was entirely dependent on an audience's willingness to pretend a trick could be so much more than it really was. But that was before she'd stood at the foot of Lo's hospital bed, wiping the tears from her eyes as the doctor left the room, his departing words echoing inside her head.

A miracle. This is nothing short of a miracle.

Her still-breathing sister on the right side of the divide.

All because of him.

Lev. Hebrew; Russian. Heart; Lion.

Bea shivers.

The air on the Garrett Farm is cold and she's as far from the hospital as she's ever been since the accident. Lo is on the cusp of awareness after so much time kept beyond the borders of herself from trauma and drugs. Bea wants to be there when Lo opens her eyes, but Lev wants her here, to see what he sees, to know what he knows. She'd refused the first time he asked. The thought of being anywhere but next to her sister was so unbearable to Bea it hurt. Lev told her he understood but he'd also said, *It's the only thing I'm asking of you.* It overwhelmed Bea with shame; how could she deny him, after all he'd done?

The next time he asked, she didn't.

Now Bea aches for Lo and is trying so hard not to show it. She's been put in Casey's charge and Casey, Bea realizes, is someone very important to Lev. There's a way she carries herself—so graceful and so assured—that Bea would one day like to emulate but for now she's awkward and small beside Casey, nervous under her watchful gaze.

They stop at a fence along the property, observing members dragging benches into the barn. In another few hours there will be, Lev called it, "a family meeting." He asked Bea to come early because he wants her to meet his family, to see herself among them. Bea marvels at the thought, her mind never far from the nights she leaves the hospital for her empty home where her own family isn't and will never be.

Do you know about Lev? Casey asks her. *Beyond what he's done for you?*

Bea knew about Lev and The Project in that abstract way you know about something that exists outside of your own needs, their mission far removed from the kind of person Bea understood herself to be. She remembers the girl on the bridge over the summer, remembers watching some of the scene unfold on TV before—it embarrasses her to admit this—changing channels. She knows more than that now, was eager to learn if Lev Warren entered everyone's life as dramatically as he did hers and how many miracles followed with him. She found the *Vice* article. She doesn't know if she should bring it up, not because she believes it—she doesn't—

but because it strikes her as rude and she wants Casey to like her. She glances at Casey, who gives her an encouraging smile because she knows what Bea is thinking.

Of course she knows.

If the Vice *article revealed anything,* Casey says, *it's that people get so comfortable in the prisons they make for themselves, they instinctively reject what will set them free. Their scrutiny of The Unity Project represents a failure of its people to look inward. Do you agree?*

Bea nods.

Then let me tell you about Lev, she says, *the way it's meant to be told.*

And Bea hears it, for the very first time, out there at the Garrett Farm.

1980, Indiana. A boy is born.

His mother doesn't love him; she shows him so with her fists.

He's hurting, angry and alone. He yearns to be seen.

He's seventeen when he wanders into the church and feels the pull of God before he has the language for such feelings. The place is warm. The place is love. As he joins the congregants in prayer, a miracle occurs: he is no longer angry. He is no longer alone. The boy is filled with a sense of purpose he's never felt before. He sees that he is God's instrument.

God calls on him to follow, and he does.

Their fingers entwined, Casey takes Bea down the path to the barn.

The boy becomes a man. The man's faith takes him to the seminary, where he will give his life over in service of the Lord, but he soon realizes there is no God in church, only men who hide their sin behind its walls. The man feels its sickness, can feel God's grace smothered by its sickness, so he turns to the world and finds still more sin-sickness there: for-profit wars, people without, pockets bared by recession, hands outstretched, no hands to them extended. The man is not on the path he thought he was. He no longer knows what the path is. He returns home, to his hateful mother, where she strips him of his ego and he kneels. He prays. He prays for thirty hours and he does not sleep, eat or drink.

They come to a stop in front of the barn doors. Inside, Lev stands in the middle of a circle, his family gathered around him.

All of them, Bea realizes, waiting for her.

In the thirtieth hour, Casey says, *God sent Lev a vision. He's chosen to share it with you.*

Casey lets go of her hand and fades gently into the background as Lev makes his way over to Bea, coming to a soft stop in front of her, his eyes only on her. He presses his palm to her face and it is warm, and it is love.

Are you ready to receive it? he asks.

Bea stands in a field alone, tears silently streaming down her face as the walls of a church build themselves around her heart. She is not sad. She is not afraid. She's *awake.* Everything is different than it was before. She stares up at the sun, the sound of bells ringing faintly in her head until she realizes it's her phone. Texts from Patty.

Lo's awake, the first one reads.

And the next: *Lo's awake and she's calling for you.*

OCTOBER 2017

There's a stretch of road between the towns of Chapman and Auster that was once covered in my parents' blood. They were spread all over the highway and breathed their last breaths there. These days, people drive through it as though it's not a sacred place—just the distance between where they started and wherever it is they hope to end up. Now I stand where Jeremy stood as travelers hurry to their platforms, unaware of what happened here a month ago. Or, if they remember, they've moved on quietly from it to go about their lives.

I wish I was built like that.

I stare down at the flyer in my hand.

THE UNITY PROJECT WELCOMES ALL TO ITS ANNUAL PUBLIC SERMON AT THE GARRETT FARM.

Bea is almost guaranteed to be there. If I want to talk to her, I need to be there too—unannounced, of course, because when Bea gets word of me, she has a habit of disappearing.

I haven't tangled with The Unity Project in a long time. The last time was supposed to be just exactly that. Since then, I haven't tried to talk to Bea. I don't even talk about her. If I'd had to place a bet on which one of us was going to break those rules first, it wouldn't have been her.

So why, after all these years, did she put my name in a dead boy's mouth?

And what was he telling me to find?

I step back inside the station to check the time.

Fifteen minutes.

No delays.

"I'm headed there too."

A woman with deep brown skin with amber undertones and warm brown eyes stands nearby. Her hair is in braids that fall halfway down her back. If I had to guess, I'd put her in her late thirties or the first blush of her forties. She smiles, looking to the flyer clutched tightly in my hand. "To the sermon, I mean."

"You a member?"

"I am." No small hint of pride in her voice.

I glance around the station, wondering how many others might be here to scope out potential marks. I should've anticipated it. Members of The Project lack enough shame to seize any opportunity. I turn back to her, and push my hair away from the left side of my face for an unobstructed view of the scar. Certain members would know me to see me, and I them. Jeremy shouldn't have been one, but now I wonder if he was the exception or the rule.

Probably better to find out before boarding.

But the scar doesn't seem to light on the woman the way it did Jeremy. She registers it, but in that subtle way decent people do. She asks if I've ever been to a sermon before. I tell her I haven't and she says, "You'll have an amazing time."

"And what if I don't?" I crumple the flyer and toss it in a nearby trash can. "I don't know. I'm not sure it's my kind of thing."

"What else have you got to do today?"

I grimace.

"I'm not going to pitch you, but we've got time before the train if you want to get a coffee and talk about it, or if you have any questions you want to ask." I hesitate. She shrugs.

"It's cool if you don't, but . . . I just have to tell you, I was in the same spot you were, like, literally. I was right exactly there deciding whether or not to take the train to the sermon. A Project member found me and helped me make my choice. I felt like I had to say something."

"I don't even know you," I tell her.

She holds out her hand. "I'm Dana."

We end up across from each other at a small table next to an even smaller café stall. I wrap my hands around a steaming Styrofoam cup and sip the scalding coffee inside. It's bitter, strong. Awful. I don't know where to start this conversation. I try to shed the questions I really want to ask for ones that will arouse less suspicion. I'm also curious; I want to hear what answers could tempt sisters away from sisters, tempt lost boys in front of oncoming trains.

"It's weird, right?" Dana asks before I can say anything. "The Project? On paper it sounds either too good to be true or just really, really—"

"Crazy."

"Yeah, crazy. There's no in-between. But I think there's hearing about it and there's being in it and those are actually two very different things. I mean, I wanted to do some good and now that's all I'm doing, so I'm happy. What interests you about it?"

"Warren's Theory. I'm looking to be Redeemed."

It comes out of my mouth with just a little too much derision. She studies me for a long moment then decides to call me on it. "Or are you looking to prove some kind of point? This sermon isn't weekend entertainment for you to laugh about with your friends on Monday. It means a lot to a lot of people and it deserves to be met with respect."

"Honestly, Dana, I'm looking for anything better than

what I've got," I say, and she relaxes a little. "But I have to admit Warren's Theory might just be the craziest-sounding part of the whole damn thing."

"I think it's the most beautiful. Let me tell you something actually crazy."

"Okay."

"I was in the army," she says, and when I don't reply: "That's it, that's the crazy thing."

"Thanks for your service." It ends up sounding like a question.

"You're welcome. Now let me tell you what that's like: I did what I was told and I didn't question it, because you don't," she says. "You're not there to question anything. You're ultimately there for your brothers and your sisters who are in combat with you. By the time I was honorably discharged, I would've died for any of them and I damn near did—damn near tried—on more than one occasion."

She exhales slowly and I see a story unfolding behind her eyes, one she chooses not to share—or can't, judging by the amount of pain ghosting across her face.

"I lost . . . so much. I came back, and I felt lied to. And the places I'd been, the things I'd seen, the things I—the things I did . . . I lost my faith. No idea how to begin again. And no one was giving me what I needed. No one.

"So I go to one of the public sermons and Lev Warren sat next to me and I said, 'I don't know how to start over. I don't know how to put good things back in the world, when I feel like I've been part of so much that's wrong with it. I don't know how to atone for the things—the things that I've done.' And he looked at me, and he said, 'The Unity Project has already atoned for you. This is our gift. All you have to do is accept it.' And"—she swallows—"and I did. And The Project has been looking after me ever since."

"'Its good works will atone for the world's sins and bring salvation to the ends of the earth,'" I say. "You really believe that?"

She leans forward. "When you become a member, you're accepting your atonement. You accept Lev as God's Redeemer and in him, you're redeemed. Your redemption allows you to participate in giving the gift of atonement. If everyone accepts that gift and works together to make this world a better place, what else could it lead to but our salvation?"

"And you've always believed in God?"

"Yes."

"But what if you didn't? What would you have done then? What about all the people who want to do the good things you're doing, but lack that faith? You ever think you could probably save the world sooner just by leaving the God parts out?"

"You think Lev should betray his faith and conceal his calling, his appointment from God, to make others more comfortable? You realize in any other context, asking someone to deny a fundamental part of their identity would be very problematic, right? We'd also lose credibility as an organization if we weren't fully transparent in all aspects of our mission."

"Then why haven't you confirmed or denied that Lev Warren sees the future and brought a girl back from the dead?"

There are whispers about Lev Warren. I've heard them all, found them in Reddit threads, comments sections, read between the lines of various write-ups. Most people tend to accept

Lev as a good man, but leaked audio of a late 2014 sermon where he seemingly predicted the outcome of the 2016 presidential election had them asking, sincerely, whether or not he could be a holy one. *I received revelation,* the sermon began, and it traced a path to our miserable present. It tends to resurface every time something new and terrible happens under the Trump administration, which is just about every day, these days.

Lev Warren warned us.

That he's resurrected the dead feels like it must have been hyperbole at some point, but every year it becomes more and more reclaimed in the whispers between believers and would-be believers alike. The Unity Project refuses to engage with any of it, allowing instead for that faint shimmer of something more to attach itself to them. It's one less ad they have to take out on Facebook.

"We don't participate in that kind of rumor or speculation," Dana says, "because it would begin a conversation that would detract from the work we're here to do. Where did you first learn about The Project, Gloria?"

"*Vice.* They think you just might be a cult."

She sips her coffee. "They do."

"And?"

"And . . ." She sets her coffee down and starts ticking it off on her fingers. "The Unity Project has never asked me for more than I was willing to give. They've never asked for more from me than was fair to ask for. They've never asked me to participate in their cause under false pretenses or used me as a political pawn. I have never once felt unsafe or threatened in The Unity Project and I've *always* felt and have been free to leave, should I ever want to." She pauses. "I couldn't say the same for the army."

Her eyes travel over my scar in a way that makes me brace myself for the *gotcha,* but it doesn't come. Instead, her gaze becomes more intent, as though she's trying to see what might be beyond it. It gets to be too much. I look away.

"I recognize your tone, you know," she says. "I've heard it many times."

"And what's my tone?"

"Skeptical. Dismissive."

"You think you're chosen by God."

"I *was* chosen by God."

"Just so long as you pay the membership fee."

"Actually, whether or not you become a member," Dana says, and the brief look of confusion that crosses my face seems to satisfy her. "See, that's what many people don't really understand about The Project, Gloria. We have all been Chosen by God. His sacrifice was our calling. Over time, we lost the ability to access it. That's the gift God gave to Lev: he sees it in us and enables us to see it in ourselves. That's what's going to happen to you today and you may reject your gift. You may embrace it. But it will always be your choice. And if you judge us for ours? That's not our failing." She appraises me. "You're young . . . still in high school?"

"Nineteen. Dropped out. Got my GED, though."

She nods knowingly. "Ah."

"What?"

"We have a few members who eschew institutional, traditional paths. They all share a similar—edge, I guess." She clarifies before I can invite her to: "An aversion to group work. A skepticism of the system. A need to buck it. It's a certain type. You're not quite a joiner, but you definitely want to make an impact, and that's the part of you that can't help but wonder what will happen if you get on that train today."

A sharp burst of static crackles over the loudspeakers.

"Attention passengers: train forty-one from Morel to Bellwood, with stops at Peekskill, Croton-Harmon and Ossining, will be arriving in five minutes."

Five minutes.

I've thought about all the ways this could turn out to be an unmitigated disaster. That's the easy part, knowing that even if this whole experience ends with me feeling so helpless with rage I end up going back to my apartment and breaking everything inside there is to break—it still wouldn't be the worst of what I've lived through. The hard part is this: the small, broken girl inside me clawing against the wall I've built to keep us separated. The one who still wants so much for certain things, despite all she knows.

There are more people on the platform now, all of them awash in the golden glow of a beautiful October morning.

No Jeremy Lewis around to enjoy it.

"There was a jumper here last month," I say.

"What's that?" Dana asks.

"A boy jumped in front of the train. He died." I turn back to her. Her eyes widen politely in the once-removed way they do when you've heard something bad has happened and you know that's how you're supposed to react. "You hadn't heard about it?"

"No." She looks me right in the eyes when she lies. "I hadn't."

———

The silhouette of a weathered barn stands tall against the backdrop of a cloudy sky.

Eight years ago, the Garrett family gave Lev Warren use of their land in exchange for free labor, and it was there, in that barn, where he gathered a small group of people and asked them to imagine their part in the work he was only calling God's will at the time. A large white tent stands at the front of the property now and I shadow countless bodies navigating the maze of vehicles parked in the mud as they make their way to it. It calls to mind a tent revival, the air thick with easily corrupted, foolish belief.

And my sister, here.

My sister has been here.

I have to push my soul past that reality, through it, just so my body can exist within it. I've wasted enough time trying to see all of this through Bea's eyes, to understand it with her heart, and I can't. I see it for what it is: the dirt-stained edges of the tent pinned to the ground, the sick scent of desperation in the air, cow shit mapping its edges, Project members moving through the crowd, sizing up the weakest to bring into their fold. Bea was weak. I'm not.

That we're both here today proves it.

"Amazing, isn't it?" Dana asks.

I swallow hard, find my voice somehow.

"How many here are already members?" I don't believe half the attendees are unique hits. They're card-carrying. They know belief is contagious and the most important thing they can do is show up en masse to clap their hands and shout *amen*.

"Fewer than you think."

There's a cold bite to the air that makes me rub my hands together. I see a gap among people and imagine Jeremy there, a smile on his face like in the pictures. I scan the crowd and wait for a sick jolt in my stomach to signal Bea, but it doesn't come.

"You won't see Lev before the sermon starts," Dana tells me.

"Right," I say, like that's who I was looking for.

I pull my collar farther up. We continue our way to the tent and I catch threads of conversations as we move. Quite a few people are here at the behest of friends and family. There are several who have left their church recently and are trying to find something that feels "right" and hope this is it. A little girl complains to her mother of the cold, and a stranger assures them the tent is heated. Before I can find out, a man stops me at its entrance, raising his hand and sending my heart crashing to my feet. He's tall and thin. He has strawberry-blond hair tucked behind his ears. It falls to the nape of his neck, curling at the ends. A tidy ginger beard frames his pale white face. He wears blue jeans, a gray Henley, a camo puffer vest and black gloves. He stares at me for a moment that feels longer than necessary. I stare back because it's all I can do.

"Foster," Dana says.

"Dana." He nods at me. "Who's your friend?"

"This is Gloria."

"Step forward, hold your arms out." He gestures me toward him, then leans half into the tent and calls, "Amalia." A moment later, a young woman with curly black hair and light brown skin appears. She's wearing the same kind of outfit he is: jeans, Henley, camo vest, gloves.

"What is this?" I ask.

"Security," Dana says. "Pat down, then you're free to go in."

"Are you serious?"

"We do it for everyone and I'm right after you."

I step forward and stretch out my arms. Amalia gives me a very small smile before her hands feather over my body, my arms, my legs, my back and my sides. It doesn't stop there; they open my bag, riffling through it, and then Foster plucks my phone from one of the inside pockets. I make a grab for it, saying, "I don't think so."

"We'll keep it safe."

"Give me my phone."

"I can't let you into the sermon with it."

I turn to Dana. "What *is* this?"

"We don't allow people to bring in any electronic devices that could record audio or video of the sermon," Foster explains, his tone clipped. "It was on the website."

"What does it matter? Doesn't Lev stand by what he says?"

"Of course he does. And if he could ensure that his words would not be manipulated or edited to discredit us, he would allow it. If we can prevent the potential spread of misinformation, that's what we choose."

"Where do you keep them?"

"In the house."

I exhale slowly through my teeth and then I tell Foster I want to turn mine off, at least. They wait while it powers down, and then he puts my Samsung in a container with all the other phones he's gathered. Next, it's Dana's turn. I watch Amalia pat her down the same way she did me and I realize it's a trick, a way to keep onlookers less certain of who is and who isn't a member. Dana doesn't have to give up her phone. When we're finally cleared, Foster steps aside.

"Welcome, Gloria," he says.

It's stuffy inside the tent, to the point of near immediate

nausea. Rows of benches make up both sides but there hardly seems enough room for everyone who's come. At the back of the tent—or I guess, the front—a transparent, plastic window lets gray light in. I expect a pulpit, but there's none. Dana keeps close to me.

"Can't remember being frisked at the last church I went to."

"You know what history shows us happening to men like Lev?"

I try not to laugh. "Someone wants to *kill* Lev Warren?"

"Look around you. Look at how many are here. The current administration and its supporters think the greatest threat to national security are the kind of principles The Project is built on and they know Lev saw them coming."

I glance back at Foster. He's working over a middle-aged man while a family of four waits behind him. An uneasy feeling washes over me.

"Are Foster and Amalia armed?"

"Let's sit there." Dana points to a bench five rows from the front. We're about ten minutes out from the sermon, the room filling in a halting fashion as each person is processed by security and I keep looking for her—but I still don't see Bea.

The energy continues to build as people seat themselves and once the tent is full, the frenzied, fevered pitch of voices becomes dangerously taut, marching toward a crescendo I'm afraid will somehow snap us all in half. And then, in what feels like the second before it would, a quiet descends. Something happening at the back of the room. My palms sweat. Lev Warren may be inextricably tied to my life, a stain on it—but I've never actually been in the same place as him before. I twist around in my seat.

It's not him.

Not yet.

A tall, lithe white woman with long, crinkly red hair stands at the tent's opening. Casey Byers, Project spokesperson. NuCola heiress. Rumor is her trust fund got The Unity Project off the ground before membership could sustain it. She wears a white dress that drapes softly over the curves of her body and a gentle smile on her face.

All I see is teeth.

I sink down low in my seat as she makes her way up the aisle.

She reaches the front of the room and surveys us all warmly.

"Welcome." Her voice is soft, demanding the absolute silence of the crowd just to hear it. "My name is Casey Byers. I've been with The Unity Project from its earliest days. It was only a handful of us back then. Bunch of kids, really. We'd gather in the barn you see up the hill to talk about Lev's vision. God's vision. I imagined you all here with me then and now . . . here you are." She pauses. "It's a certain type of person that finds themselves at this sermon. Perhaps you're hurting, angry, confused or alone. You yearn to be seen. I want you to know that I see you. I see you because I *was* you."

She holds for an appreciative—if a little bit extended—round of applause.

"My life was without meaning before The Unity Project. I had everything and wanted for nothing but I was incomplete. I was empty and I wanted to be free of my emptiness. I escaped into sin, numbed myself with vice. I hoped—" Her voice wavers a little. "I hoped that I would die before anyone realized how worthless I knew myself to be.

"But then Lev Warren Saw me."

She closes her eyes.

"And I realized how starved my soul was and how desperate it was to believe in something greater than myself—and to be believed in. I can't talk you through what you're about to experience. No words could do it justice. Lev Warren witnessed me through God's eyes and I was no longer afraid, I was no longer hurting and I no longer felt alone. I walked the path of Warren's Theory and I am redeemed. My life has purpose. I live with hope. I am complete. The Unity Project now offers that same opportunity to you. Faith without works is dead. Our faith is vibrant and alive."

She opens her eyes and her gaze shifts just slightly past us.

"Let him show you," she says.

A hushed, heavy awe settles over the room and then someone starts to wail—a keening sound above all else. What happens next is chaos; people fold themselves around him, hoping to be witnessed. I don't even glimpse Lev before he disappears into their collective faith. I can only track his progress by the rippling of bodies as he makes his way slowly toward the front. As soon as he's close enough for me to parse, a hand grips my arm, pulling me violently from my seat. I instinctively reach for Dana but her back is to me; I call her name but she doesn't hear. Lev's devotees pay no mind to the girl struggling to break free of this punishing grip and I have this thought that if I died right here, right now, no one would notice.

It's Foster. He guides me roughly down the outside row until we're through the tent's opening and back outside, where the cold air shocks my skin and burns the inside of my lungs, waking me up to just how sick with its own revelry it was in there.

"Get your fucking hands *off me*—"

He says nothing and he doesn't take his hands off me until

we're far enough away from the tent. By then I'm ready to tear his throat out with my teeth.

"*Fuck* you. Don't *ever* touch me—"

Stop. I close my eyes and take a deep breath. I've been a feral and tearstained girl in The Unity Project's presence before. I will not be her today.

"Lo."

I open my eyes, quickly passing my hand over my face. Casey.

Foster moves aside, and there she is. I'm such an emergency, she didn't even have time to grab a coat. She doesn't look cold. She looks like a painting. The wind pushes her hair away from her face and if the sun was just so and the sky was clear, the light would halo her head and make everything about this moment even more of an insult.

"I want to see Bea." It's pointless to say anything else.

"Does she want to see you?"

"Bring her out here and let's ask."

Casey doesn't say anything.

"Bring her out here."

"I can't do that."

"Then point me in her direction."

When Bea stopped talking to me and wouldn't take my calls, Casey was left to deal with my aftermath. I never made it easy on her and I'm not sorry that I didn't. I was beset with a kind of fevered persistence it's hard for me to imagine being led by now. It was a pure, raw fire. The calls, the emails, a final, painful confrontation that should have only been between me and my sister but left me begging for my family to a proxy instead . . .

"Foster." Casey turns to him. "Lo is leaving. Can you get her phone?"

He nods and heads to the house. Casey's eyes slowly travel up and down my body, and I hate the way it feels. She can be unsettlingly parental at times; nails the classic Mom 'n' Dad mix of patient disappointment I barely got a taste of before my own mother and father died.

I raise my hands, as if in surrender.

"Look, I'm not here to make trouble."

"Oh, really?" she asks. "Is that why you're telling your boss to poke around, exploit our grief, our pain, our loss?"

My heart stops.

"You keeping tabs on me, Casey?"

Or is Bea.

"I have to say, despite all I know of you, Lo, I never imagined you'd be capable of something so ugly and so cruel—sensationalizing Jeremy's death to get Paul Tindale sniffing around here, hoping to sell a few more subscriptions to his failing magazine—"

"If people are dying in The Project it might be worth a feature."

Hearing Paul's name out of her mouth sickens me.

She glances beyond me, at the sound of the screen door as it opens and rattles back into place. Foster is heading back to us now, my phone clutched in his hand. As soon as it's passed back into mine, I know this conversation will end and I haven't gotten anywhere close to what I wanted. Casey returns her attention to me.

"He didn't find any wrongdoing and you know it," she says.

"That was before he found out I saw Jeremy die." It might be the only time in my life I've caught Casey off guard. Her face slacks and pales, but only for a second before her carefully constructed mask returns and her eyes shutter. I keep pushing. "I was there the day it happened, Casey. I saw it all and now Paul's real interested in what I have to say about The Project."

"You're lying," she says.

"No, I'm not. But let me see Bea—" I make one last grasp at it all, throwing cards I don't have right on the table. "And you won't have to read about it in *SVO*."

She sizes me up, looking for cracks, but I hold steady.

"We don't negotiate with threats," she finally says. "You're not welcome here, Lo."

"But The Unity Project welcomes all."

"We welcome open minds and open hearts." A chorus of perfectly timed *amen*s float from the tent. It all sounds so hollow out here. "And all you've proven today is you're still as angry and insolent as you always were, that you only want to ruin what you haven't earned the right to be a part of." She crosses her arms, shivering as the cold finally reaches her. "If you insist on continuing this attempt to expose us, you will fail. We have nothing to hide."

Foster finally rejoins us, holding out my phone. I rip it from his hands without meeting his eyes. My eyes are only on her. She turns, making her way to the tent where her God and his worshippers—and my sister—are waiting.

"Go in peace, Lo," Casey says without looking back at me.

And then, to Foster: "Make sure that she does."

At the office, on Monday, I open Google and type "Bea Denham" into the search bar.

No results.

There used to be some—our parents' obituaries, her neglected Facebook page, a couple of mentions of her in her old high school's newsletter—but a little over a year after she joined The Project, it was all just gone. Like her. I type "Lo Denham" into the search bar next. No results. It's enough to make me wonder if either of us exist.

The phone rings and the brief silence on the other end of the line ahead of the usual heavy breathing suddenly exhausts me. I press my fingers against my forehead.

"Don't you have anything better to do?" I ask wearily.

No answer.

I hang up, turning back to my screen.

"Denham. My office."

"Why?" I ask distractedly, and it isn't until I hear Lauren snicker that I realize what I've said. I swivel around in my chair and Paul stands in his doorway, his eyebrows up. He steps back into his office without a word, leaving the door open and I rub my eyes, trying to muster the energy to be there for this, whatever it is, before heading in.

He's already back at his desk by the time I'm in front of it.

"Have a seat." He rests his chin in his hands while I sit across from him, then gets right to slapping me in the face:

"Something's been bugging me since we last talked about this. I just want to make sure I was clear and that I established a reasonable baseline for any expectations you might have working here." He pauses. "I don't know what kind of impression I might have given you when I hired you, but I'm not looking for another staff writer right now, Denham, and your lack of education and experience would be a considerable obstacle if I were. I thought I made it plain, but if I gave you another impression, I'm sorry."

I try to keep my face blank.

"Lauren started out as your assistant."

"Lauren was overqualified for the job," he replies. "It was the best I could offer her at the time. Advancing to staff was always on the table. What I offered you was this and only this—"

"I mean, you can't even throw me some proofreading or fact-checking or *something*?" I throw my hands up in the air. "I'm not even a *glorified* secretary, Paul."

"Do you want to keep working here, or what?" he asks, but the tone of his voice says he genuinely wants to know. "Because I like having you here, Denham."

We stare at each other for a long time.

"Yeah. I want to keep working here," I finally say. I get to my feet before he can push for further confrontation because that's a thing he sometimes does. "Anyway. Turns out you've got nothing at three. Bob Denbrough canceled—"

"What? What else has the chief of police got to do all day?"

"I'm trying to reschedule it now, I'll let you know."

"Perfect. Gives me time for a nap."

Fuck you, Paul.

I leave his office, closing the door softly behind me, trying hard to tamp down the rage and disappointment threatening to overtake me. I stop in front of my desk and look at it long enough that if Lauren's looking at me she knows what I'm thinking.

"I'm taking an early lunch," I say to no one.

I grab my coat and leave, shoving my hands into my pockets as soon as I step outside. Morel is dressed for Halloween tomorrow. Paper jack-o'-lanterns, ghost and witches in storefront windows, creepy-looking scarecrows mounted in the empty flower beds at each corner. I cross the street and grab a coffee at Betty's, where I sit at a table and nurse it, staring out the diner's front window, which gives me a perfect view of *SVO*.

It used to make me happy, seeing it.

I was fifteen when I first read Paul's profile in *The New York Times*. There was this part that kicked me right in the teeth, but in that perfectly timed way you need one. They asked him about what his work meant to him and what his life meant because of his work and he'd answered, *You know, I don't have a kid or a partner. My work is how I make myself permanent in other people's lives and I only write what's real and what's true because the truth endures. The closer you get to the bone, the less you can be denied.*

It was the first thing I'd come across after the accident that made me feel like my life could mean anything. I wrote, loved to write, it was the one thing that survived the wreck— and that revelation, that I could use my writing to be real here, to matter here . . . and then to have Paul Tindale himself hand-pick me out of his lecture . . .

It all seemed so fucking fated.

I chug the last of my coffee and check in on the office Slack. Paul sends out a call for drinks at McCray's after work and I watch the confirmations roll in with a knot in my throat. I could go, stick to Coke or water, but when I'm there, I kill the vibe. No one wants to talk about the worst thing they ever did for a story or who they've fucked—literally and figuratively—in this biz with a nineteen-year-old "kid" at the table.

At the end of the day when they all head down, I stay in the office, telling Paul I want to make a dent in my inbox. He tells me to be sure to lock up. When the coast is clear, I let myself into his office and sit in his chair for a long, long time with my palms flat against his desk, trying and failing to imagine any other life I could settle for.

The ringtone I've set for Paul has a demanding pitch to it, so I know it's him before my eyes are open. I fumble for my cell, faintly registering my open laptop hovering precariously on the edge of the mattress next to the half-eaten Lean Cuisine I served myself for dinner last night. It's barely morning and he apologizes for waking me before asking if I saw anyone hanging around the office when I left. I rub the sleep out of my eyes, confused.

"What? No."

"So you just locked up and left?"

"Yeah. What's going on?"

"Someone broke in and trashed the place."

I bolt upright and grab my laptop before it can topple to the floor and then I climb off the bed and head for my clothes rack, blindly pulling a pair of jeans from a hanger.

"Holy shit, Paul. I'm coming down there—"

"*No*, Denham—it's a mess and I'm too hungover for any more input. I just called to tell you and to tell you not to come in. It's going to take a hot minute to get things cleaned up. I already had the cops down, filed a report—"

"What's the damage?"

"Busted in the doors. Broken glass everywhere . . . probably some wasted fuckers down at the community college getting a head start on Halloween." I keep my phone wedged between my chin and ear while I pull on my jeans. "My office is a goddamn disaster. My computer's fucked. I've got to get a tech guy down to look at it, see if it's salvageable." I start saying *oh my God, Paul,* but he cuts me off. "I have backups, but it's a bitch of a thing—"

"What about the rest of our data?"

"Looks to be intact, but I'm going to have everything looked at just in case." I can practically hear him pinching the bridge of his nose. "The worst part is, it's *just* on that line between fucking around and fucking with me and the magazine specifically, which is going to bug the shit out of me until the day I die, which makes me think that's exactly the point. But nobody else on the street got hit like this . . ."

"You really think it was college kids?"

"I don't know. Were you feeling particularly pissed off at me yesterday?"

"Are you fucking kidding me?"

"Relax. It's a joke. But don't think I can't tell when you're pissed at me."

"Like right now? I locked up, Paul. Jesus."

"Yeah." He sighs. "I know you did. Anyway, if you got any ideas, tell me, Denham, because I got nothing but a new fuckin' mess to clean up . . ."

I hesitate. I don't have to guess what Paul would do if he knew I was going behind his back to look into The Project or that Lev Warren and Casey Byers now believe *SVO* is intrinsically tied to my desire to see them burn to the ground. Or that they believe I have information about Jeremy's death that they don't.

Or that this is probably the consequence of all of those things.

So I don't tell Paul.

"Just let me out here."

I look up from my phone; I'm exactly where it says I should be. A glance out the window confirms it. The cab driver peers at the road and asks, "You sure? It's a long way up."

I dig his fare from my pocket and pass it over the seat.

He frowns as he takes it and says, "I can get you closer."

"It's fine."

I let myself out. A few fat snowflakes drift from the sky as I shove my hands in my pockets and begin the trek down the dirt road stretched in front of me. The cab pulls back onto the highway and I listen to the rush of its wheels as it drives away until it's gone and I'm alone.

The Garrett property looks different without the tent commanding its landscape and all the cars parked haphazardly nearby, without its desperate crowd of revelers. But there's still the ghost of that energy here, as if awaiting its next holy moment.

The ground is hard beneath my feet, the air painfully bitter. I try to steel myself against it, but I can't. My mended bones make themselves known in bad weather, in the cold. They feel like a bruise wrapped around a toothache. Patty had so many years on me, but my body had so much wear on hers, so many more weaknesses. In that way, I was the elder between us. I hunch my shoulders and push forward, trying to ignore my churning gut. The house is at the farthest end of the farm and by the time I reach its edges, the beds of my fingernails are purple.

It's a nostalgic-looking two-story with white siding and stormy blue accents. The kind of place that's known many generations. It's mostly well-kept, but there are parts of it that seem weathered just enough to keep it humble or at least maintain the illusion of humility. Jesus was born in a stable, after all. The front porch has a battered screen door blocking the hefty wooden door behind it and a raggedy wicker chair sits under a picture window, its curtains drawn.

The narrow path up is dug from the earth, flat stones pressed into it. I've just put my foot on the first one when the bulky front door opens slowly, a struggle very apparent in the tiny hands grasping its edges and forcing it open. The screen door is a much easier conquest. It swings out with a whine of protest, and then a little girl comes flying from the house before disappearing around the back. She doesn't notice me. I only really register her after she's gone, repeating the scene in my mind's eye to take it in. She was very small, with brown hair tied into a sloppy ponytail, a puffy yellow jacket, and garish pink boots. There and gone. I wonder if this is some kind of jailbreak, if I should follow the motion blur of her to be sure . . .

I turn back to the house.

She left the main door open, a black hole past the screen. I make my way up, my eyes locked on the darkness until they slowly adjust to a form: the subtle curve of person holding themselves back, keeping to the shadows. Watching me. I still and watch back, my palms tingling, neck prickling, my whole body responding to the question my mind is too afraid to ask. I swallow, wondering if she would deny me now, here, like this.

My breath catches in my throat as the screen door opens.

But it's not her.

It's Foster. He steps onto the porch, taking me in as I take him in. He's wearing scuffed-up jeans and a plaid winter jacket, less the security guard he was the last time I saw him, though it doesn't make him less imposing.

He says, "You shouldn't be here."

"You shouldn't be breaking into my office."

It catches him off guard, enough to stop his journey to me, but only momentarily. I shiver, the fury that drove me here diminishing in this wide-open space and suddenly, that question I asked Dana when I came to the sermon hangs in the air.

Are Foster and Amalia armed?

"Casey says The Project has nothing to hide," I say. My voice falters as he gets closer.

"We don't."

I raise my chin.

"You sure act like people with something to hide."

He stops just in front of me and then *I* take a step forward, bridging that last inch between us, daring him with my whole body, using it to tell him I'm not afraid, even if I am.

"I want to talk to Bea."

"Turn around," he says, "and go back to your life."

"No."

"Get out of here and leave us be."

"Where *the fuck* is my sister?"

"You need to leave before something happens."

My pulse thrums at his threat and the sheer hubris of my utter refusal to accept it.

At the way he's looking at me.

At the sound of the screen door opening slowly behind us, and the soft, new voice that follows—

And says my name.

2012

Bea dreams of him.

She dreams the kind of dreams you shouldn't have about a man so close to God, or at least that's how it feels when she wakes up in the morning with her skin taut around her body and her pulse racing. He phones her at night when she's most alone, lying in her bedroom, in her empty house—phones, but never ever texts—to check on her. Her broken heart called to him in the hospital and it calls to him now but she needn't despair; God is holding a place for her.

It's all she thinks about and it terrifies her nearly out of her mind, but she cannot deny her part in God's plan and if it seems too soon to be imagining a new future this close to the ruins of her past, what else should she do? Bury herself with her parents?

They would want her to live.

She's been asking for you for the last hour, Patty says.

The hospital is decorated for Valentine's Day, crude red and pink construction paper hearts taped to the wall connected by paper chains. Bea hates it, but not as much as she hated the hospital in December with its garish, tinseled-out trees and candy-cane lights signifying their first Christmas without their parents.

She's always asking for me, Bea snaps. She doesn't know

what it is about Patty that brings it out in her. Patty doesn't have to be here, but chooses to be here, helping Bea navigate the overwhelming amount of decision-making and paperwork that accompanies devastation like this. Patty is elderly, dignified, stoic and sharp. When Bea asked her why they'd never met, Patty had replied, *Your mother and I had different lives. It was enough for me to know you were living yours.* Patty's generation is duty-bound, answers to need. Now there is a need.

You have to be here more, she says to Bea. *Where on earth do you go?*

Nothing prepared Bea for the brutality of Lo's recovery or the space it allowed her to count her own losses. They're cast in sharp relief in the hospital where the air is so thin and hard to breathe. Sometimes she walks Morel alone for hours and sometimes she goes to the cemetery to weep over her parents' grave until the aftermath finally calls her back. She's grateful for those brief moments of reprieve she finds in Casey, who seems to appear out of nowhere, offering her coffee and a shoulder to cry on. Grateful for those nights her phone rings and it's him.

Nowhere, she tells Patty.

When Bea steps inside Lo's room, Lo is pretending to sleep. The knot in her forehead gives her away. When Lo is really asleep, the drugs smooth her face but for the hot pink scar torn through the landscape of her left cheek.

Lo can't seem to let herself go anymore, often has panic attacks when night falls and closing her eyes is the expected thing to do. Her time in the ICU, on the ventilator, muddled her reality in ways Bea didn't know were possible. Lo had hallucinations. Now she has nightmares about the hallucinations. Sometimes she gropes, blindly, for whatever hand there is to hold, sweaty and feverish, and tells Bea there's a man at the end of her bed, reaching for her face—or was. She's afraid of all the things she's not sure really happened to her.

Bea feels untethered to her body when she's around Lo, who is so trapped within her own, imprisoned by its pain. Her fractured collarbone and kneecaps and left elbow. Her broken left hand. They opened Lo up immediately after the road and ripped out her spleen, then sewed the infection in, the infection that nearly killed her and left her kitten weak, among myriad other things. And then there's the person the loss and trauma turned Lo into.

Bea doesn't yet understand the girl who survived the car accident, but quickly came to the heart-shattering conclusion that the sister she knew died with their mom and dad. The first month after Lo came back to herself, Bea tried to wrap her in the comforts of the past, would whisper memories of the two of them in her ear, tell her of her birth, of the very first time Lo said her name and Lo would listen to these stories and more, expressionless, and at the end of every one tell Bea she didn't remember, she didn't know what Bea was talking about. This resulted in scary neurological tests to make sure the accident hadn't robbed even more from Lo than they could see. But it turned out Lo could remember. She just didn't want to.

Bea sits in the chair next to Lo's bed and reaches out, wrapping her hand around Lo's bony wrist. Lo has always been small, but not like this. She's lost so much muscle and fat, she looks like death. Bea would never admit it to anyone, but it repulses her.

Lo lets the charade go on briefly before wrenching her hand from Bea's and turning her face away. She must be having a migraine, because in the wake of the movement, she chokes on the air, then whimpers, then starts to cry. Lo is supposed to tell the doctors when she feels one coming on and Bea suspects Lo let this one happen just to punish her for her absence.

Bea reaches for Lo again.

I know, honey, I know . . .

No, Lo whispers, *you don't.*

Bea thought Lo would be relieved to have one person left in the way that she was so relieved to have one person left but Lo is so, so angry. She woke up and her parents were dead, had been dead. She woke up in a body so frail and weak and on fire. She looks at Bea and Bea can see the question in her eyes: *Why?* And Bea knows no answer would be good enough for Lo.

Not even if it came from God himself.

Lev is patient.

When Bea asked him if he would wait for her until Lo was better, he told her he wouldn't have expected her sooner.

Every day, she wishes it was sooner.

Bea is tired of the hospital, where Lo is angry and in pain and there is nothing she can do and she makes no difference. She's tired of Patty's reproach, the expectation that Bea's sense of duty be greater than her own need. And then there's Lev on the phone, nearly every night, reminding her of the work ahead and how incomplete it would be without her, how essential she is to the fight. They need her ferocity, her impulsiveness and her beautiful, unselfish heart. It makes Bea feel like she can breathe to hear that, and she makes him say it to her over and over again. Patty and Lo, they both look at Bea like she's selfish.

God wouldn't choose someone selfish. God is infallible, he tells her. The first time Bea put her heart into the universe, it was for the sake of saving someone else.

That isn't selfish. It's pure.

God has given me revelation, Lev says, and then he tells Bea something she has yet to hear from the doctors herself: Lo will be discharged by the end of the month. It's sooner than Bea thought. There was supposed to be one more calendar picture to go.

But it comes to pass, as all his revelations do.

Lo's recovery will continue at home. Patty will assume Lo's care at her house in Ossining. Patty tells Bea Lo needs more than Bea can give her. Lo needs someone to make sure she's eating and taking her meds, needs someone to address the various indignities of her injuries with the businesslike affect Patty is so goddamn good at. Lo needs someone to speak for her pain when she can't or refuses to do it for herself. Patty has the time. Patty has the money. Patty has the space. Patty lives near a better hospital.

Lo will go with Patty.

You're welcome to stay with us, Patty tells her, *but I don't expect you will.*

Lo is sleeping—really sleeping—when Bea lets herself into the room. Her face is blank, her lips slightly parted, her breathing deep and even. She's so small there's enough space for Bea to crawl into the bed next to her, and so Bea does, with a lump in her throat and tears rolling down her face. She is torn between the tension of what she has been called to do for Lev, for God, and the cost of that calling. Bea loves Lo, no matter who she's become, even if she seems like a stranger wearing her sister's body. And it doesn't matter if the accident stole their secret language or leveled their secret place because these things, by their very nature, have to change because nothing can ever stay exactly the same—isn't that just how life is?

But one thing will always remain true.

Bea reaches out, running her hand over Lo's head, smoothing her hair back from her pale face. She gets as close to her as she can.

I'll always be your sister, she whispers. *I promise.*

She closes her eyes. She dreams of him.

NOVEMBER 2017

"Gloria."

He's taller than I realized, his shoulders broad. He's wearing a white Henley with the sleeves rolled up, half-tucked into a pair of worn jeans. He has a prominent nose just crooked enough to suggest his tragically violent up-bringing, made widely known through Project literature— there's nothing more inspiring than overcoming a tragic past only to be chosen by God—and his guarded, deep brown eyes suggest the same. His curly black hair is pushed from his face, and a five o'clock shadow trails the sharp edge of his jaw, surrounding his bowed mouth. The weak light catches the small silver pendant around his neck, and it glints at me, briefly, as the screen door creaks slowly shut behind him.

He's just a man.

As soon as I think it, anger courses through my veins, alighting my blood. It's a wrath strong enough to make me want to disappear the space between us just to break him into pieces.

That Lev Warren could do everything he's done to me— And be only a man.

Foster faces Lev, who inclines his head toward the back of the house. A silent order. Foster nods and goes that way, leaving us alone. The little girl must be his charge.

Lev turns back to me, his eyes meeting mine. My chest

tightens painfully because my head is full of my sister and what she might have seen and felt in a moment like this. God? *Really?*

It was nothing I could accept at the time, but at least then it was abstracted by her grief and her sudden, desperate need for faith in the face of our loss. Now that the reality is in front of me, I accept it even less and I hate her even more.

I stand before the porch as Lev stands on it, looking down on me, waiting for me to do something because whatever is next is, apparently, mine to do. I understand what is being extended to me now is unlikely to ever be extended again, so I make my way slowly up the path and the steps of the porch until I'm in front of him. His eyes search my face for a long moment, trailing over my scar, and then he leads me into the house.

I follow him down a dim hallway, its deep wood paneling swallowing what little light filters in from the windows of the door at the very back of the house. There are old, framed pictures on the wall: the farm in different days, from before The Project, when it only belonged to the Garretts. The Garretts pretty clearly don't live here anymore and I wonder where they went and if they wanted to go. If they were happy to give their lives to a God or if it was a necessity born of The Project's increasing popularity. What kind of price did they put on their lives and history to leave it all behind? Money or blessings? Lev glances once over his shoulder and then turns, leading us into a small kitchen. It's brighter in here, sun shining through the window over the sink. Beyond the glass, Foster and the little girl play in the yard. The mess of a few meals surround the table and sink, plates of half-eaten food, crumbs and cutlery. All of it speaks to more people than are present. I listen, wondering if they're somewhere in the house—if she's hiding somewhere in this house—but all I hear is the sound of a clock ticking faintly from another room.

Lev crosses his arms and faces the window, tracking the silent movie happening outside. A game of tag from the looks of it, but even from here I can see the tension in Foster's body at the knowledge that something—some*one* is here who doesn't belong. After a moment, Lev turns back to me, leaning against the sink, arms still crossed. There's no tension in him. The way he looks at me carries with it a certain inevitability.

"You look well." His voice is quiet but firm. Firm, yet somehow edgeless. "Are you?"

He once again studies my scar—then the rest of me. The question feels more personal than he has a right to ask, but anything less than my answering it feels cowardly.

"Made a full recovery," I say.

"Good. Then Ossining was the best thing for you."

I press my lips together, preventing a bitter smile. Living with Patty in her place, on her terms . . . well, it wasn't the worst thing for me, but I'd be hard-pressed to call it "the best." I remember the day I left the hospital, I asked Patty to drive us past the house. The feeling in my gut when I saw the swing in the yard—everything looked so unbearably the same that it was as though my body believed the loss was a dream I'd finally woken up from. I sobbed, begged for her to let me out, but she told me it was too much for me. She would always think it was too much for me. I'd never go home again.

It's like we talked about, Patty had said of the arrangement, but I swear no one talked to me about it. There are so many gaps from that time, so many ICU nightmares that felt more real to me than what was actually going on. Some of my memories confuse me still, and now I have no one to tell me the difference between what was and was never.

Bea called me once at Patty's. I was on painkillers and all that remains of the conversation was the last thing she ever said to me. I know *that* was real because it burrowed itself into my bones, became a life raft for the months that followed.

We'll see each other again.

Two years at Patty's and I never saw her.

Even after I made it back to Morel, I never saw her.

I blink at the sudden sting in my eyes. The weight of the moment presses down on me in this small kitchen, standing across from Lev Warren, and it wants to drown me in its truth: he's only a man, and if he's only a man, what does that make me?

Less than her sister?

"You have my time. You have my attention," he tells me.

"I'd rather hers." The words fracture as they leave my lips, too pathetic to be an insult. The look they inspire him to give me makes me feel impossibly bound to a body that has only shown him its weakness. I close my eyes, turning my face away.

"I'm not your sister's keeper and The Project has never been your sister's prison. I accept that you think of me as your enemy because it's easier than believing she made a choice that you were not made a part of." He pauses. "Gloria."

I open my eyes.

"You have my time," he says again. "And you have my attention."

"Casey said if I keep trying to expose you, I'll fail."

"She's right. We have nothing to hide."

"Then why break into *SVO*?"

He frowns. "Excuse me?"

"Don't act like you don't know."

"But I don't," he says.

"Project members broke into *SVO* last night, trashed the entire office," I tell him. "That's why I'm here. Call off your fucking dogs."

"You have proof of that?"

"Who else would it be?"

"Why are you so sure it was us?"

I open my mouth and then I close it again. Lev pushes his sleeves farther up his arms, facing the sink. He turns the water on and reaches for one of the dirtied plates, and it's so strange to see him do something as ordinary as wash dishes and I realize I can't have it both ways; that he's either a man and should do this, or he's more than a man who deigns to. He's just a man. He is just. A man. He scrubs at a plate, rinses it, and then sets it gingerly in the drying rack, gazing out the window. Foster and the little girl are no longer in view.

"The Project may have enemies, but we are no one's enemy," Lev says. "And I knew, early on, to live boldly in faith, our work would have to be our first line of defense and it would have to speak for itself. Our mission is not, and has never been, to silence our detractors but to make our work louder than them. *SVO* is free to write what it wants and we won't stand in its way. We will continue to do the work." He faces me. "I would hope a journalist as respected and committed to the truth as Paul Tindale would make sure any story he wrote about us was verifiable fact. Regardless, we didn't break into your office. An action like that runs counter to everything we stand for."

"I don't believe you."

"That's your choice," he replies.

"What you did to Jeremy—"

"Be very specific if you're going to talk about Jeremy."

"You isolated him. Held him hostage, just like Bea. Kept him from his father—"

"We didn't keep Jeremy from his father."

"That's not what Arthur seems to think."

"Then that's something about himself Arthur isn't ready to confront. Over the years, we've become a sanctuary for those looking to start over. People view their redemption as a clean slate in all aspects of their lives. No one who comes to us is forced to leave anything behind they're not willing to part with. Jeremy didn't want a relationship with his father and we respected that. We didn't intervene. If he had decided to reopen lines of communication with Arthur we would have embraced it. I wasn't *his* keeper either." Lev moves toward me. "But I know that doesn't quite serve your narrative."

I close my eyes briefly, as though I can reset myself every time I do and reclaim my hold on this situation, if I ever had it.

"I was there when Jeremy died."

"So Casey said."

"That's how I know you're responsible."

A shadow crosses Lev's face.

"How would you feel," he asks quietly, "if you made a commitment to something you believed in, and you lived and embodied that belief, only to have it perverted by someone else's refusal to accept or understand it?"

He gives me a moment to answer, but I don't.

"Jeremy did amazing work," Lev continues. He reaches

absently for his pendant, rubbing his thumb over it. "He was a part of several outreach initiatives for those in need. He was one of our leading members in youth mentorship. He loved us and we loved him. To deny his autonomy and erase his life's work, to reject his faith so you can rewrite him a victim of mine and The Project's, for the sole purpose of validating your hatred of us and your anger at your sister is . . . deeply awful."

I bite the inside of my cheek so hard, I feel the skin giving in to my teeth. The ugly taste of copper is quick to follow.

"If anyone could have saved Jeremy, shouldn't it have been you?"

"No. Because I'm not God," he says. "I'm just a man." He moves closer, taking up the whole of my vision, forcing eye contact, and his closeness activates a flight response in me, makes my mouth dry, my lips and fingertips numb. There's a vise around my heart and my heart flutters frantically against it. "Tell me what it is that you want from us."

"I want the truth."

"I've given you the truth and you reject it."

"I want my sist—"

The sound of that voice. The sound of *her* voice. That small, broken girl clawing against the wall inside me, but now the wall's gone and I feel its absence and a flood of need in its wake. *I want my sister,* the girl whispers in me and the words try to slip from my mouth whole. I bite down. *I want my sister.* It's louder than Jeremy's voice still echoing in my head. His last plea blurs into her sorry refrain until they form a whole new want: *Find her.*

"Lo."

The gentleness of Lev's voice makes me flinch but there's something else—my name. The way "Gloria" sounded on his lips earlier, as though he'd never said it before and how effortlessly "Lo" falls from them now. The thought of being spoken about between him and Bea hardens something inside me enough for my anger to rise above all my want.

"Didn't Casey tell you? It's not Paul's story anymore. It's *mine*."

"Is it?" he asks.

"Yeah. Starts with a half-dead kid in a hospital. All she's got left in the world is her big sister until The Unity Project takes her away," I say. "I remember every single call with Casey, every door she slammed in my face, all the times she told me Bea wanted nothing to do with me. What would people think of that? How you treated a *child*? A broken, orphaned *kid*—" My voice splinters. "And now Jeremy. He joins The Unity Project, shuts his dad out and jumps in front of a train. I think you're poison. I think the world needs to know."

Lev doesn't respond.

"And if all that doesn't get everybody's attention, maybe this will." I gesture between us. "Lev Warren's first meeting with the press since 2011."

I turn and step into the hall just as the little girl runs up the porch steps, giggling, Foster trailing behind her. She stops in her tracks when she sees me and watches me carefully through the screen, her face obscured by mesh.

The floor creaks quietly behind me.

"There's so much you don't understand," Lev says at my back.

"If The Unity Project doesn't want this story getting out," I say without turning around, "then Bea needs to tell me a different one and she needs to tell it to my face."

PART TWO

2012

To give the gift of atonement, Bea must first be redeemed.

To be redeemed, Bea must let go of all she knows she is.

She presses the phone to her ear, trembling, while she waits for an answer. She takes in the serene winter scene outside the window before her. Her eyes follow a beautiful blue sky down to the tops of the snow-dusted pine trees that stretch across the perimeter of the property, and, beyond them—though she can't see it—the lake, shimmering, she knows, with light.

The water will be cold.

But first, this.

Patty picks up.

Bea asks for Lo.

She took her meds a little while ago. She's in no state to talk.

Bea insists. A series of sounds follow. Patty's voice again, gentler than Bea's ever heard it, encouraging Lo to open her eyes: *That's a girl, you're fine . . .* the soft sounds of Lo surfacing, the clumsy transfer of the phone from Patty to Lo's weak grip and finally, her sister's voice in her ear, thick as molasses: *Hello?*

When Bea says, *Hey, Lo,* Lo replies, *Mom?*

The silence that follows is painful, but much less painful than it would be if Lo were more aware. It's better this way, Bea tells herself. Better to have Lo blunt at the edges and open instead of angry and closed off, blaming her for things so far out of her control.

Bea. Lo corrects herself. *Is it really you?*

She ignores the pang of guilt the question inspires and asks one of her own. She wants to know how Lo is feeling. Lo's answer is slow to travel the distance from her head to her mouth to Bea's ear: *Tired.* She's so tired. Healing is exhausting work.

Bea swallows hard, an ache spreading outward from her heart. As much as she wants for what's in front of her, she also wants to stay on the line like this forever, exchanging as few uncomplicated words as she can because it's been so long since it was easy with Lo.

She feels a reassuring hand squeeze her shoulder and focuses on the warmth of it through her shirt. She thinks of the water past those trees and how it will be cold.

I gotta go to sleep, Lo mumbles and Bea begs her to wait, to hold on, she has to tell her something important. *Okay,* Lo breathes and Bea steels herself to say it, but what comes out of her mouth instead is, *I remember the day you were born.*

No matter how far time pushes her from it, Bea will always remember it like it was yesterday. She tells Lo of her anger and fear, how selfishly she resisted Lo's arrival until the point she was asked to give her new sister a name. Bea didn't want to do it but then she heard a voice inside her. Years later, she'd come to understand who it belonged to.

It was you, Lo. You gave it to me, somehow.

Lo, faint over the line: *I like my name.*

Bea laughs a little, wiping at her face.

They told me you were going to die. They told me I was going to have to bury you.

But I'm here. Lo breathes. She's fading fast. *Why aren't you here?*

Bea closes her eyes. She wants Lo to understand that night in the hospital, what was supposed to be Lo's last night on earth. How it brought Bea to her knees and how it split her heart in half and how its break called forth a miracle. She wants Lo to understand how it felt to be there, to feel death so imminent, a palpable rot, and then to have Lev stand over Lo's prone body and take it all away. To see him lay his hands on her, to feel the electricity that filled the small space. It was an electricity that traveled through all of them but none more than Lo. The lights flickered just a little, Bea remembers . . . didn't they? She thinks that must be the moment it happened. The moment he gave Lo life and death fled from her.

She never told her sister what happened that day because Lev told her not to; when Lo was ready to know it, God would reveal it to her. But Lev's energy, God's energy, must have imprinted on Lo's unconsciousness. When Lo whispered of the man at the end of her bed, the one she mistook for a nightmare, reaching for her, there was only one person it could have been. Bea wants so badly for Lo to understand that everything now stems from this miracle, but she keeps it tucked safely in her heart. Lev promised Bea that Lo would one day understand.

Bea has to trust in that.

Lo, I need you to know something, Bea says quietly into the phone. *This is where I'm supposed to be. One day, you'll walk the same path. We'll see each other again. But for now, you need to know that I love you so much.*

Lo doesn't respond. Bea listens to her breathing.

And then Patty's voice on the line: *She's asleep. Let her sleep.*

With a shuddering breath, Bea hangs up the phone and then she starts to cry.

Casey wraps her arms around Bea, her hands meeting across Bea's chest, resting lightly at the point of her heart.

The water will be cold, she says.

He stands at the edge of the lake, ice edging its shore, the sun just edging the horizon as it slowly sets. He senses her there and turns. He holds out his hand.

Go to him, Casey says softly at her back.

Bea makes the walk to Lev alone.

She takes his hand. It's warm. They face the lake together and he silently urges her in ahead of him. As soon as her skin makes first contact with the water, she gasps. Her body arches and her knees almost buckle. The cold cuts into her bones. Lev walks in beside her, the water lapping his clothes. He doesn't flinch.

Merciful Father, your daughter has heard our calling. She accepts your gift of atonement and renounces all sin. In your name, I shall redeem her, so that she can be sanctified and reborn in our image to take her place among our Chosen—and to do your good work.

He moves closer, pressing his body to her body, pressing his mouth to the side of her face before moving to the shell of her ear. He tells her to repeat after him.

She does.

I believe Lev Warren has been called by God. I believe I am his Chosen. I believe he is my refuge and his faithfulness, my shield, and that to dwell in His shadow is to live in the light of the Lord. The world will fall around his fortress, but all inside will remain untouched—for no evil shall happen upon those under the cover of Lev's wings. In return for setting his love, grace and protection upon me, whenever he calls, I will answer. I will guard him in all his ways. I will honor, uphold and exemplify my salvation in my commitment to God through the workings of His Unity Project and in obedience of His One True Redeemer, Lev Warren. I free myself of my sins, of my past, and of my life before The Unity Project so that I may allow true faith to take root. I understand the sacrifices this asks of me and will continue to ask of me. Amen.

He cups the back of her neck with one hand, the other pressing gently against her chest as he eases her into the water and holds her there.

Her lungs burn for air.

She realizes, faintly, that she doesn't feel the cold anymore.

He breathes her name.

She lets him in.

NOVEMBER 2017

The surviving letters of *SVO*'s motto—ALL GOOD STO-RIES SERVE A PURPOSE—assert themselves amid hap-hazard slashes of red paint, telling us something new.

A   G OD   A   R OSE

The office is different since the break-in, in those small and crucial ways that leave you fumbling and unsettled. The doors were replaced, their familiar creaking announcements of all comings and goings, silenced. Surfaces bare where breakables once were; every so often one of us kicks around a stray piece of glass that got missed in the cleanup. A mismatch of plates and glasses now in the kitchen cupboards that I suspect Paul volunteered from home. I keep reaching for his favorite coffee mug, then remembering.

The plants didn't make it.

Paul's office was completely trashed, his computer turned to pieces. His hard drive was ultimately recoverable but even if it hadn't been, it's all on the Cloud. And then there's the incongruities: everyone else's stuff was untouched. It was all the evidence Paul needed to rule out the Halloween-high of some asshole college kids.

This was personal.

I stand in front of his door and knock.

"Come on in," he calls.

He's wearing his glasses today, frowning at his new computer. He only wears his glasses when his eyes are too tired for his contacts and that only usually happens when somebody's fucking something up. Today, at least, I'm reasonably confident it's not me.

"What's up?"

He gestures to the chair across from his desk. I don't sit down.

"What if I had a story?" I ask.

"What?"

"If I had—I don't know, if I had this amazing, huge, exclusive story that even you couldn't deny. Just play along: what then? What would you tell me? Would you run it?"

"The odds of that are—"

"It happened to you. That's how you broke out."

"Breaking in and breaking out are two different things," he says. "It's hard enough to do one, let alone the other, and rarer still to do both at once. That was a lot of luck and timing and I wasn't seeking it out as a shortcut." I raise my eyes to the ceiling and he relents. "If you had a 'big' story, yes, of course we'd try to figure out how *SVO* could facilitate its release."

"What does that mean—does that mean you'd let me write it?"

"If that was the best of the available options, yes."

He would never think it was, though. I'd have to prove it. I glance at the river outside. Every day is some kind of gray, the weather constantly on that tipping point between unpleasant and awful. The Unity Project hasn't made contact since I went to the Garrett Farm and each day that's passed since somehow feels more and less urgent for it. But I've looked Lev Warren directly in the eyes and told him I was going to be the worst thing that ever happened to him. I *have* to make good on that and the only person who could help me wants to stand in my way.

"What?" Paul asks at my silence.

"Do you think I showed up at your lectures because I wanted to be your assistant?" I cross my arms. "And what about me made you say, 'I want *that* to be my assistant?'"

We stare at each other for a long minute.

"*That*?" Paul asks. "Denham, why do you think I hired you?"

I run my fingers across my lips and look past him, at the window, but I don't really see anything there. I've been asking myself the same question since he told me I had no hope of moving up and every time I get close to the answer that feels the most plausible, I have to shut that part of my brain off. "I don't know."

"You sure about that?"

"I mean, come on, Paul. I was like, this little kid compared to everyone else at your lectures and if it wasn't that you thought I could . . . that you thought I could—" *Write.* I can't even say it. "Then it has to be because I have this— because I look fucking tragic, that's all."

He stares openly at my scar, but I've more or less put it on the table, so I can only blame myself for how bad it feels.

"It was a car accident, you said? Took out your whole family?"

It's only come up once before, briefly, awkwardly, when I started here, after one of Lauren's intrusive lines of questioning. I was snappish about it because I didn't know That's Just the Way Lauren Is. I remember the fleeting silence that followed, not being able to meet a single pair of eyes until an hour or so later, when it felt far enough away.

No one ever brought it up again.

"Yeah."

"That's really—rough."

"Yeah."

"Look, Denham, as much as I handed you a job, I didn't hand it to you because I felt sorry for you. Lauren was pulling double duty forever, and it wasn't fair to her, and I'd been interviewing for an assistant for over a month—"

"So you were desperate," I finish.

"That's not it either. Would you let me talk?" he asks, laughing a little. "You know, that was the main reason I pegged you for the job. You wouldn't let me talk in my lecture. Every time I said something, you had your hand in the air. Because I usually coast on these things. People come, they don't engage. You kept me on my toes. I thought if she's game, she'll keep me on my toes. And I was right."

I swallow hard. I know Paul thinks he's giving me a compliment, that there's nothing inherently wrong with what he's saying, but it's hard to hear myself recast in a role I never envisioned for myself. And I feel stupid for not realizing it was all I was being offered all along. I change the subject because I can't bring myself to thank him for making me feel so worthless.

"You gonna get that wall repainted?"

"Lauren wants me to keep it. Says it looks like blackout poetry." He pauses. "I hate it. But I'll let her enjoy it until the New Year. Maybe. Probably not."

I leave him to his work and go back to mine.

The phone rings as soon as I sit down.

"*SVO*. Paul Tindale's office."

This time, the silence on the other end feels more like a puzzle piece fitting into place. I turn away from Lauren and bring my mouth closer to the receiver, lowering my voice.

"Casey?" I pause, listening to the breathing on the other end of the line. "Look, if this is someone from The Project—"

They hang up.

It's the first time they've hung up on me.

I put the phone back in the cradle and get back to work, opening the feedback inbox, sifting through the usual bullshit. One email from Facebook catches my eyes.

Arthur Lewis wants you to join the group THE TRUTH ABOUT THE UNITY PROJECT.

"Oh, shit," I say softly.

Lauren glances at me. "What's up?"

"Uh—nothing. Thought I deleted something I shouldn't have."

It seems to satisfy her. I click the link and wait for the tab to load.

The page's banner image knocks the wind out of me. It's one of the pictures from the series Arthur showed me on his phone . . . Bea is in this one. She stands close to Jeremy, gazing at something to her left. I enlarge the image and study it in the way I couldn't sitting across from Arthur in the bar without giving something of myself away.

When I was a kid, there was no one more beautiful to me than Bea. She reminded me of the princesses in Disney movies; the light always catching her just right, bringing out the sparkle in her warm brown eyes, reflecting off her shiny, wavy brown hair, which always settled around her head so perfectly, never a strand out of place. Mom always said Bea had a *lovely spirit*—her Busy-Bea, so impulsive and free—and her loveliness made it almost impossible to see past that veneer of prettiness to her flaws. But she did have them. I was eleven when I got little-sister jealous enough to start cataloging. Her mouth was a little too small for her face, her eyes set a little too close together, her right eyelid a little larger than the other, so sometimes, if you looked at her at the exact right moment, you could see two different expressions playing out on her face.

There's a world of difference between nineteen and twenty-five, is what I'm seeing. The Bea I keep in my mind is forever frozen in the body, in the state, I saw her last. The wear of the hospital on her, the wear of looking after me on her. It's gone in this photo. She's settled into her features. She's completely at ease. It makes my stomach ache to think how much farther she is from me than I've ever been from her. I scroll past it, to the group's solitary post from Arthur, a caps-ridden, grief-stricken plea for help.

I AM SEEKING ANSWERS REGARDING THE DEATH OF MY SON, JEREMY LEWIS,,,, JEREMY WAS 23 YEARS OLD AND HAD HIS WHOLE LIFE AHEAD OF HIM UNTIL HE JOINED **THE UNITY PROJECT**. JEREMY DIED CUT OFF FROM HIS FAMILY AND FRIENDS WITH NO MONEY, NO PROPERTY, AND NO HOPE AND I BELIEVE LEV WARREN'S CULT (YES IT IS A CULT!!!!) IS DIRECTLY RESPONSIBLE. IF ANYONE HAS ANY INFORMATION OR STORIES OF THEIR OWN ABOUT THE UNITY PROJECT PLEASE SHARE THEM HERE,,,,, I NEED SOMEONE TO HELP ME EXPOSE THE TRUTH AND TELL THIS STORY!! LEV WARREN IS A MURDERER!!!! HE MURDERED MY SON!!!!! **VICE, NBC, CNN** LOOK INTO THIS CAN YOU HELP ME

His profile picture is the photo of Jeremy he keeps in his wallet. He's tagged The Project, tagged the media. He's commented on his own post; a single word: *jeremy*, as though he'd started typing something and hit enter before he was finished and walked away from the screen, leaving it for the rest of us to complete. It's almost sadder than I can bear.

I scroll back up to the photo again, to save it. They're so close, Bea and Jeremy. They look like good friends. I think of the other photos I glimpsed on Arthur's phone, her whispering in his ear and wonder, for the first time, what else she might have been saying to him beyond my name. When I think of Bea, I think of a girl held hostage by both her grief and the people who took advantage of it. But where is the line between what circumstances have turned you into and who you choose to be?

A couple hours later, I refresh Arthur's page to check for new activity. It's gone.

It's freezing rain by the time I leave work. I'm walking back to my apartment, shoulders hunched to my ears, when my phone rings. I step aside while people hurry past, digging into my pocket. I check the display. CASEY BYERS. I let the phone ring just a little too long, then bring it to my ear, hovering under the awning of Roth's Baked Goods, the rich scent of bread cutting into the cold, dirty air.

"Hello?"

"Hi, Lo. It's Casey."

"Where'd you get this number?"

"You're not that hard to find. I'm calling on Lev's behalf," she says. "He's decided there are certain things that need to be discussed if we're ever going to move forward in understanding."

I stare out at the road and watch as an SUV hits the brakes

and skids just a little before stopping at the light. "I don't want to talk to Lev. I want to talk to Bea."

"You need to understand that what's about to be offered to you has never been offered to anyone before and if you refuse, then . . . I suppose we'll each proceed in the manner we think best."

"Are you threatening me?"

"No more than you've threatened us."

"I thought The Project let their work speak for itself." I lean against the building, watching as a couple moves past, a girl's arm laced through another girl's arm, two pairs of eyes only on each other. I wonder what that's like.

"We do. And you are more than welcome to take it on."

I clear my throat. "What exactly is this offer?"

"Come to Chapman House. Talk with Lev. He'll tell you everything you need to know."

"And Bea?"

"Bea has other obligations."

I shake my head, as though she could see me.

"That's not good enough—"

"Look, can I tell you something, Lo?" she interrupts. "And it's nothing I've been told to say, but it's something I think you need to hear."

I close my eyes. "Go nuts."

"You're approaching this from a place of . . . of finishing something. I think it's going to make a world of difference for you if you approach this as its start. I really, truly believe you'll get so much more out of it if you do that."

"It's just strange how you wanted nothing to do with me when I was too young and too powerless to fight back," I say, opening my eyes. "Now I've got you and suddenly The Unity

Project has room for me? Last we talked, you were calling me angry and insolent, Casey."

"That's because you are," she returns calmly. "But you were never powerless. You just weren't ready for the truth. So will you meet with him to hear it or not?"

". . . When?"

"He can make the time midweek."

"Chapman's pretty far out," I say. It's downstate, Dutchess County. I'd have to hit Poughkeepsie just to get to it. "There's got to be something halfway."

"That part's not negotiable," she says. "I'll pick you up at the train station. We'll make sure you get home safely. Now, will you meet with him or not?"

Casey waits for me at the Poughkeepsie station.

She's dressed in jeans and a black wool jacket, a messenger bag slung over her shoulder, her hair in a tight knot at the back of her head. She's far from the woman in the white dress with her red hair flowing over her shoulders, wearing her faith in Lev like an accessory. This is more the Casey I know. The one who constantly stood in my way.

"How was your train ride?" she asks.

"Uneventful."

"Better than the alternative."

She gestures for me to follow her. We navigate the crowded station to the parking lot, where a dirty white SUV awaits us. Casey takes out her key fob, pushes a button and with a light chirp, the doors unlock. She gets behind the wheel and I climb in beside her, buckling my seat belt as she turns the ignition on, then the heat. As the car slowly warms, she digs into her bag.

"Before we get there, I'll need something from you."

I eye her warily as she produces a piece of paper. She holds it out to me and when I make no move for it says, "I can read it to you, if that's what you want."

I take it from her none too gently to look over.

As a guest at The Unity Project's Chapman House on November 22, 2017, I understand that I may have access to confidential information about The Project, its history, its members, its inner-workings and daily operations . . . a space at the bottom for my signature.

"You want me to sign an NDA?"

"It's for the duration of your visit today."

"And if I don't?"

"Why do you think we haven't left the station?"

"This is a goddamn gag order."

"We're protecting our membership."

"Do you treat all your guests this way?"

"We pride ourselves on our transparency as an organization, but our members are entitled to privacy. You are a member of the press—and you're headed into their home."

"Do you treat all your guests this way?" I ask again.

She looks at me. "We don't have guests at Chapman House."

I bite my lip, furious, and turn away from her, staring at the cars pulling out of their parking spots, onto the next leg of their destination. Clever, bringing me all the way to Chapman and then shoving this in my face. Most people would rather hold themselves hostage than feel like they wasted their time. The NDA forbids me from sharing my experiences within the walls of Chapman House without prior written permission from Lev or Casey.

"Only for today," I repeat.

"Yes."

I reread it, making sure that's all it holds me to. After a long moment, I ask Casey for a pen. I hesitate before signing my name on the dotted line.

Gloria Denham.

"Thank you." Casey tucks the paper away. "I know it wasn't easy for you."

She pulls out of the lot and into traffic. I swallow hard and look at my hands.

"You don't drive, do you?" she asks me.

"Sometimes I do." Patty forced me to learn. *I don't care if you ever get behind the wheel after this, you should know how if you need to.* "Just try not to make a habit of it."

"That's fascinating. Because of the accident, I presume?"

I don't answer her.

"You were a passenger, though," she says.

I still don't answer her.

As often as I can stand it, I glance out the window. Chapman is one of the smaller cities in the valley. Has that pretentiously artisanal vibe, the kind of place made for professional Instagrammers, but if you drive long enough that part of it slowly fades away, stretching into wilderness. That's where you'll find The Unity Project's Chapman House, far removed from the world's main feed.

There are fewer and fewer cars the farther we drive. A sparsity of houses dot either side of the highway, eventually giving way to no houses, to forest, to rougher road. It begins to snow. After some time, Casey turns onto a road I can only assume leads to our destination, judging by the small smile that lights her face. And then:

"Chapman House."

It's not a house. It's a lodge. Two stories and wide enough to stretch beyond the view of the windshield. It's beautiful and its beauty is something I hate about it because it's impossible to ignore. The trim and roof are a deep, forest green. Its angles, modern and pleasing.

The large, timber frame entrance is illuminated by the inviting glow of a light overhead. Narrow windows on either side of the door hint at what's beyond, though from here, it's too far to see. Casey parks alongside a handful of snow-covered cars.

"How many live here?" I ask.

"Here in Chapman, or here in Chapman House?"

"Both, I guess."

"We're at a little over three hundred members in Chapman. They're spread out across Project residencies in and just outside of the city. We have fifty members living here—staff. We develop and oversee Project initiatives, tend to members' needs individually and as a whole. Depending on what's happening within The Unity Project, we can have upwards of a hundred members in and out at one time. The house also serves a similar function as the farm; we host gatherings, meetings and sermons here, particularly when the weather's nice. Past the house there's a lake. It's quite beautiful."

"Who paid for this?"

"My father donated this property. He used to hold company retreats here," Casey answers. "He's a huge proponent of our work. It cost The Unity Project nothing."

"He's a member?"

Jerry Byers is the CEO of NuCola—the best-tasting zero-calorie soda on the market—and he's swimming in cash. Whenever Casey's in the news for Project work, they don't leave the fact of her parentage too far behind. But I've never heard Jerry Byers identified as a member, or even a fan, and I'd remember something like that.

"No. Not officially." Casey pulls the keys out of the ignition. "Come on."

She exits the car.

I stare at the house, knowing Bea won't be there, and letting myself imagine her there anyway, imagine her keeping herself from me somewhere inside.

My cell phone rings. I take it out of my bag.

I don't recognize the number.

"Hello?" The slow, familiar sound of breathing reaches my ear at the same time Casey turns to me expectantly. My blood goes cold. "Who is this? How did you get this number?"

Nothing. Casey's expression turns impatient and I disconnect, try to shake it off. I get out of the car and make my way to the front door. She pushes it open and gestures me in ahead of her. After I step over the threshold, she takes the lead again and we enter a wide-open living space.

"This is the Great Room," she says, her voice echoing slightly.

It's huge. The opposite side of it is a wall of windows, a door tucked neatly at the heart of them, and the view beyond is breathtaking, like a Bob Ross painting. Snow swirls through and around the magnificent pine trees and the lawn extends toward them, an expanse of pure white. All the furniture in the room points toward the scene and all the furniture looks expensive. No doubt it came with the place. The ceiling is tall, beautiful wooden beams and hanging lights. I turn around and stare at the second-floor balcony above us, facing the windows. On either side of the room are heavy wooden doors shut tight, leading to parts unknown.

"Where is everyone?" I ask.

"It's the middle of a workday, Lo."

I know, I want to snap. *I took one of my sick days to be here.*

It's hot, reminding me of the suffocating tent on the Garrett Farm. I pull at my collar, feeling Casey's eyes on me as I absorb my surroundings. I move slowly around the room, tracing my fingers along the edge of a sofa, a mahogany chair. I come to stop at the windows. The snow falls harder now.

"You can't see it at the moment," Casey says, joining me, "but there's a path between those trees leading to the lake. In the summer, the sky out there looks like it goes on forever. I love it out here. It's so peaceful. Quiet enough to gather your thoughts and be truly alone with yourself. To be truly alone with God. Like a place at the end of the world."

"Looks it," I say. "Where's Lev?"

She stares out at the trees before moving to a small table in the corner, where a pitcher of infused water sits next to some glasses. She pours one for me. For a moment, it seems she's awaiting my thanks but I never give it to her and it's times like these I wonder what my mother would have made of me. If she would have been disappointed in how bitter and obstinate I've become. I'm less afraid than I used to be but I'm not sure it was worth the cost. I take a drink of the water. It tastes citrusy, clean.

"Make yourself comfortable," Casey says, "and I'll tell him you're here."

She leaves, disappearing behind the door at the far left side of the room. She closes it gently, then there's a telltale *click*. I wait a minute and then I trace her path out until I reach the door. I test it and find it locked. The same holds true for the door at the right side of the room. I face the windows and I have that same thought I had at the sermon—that if I died out here no one would know.

I wait a long time. I expect to. Lev Warren has made a compromise for me and the cost of it will be whatever The Unity Project believes they can make me pay. I sit in one of the chairs and what remains of the light surrenders itself to the later afternoon. Every so often, I hear the sound of movement upstairs but its source never reveals itself to me. I take my phone out. NO SIGNAL. Really? I get to my feet and move slowly around the room, my arm held up, watching the bars.

I've just about done a full circle when a couple finally appear. Good to know if this whole thing goes horror movie, all I've got to do is make sure I'm standing exactly in this spot to call 911.

The sound of the door opening on the right side of the room startles me, my heart thrumming a *this-is-it* kind of time because however ready I pretend to be, I'm not.

I swallow and turn.

A dog stands in the middle of the open door.

It's a gorgeous white husky. It stares at me, its mouth hung open, panting slightly, one eye a vivid sky blue, the other a rich amber. Beyond it, a hallway with a staircase leading to the second floor. The dog moves forward, sniffing the air, toenails clacking along the hardwood. I still, nervous. I like dogs on a case-by-case basis, mostly depending on whether or not they like me. This one doesn't seem to pose any immediate threat so far.

I glance at the door behind it, still open, tempting me to walk through, to find out what secrets lay hidden beyond. There have to be secrets; they wouldn't have locked me out, otherwise. I make my way over and when my intention becomes clear, the dog positions itself in front of me, blocking my path. Or is it? I take a tentative step forward, and it lets out a disconcerting whine, teeth flaring a little: a warning . . .

"Easy," I whisper.

It growls.

"Atara," a voice says sharply behind me.

The dog—Atara—backs down, languidly moving past me to its master.

I turn.

Lev stands at the opposite side of the room.

Atara stops at his feet and he rests his hand atop her head

before she pads away from both of us, slipping out the door he came through. We regard each other for a long moment. His hair is pushed from his face, the stubble along his jaw more pronounced than when I saw it last. He wears a brown sweater and worn blue jeans.

"Where's Bea?" I ask.

He lets the silence build, because he can, and when he finally speaks, he offers no answer. He only points to a pair of chairs near the window and tells me to take a seat.

I stay where I am.

"Have it your way," he says.

He crosses the room toward me and then past me, his arm brushing against mine. I exhale quietly as soon as he's clear. He stops at the table with the water and pours himself a glass. I watch as he raises it to his mouth, taking his time, and when he's finished, he brushes his thumb slowly across his lips.

"I'm so used to hearing about you, Lo," he finally says, "about your misdirected rage at The Project. Your assumptions about us. Casey kept us apprised of your exploits over the years."

"Us," I echo.

"It was one thing to hear about you and another entirely to witness." He holds the top of the glass between his fingers, studying its distorted reflection of the room before setting it gently back down. He turns his head to me. "I told you the work is our first line of defense against our detractors. I stand by that. But you represent a type of false impression about us I've come to realize would be better addressed before it takes root."

"And what's that?"

"That we're a cult."

"The shoe fits."

"You think we do what cults do?"

"Yes."

"That we indoctrinate? Brainwash? Isolate?"

With every question, he closes the distance between us until he's inches from me. I keep myself rigid, forcing myself to meet his stillness with my own.

"You can deny it all you want," I say. "I know what you did to Jeremy."

He stares down at me through his eyelashes. "His death is one of the most devastating things I've experienced. And the idea of his memory used as a platform for the worst of what you think of us—and what you want others to think of us—is unacceptable to me."

"You saw Arthur's Facebook group."

"I was made aware. It hurt me, deeply."

"It hurts Arthur too," I reply. My body aches, tense, every part of me trying to anticipate his next move. This stillness between us won't hold and I have no idea what it will turn into, but I feel its energy growing. "Did you have it taken down?"

"I didn't," he says, and then, at the skeptical look on my face, "I suspect some members might have reported it of their own volition—"

"And which tenet of The Unity Project is that?"

"We're human, Lo, and I've never been called a murderer before."

"Are members calling me?"

"What?" he asks.

"My office, my phone . . . hang-up calls . . . intimidation tactics."

"Of course not." I'm not sure I believe him.

"Where's Bea?" I ask again.

His hand reaches for the pendant at his neck, directing my attention to that small piece of silver. It glints from light I can't source. There's an etching on it I can't quite make out as he carefully rubs it between his forefinger and thumb. There's no absence of intention in anything he does, not even this small movement.

And then the wind picks up, rattling the windows, pulling our attention from each other for the view outside. I watch the trees sway back and forth, the gray cast of the sky suggesting the possibility of a storm. Lev frowns and the wind stops as suddenly as it started, like a breath, caught, and some small part of me could think he did that.

But the rest of me knows better.

"Arthur convinced Paul there was something here worth looking into, had him poking around. I thought it had been taken care of, and now you . . ." He turns his face to me, his eyes locking on mine. "I've no doubt what you could inspire in others, if given the chance."

I swallow. "What do you mean?"

"Refusing to engage with the press was the right choice for a very long time, but now it's time for us to make a different choice."

"And what does this have to do with me?"

"I want you to write a profile for *SVO*. On me. On The Unity Project."

I step back. ". . . What?"

"I'll give you unprecedented access."

I open and close my mouth several times, still not grasping what he's said. A Cease & Desist would have made more sense than this.

I want you to write a profile . . . I'll give you unprecedented access.

"You're not serious," I finally say.

"I am."

"And by unprecedented access you mean . . ."

"I'll sit for interviews. You may talk to and interview any willing members, tour our properties, learn about our daily operations, our future plans . . ."

I bring my hand to my mouth. What Lev is offering is—like he said—unprecedented . . . it would take up the whole front page of *SVO*—and Paul would *have* to give that to me. Wouldn't he?

I'd write it first, just to ensure it . . .

A byline flashes in my mind's eye and for the first time, it doesn't feel like a wish, it feels like it's the future.

By Lo Denham.

"Me," I say.

"I don't think it could be anyone else, do you?" Lev asks. I can only stare in response, still reeling. "You've dug into a misconception of us for the last six years and I know you'll do everything in your power to prove it."

"You don't think I'll prove it," I say.

"I'm confident you won't," he returns. "But I know your attempt will produce a profile that can't be denied."

I stop breathing. It's practically those words of Paul's I'd live and die by, if he ever gave me the chance: *The closer you get to the bone, the less you can be denied* . . . but Paul was never going to give me that chance.

I shake my head slowly. It still seems impossible . . .

"I don't . . ."

"You wanted the truth, Lo."

"Yeah, but—"

"Or are you afraid of it now?"

I look out the window. This place is beginning to have

that inside-a-snow-globe quality, making everything seem more unreal than it already is.

"What about my sister? Does my unprecedented access extend to her?"

For a long time, Lev is silent.

"You need to know we've always acted on Bea's behalf as far as it related to you," Lev says. "She made clear how she wanted us to proceed and we honored that. Every way we dealt with you, Lo, was what she told us to do."

I look at him, hope in my heart, my heart suddenly in my throat.

"Does that mean she's changed her mind?" I whisper.

"It means," he says, "that your sister is no longer a member."

2012

I'm eager to prove myself, Bea whispers.

She watches the timer on the Tascam, feeling strangely vulnerable. She pushed record sixty seconds ago and waited for whatever words would find her.

Now they're out, and she can't take them back.

This is her first Attestation. Each week, members are expected to go into the Reflection Room alone and lay their souls bare to a microphone: to share their triumphs and setbacks, fears and hopes, how they feel about Lev and The Project and The Project's path forward, how they feel about each other. Lev then listens to the recordings and addresses what he's heard at family meetings. Bea loves those meetings more than anything, more than sermons, even. They leave her in awe. The way Lev calls out their names and stands before them, making sure they feel seen, letting them know they're heard. He asks questions, offers solutions, shifts roles so effortlessly depending on the demands placed on him—and those demands seem endless. At the meetings, Bea watches him become father to some, friend to others, therapist, shoulder, arbiter, savior . . . and that was another miracle, wasn't it? To see someone be so much to so many, yet never the same person twice? He met them with an incredible specificity that not only assured her of his specialness to the world—but of her own specialness to him.

Bea managed to avoid Attestation until Lev pulled her

aside at the end of the last meeting, sunrise creeping up the horizon, and told her he'd missed her voice. It made her shiver to think he should miss hearing it, that he should *want* to hear it at all. She didn't want to burden Lev—she had nothing important to say—but Casey told her that would be impossible.

He never wants to feel distance from us. Movements like ours depend on this level of connection. Attestation is, at its core, prayer. You may understand prayer as an asking or a giving of thanks— and it is. But we also want you to think of prayer as an expression of your heart and soul. Lev wants to hear you pray, Bea. Pray to him.

She led Bea to the Reflection Room. It was spare, with a solitary window pointed in the direction of the baptismal lake. There was a list of prompts taped to the small table next to the Tascam, if Bea needed a guide. She didn't. She pressed the record button twice and waited until her devotion found her.

There are six hundred active members in The Unity Project. Their primary objective is growth, expansion. Lev is establishing a concentrated presence in Morel, Bellwood and Chapman, cities and towns along the Hudson Valley that are just small enough to quantify the difference The Project can make and big enough that such differences won't go unnoticed. There is a point when their message will propagate itself, but for now *we're building an army.* If they don't have the numbers, they will never be a movement and if they do not become a movement, they will never be able to show people the path.

Lev sends Bea, with Casey and a handful of other

members—Jenny, Aaron and Dan—to the May Day Protests in New York City. They spend the night at the Garrett Farm in Bellwood, then take the Hudson Line from Tarrytown to Grand Central. They're armed with literature about The Project. Casey reminds them to be careful, thoughtful in their approach. Look for people who are open. Be real. No one wants to feel like they're being sold something—not even salvation. She tells them to remember they're guests to this demonstration and to emphasize the overlap in The Unity Project's values.

We're offering what's left of the Occupy Movement a way to continue their mission. We join their rallying cry against inequity, against the 1 percent, against keeping institutional power unchecked, against those who would burn the world to preserve their wealth.

Bea suspects her presence is a direct result of her Attestation. Lev saw them off and she doesn't think she imagined that he held her a little longer than everyone else, doesn't think she imagined the way he squeezed her shoulder and how deeply he looked into her eyes before she got into the car. If she comes back to him empty-handed, she will have failed.

On the train to the city, Bea's mind flows through the script Casey gave them. *What The Unity Project offers people, in its simplest terms, is food if you're hungry, water if you're thirsty, clothes and shelter if you need it, and family if you lack it. All it asks in return is being part of, and upholding the tenets of, a revolution that pays it forward.*

It's raining when they get to Grand Central. Casey acts as guide; she knows the city well. Some of her childhood was spent here, in her father's brownstone, and her familiarity shows in the indifferent way she navigates them through the everyday commotion of the city. Bea can't imagine feeling indifferent to it. She hasn't been to New York City enough to not be overwhelmed by all this *life*. She loves to be where the action is, and here there's so much, so many different bodies moving in so many different directions, so many people breathing and so many hearts beating at the exact same moment in time. It's magical.

With a sudden twinge, she thinks of Lo. Lo's been to NYC twice. Once, when she was too young to remember and again when she was twelve, the year before Mom and Dad died. They'd gone to Rockefeller Center to see the Christmas tree and the sisters' individual responses ended up disappointing their parents. Bea, at eighteen, felt small and touristy and hated it because that was the year she wanted to be cool. Lo had found the tree's awesome display much less interesting than all the people who had come to see it. She stared openly at everyone.

Look at all the stories, she'd said. That was how she saw them. Stories. Bea wonders if Lo still thinks of people that way. If she still wants to write.

Are you all right? Casey asks her, and it shouldn't surprise Bea, but it always does, how attuned Casey is to her moods. Bea nods and tells her she's nervous because this is true. Casey grips her hand and doesn't let it go and Bea feels stronger for it. She senses the others nearby and feels stronger for their presence too.

Together, they make their way to Bryant Park, which is beautiful and green and wet. Bea doesn't mind the rain because the energy feels so good. She's in the heart of a gorgeous cacophony of music and chants.

Mind the cameras, Casey tells them, nodding to various camera crews. Bea eyes them warily, imagining tonight's news reducing these protests to millennial burnouts looking for a day off work rather than presenting it as it really is. The media loves to distort the truth, but like Lev says, *The world is falling around them—and they will fall with it.*

Bea takes in the protest signs, loves them all.

OCCUPY WITH ART!

TAX THE MILLIONAIRES!

WE ARE THE 99%!

She bumps into a woman dressed as a zombie.

What do you represent? the zombie asks, though Bea thinks the question should be the other way around. Bea clumsily shoves a pamphlet in the zombie's hands. The zombie sneers and tosses it to the ground and Bea feels like an idiot as she watches it get trampled by protesters. She feels even worse when her next few encounters prove to be as fruitless. She can't seem to find the words to make people listen to her for long. She should be able to connect with their skepticism, to break through it, because she too was once a skeptic—but she can't remember what that felt like. If they could see inside her heart, they'd run to her, ask her to speak it.

She watches Casey and the others work the crowd effortlessly, handing over as many pamphlets as they've brought. They seem to know exactly who to approach and how. They preach Lev's gospel without making it seem like preaching. Bea spends more time watching Casey than doing anything herself.

Have you heard of Lev Warren?

We're a group based out in the Hudson Valley . . .

I like your sign. I know someone who'd agree with it . . .

What The Unity Project offers is a lot like this . . .

How is Bea so bad at this?

Doesn't she believe enough?

She can feel Casey's eyes on her, assessing her, so Bea folds herself into the crowd, moving toward two girls who look as uncertain as she feels. They're holding hands.

Here, Bea says stupidly, thrusting a pamphlet at one of them.

They don't take it. They wordlessly move away from her.

Hey, what's that? Can I have one?

A man materializes from nowhere and Bea can tell by the way his eyes greedily roam her body there's only one thing he's really interested in. She wordlessly hands a pamphlet to him. He studies it for a moment and then makes a face.

Lev Warren? That cult asshole who thinks he's God?

Bea takes a step back, as pissed as she is embarrassed and then ashamed for being embarrassed. Embarrassment is supposed to be beyond those who know God's truth.

He's not an asshole, Bea snaps. *He's real.*

Sure.

The man rolls his eyes. Casey moves toward them and Bea feels her face get hot in the wake of still more failure. She ends up blurting out, *He brought a girl back from the dead!*

The man stares at Bea and then bursts into raucous laughter, reaching out and grabbing someone as they pass.

Hey, you'll never believe what this chick just told me . . .

It's true! The hot fury invading Bea's body is greater than all common sense. *Lev Warren brought a girl back from the dead!*

Bea, Casey says sharply, grabbing her by the elbow. They move away from the immediate crowd and Bea's anger disappears, a series of apologies falling from her lips, which feels worse than anything has felt so far—like she's denying Lev.

Do not give them a reason to discredit us, Casey says.

But it's true, Bea replies weakly.

People aren't ready for the truth.

During the march to Union Square, Jenny gets trapped in a wave of protesters and the push and pull of the crowd sends her to the ground. She lands hard on her wrist. She says it's fine, but by late afternoon, is surprised to discover it swollen and purple—broken. Bea volunteers to take her to the hospital, hoping to seize at least one opportunity to be useful before the day is over. Casey is happy to let her have it. In the taxi, tears stream silently down Jenny's face and Bea realizes Jenny probably knew her wrist wasn't fine long before she ever said something. Bea asks her why she didn't say something.

The work is more important, Jenny whispers. And then, *Maybe it's because we're too far away from Lev. Something bad was bound to happen.*

A chill courses over Bea's body. Jenny has articulated something that cuts straight to everything Bea's been feeling. The inherent warmth, love and safety of Lev's presence is absent here. She felt something akin to it in Bryant Park, but it was incomplete and in its incompleteness, they were left vulnerable and harm happened to them.

She wants to go back home.

The feeling intensifies at the hospital. She hasn't stepped foot in one in what feels like a longer time than it's actually been. Her body rebels; she's instantly nauseous, overcome with sense memories. The antiseptic smell, the crude overhead lights, the almost-music of the place; the oddly respectful hustle of it interrupted by moments of chaos signaling someone's worst nightmare, followed by the altogether surreal reconstruction of peace once the emergency has passed. Her soul moves back through time and ages another thousand years. She splits in half. The Bea of her present, the Bea of her past.

When they admit Jenny, Bea sits in the waiting room, lacing and unlacing her fingers, breathing slowly in through her nose and slowly out through her mouth, trying hard not to throw up. She's thinking of Lo again, but in a way that's crushing her. She leans back in the uncomfortable plastic chair and hears her sister's plaintive, drugged voice in her ear.

I'm here. Why aren't you here?

Bea hasn't spoken to Lo since that call in February, but Lo has called for her since. Each time, Casey answers the phone. Bea hid in the hallway once to eavesdrop and found Casey's cold rebuffs so devastating, she vowed never to eavesdrop again.

It's part of God's plan, Lev promised her.

It is all a part of God's plan.

You are transitioning into faith. You must become secure in it. You cannot be weak. I'll tell you something now: your sister will join The Project. I've seen it. Her path to us cannot be known to you, but I promise you'll be waiting for her at the end of it—but only so long as you do not intervene. Her faith depends on yours.

Would it be intervening to call Lo just to hear her voice? Bea wouldn't have to say anything herself. Her hand slips into her pocket for the cell phone Casey issued her and she has Patty's number half-dialed when a flurry of orderlies hurrying past shock her back to her senses. She's horrified with herself. She lets go of the phone and buries her head in her hands. She shouldn't have been the one to bring Jenny here. She didn't realize how close to the surface everything would be here—that every hospital would become *that* hospital.

She clasps her hands together and prays to God to give her strength.

Please.

The words of her prayer are fraught, desperate, as she awaits God's hand to lift her past her weakness. When it doesn't happen, she gets to her feet. She paces the waiting room until such restlessness gives way to roaming and she roams the halls until she reaches areas of NO ADMITTANCE at which point she forces herself to carve new paths back to where she came. She presses her palm to her chest, feels a curious fluttering there, a lightness taking hold, one she typically attributes to Lev, to being close to his grace. She closes her eyes and listens to her heartbeat. The hospital sounds slowly fade away until it's only her heartbeat and then— another, resonating somewhere beyond her own.

She opens her eyes and makes a small circle, ignoring the strange looks it earns her, until she feels a pull in her gut and heads in that direction. She reaches a crossroads, and then does that small turn again, letting the pull guide her to where she needs to go next, through one hallway and down another, past rooms holding the young and old, the sick and convalescing, their friends and family, doctors, nurses, past a double set of doors and into—

The chapel.

It's moments like these that make Bea feel foolish for going so long without believing in God. To think of everything she could not See before her heart was willing to give itself over to a power greater than her person. It terrifies her to know she almost jeopardized everything tonight with a single call. But she resisted.

And now, as reward, she's received a call of her own.

In the pew at the very front, a person.

The heartbeat she hears that's not her own belongs to this person. It's so loud, so uncertain, so lost. She moves her way slowly up the aisle until she's at the pew's edge. A man is slumped forward, his arms rested against his knees. He's wearing scrubs, a badge. Bea puts her hands in her pockets and sits beside him and from this angle, she can see his face is wet with tears. There's a sadness coming off him and it's so strong she feels it in her bones. The prickling over her body intensifies. He stiffens at the audacity of her closeness but she pays it no mind. God brought her here. She just needs to wait for the man to realize it.

After a time, it happens.

Foster, she says softly. His name is Foster, and she doesn't know how it comes to her, if she had glimpsed it on his badge and it took this long to register, or if God was waiting for the perfect moment to whisper it in her ear.

She knows what she chooses to believe.

Foster's breath catches in his throat.

He presses his palm against his chest.

Bea often wonders what it would be like to be inside Lev's mind, to parse his divine mystery.

How does God speak to him?

What does it feel like when he does?

Bea's only received a taste. The magnitude of his own calling must be beyond comprehension, but those nights when his urgency flows like a current from him, electrifying them all, almost enables her to imagine it. They're sitting outside Chapman House, on the ground, a bonfire crackling at the heart of the circle they've formed, Lev next to it, his beautiful dog, Atara, next to him.

The early spring air is a little bitter, but it's hard to mind being cold in Lev's presence, especially when Lev himself doesn't seem to mind being cold in theirs. He stands before them and tilts his head back, as though he can see past the starry sky and into eternity.

He's received revelation.

In October, the nation will blanket itself under the false

security of the election and hate will take root in the gaps created by that complacency. Their Father has shown him the signs; this year will herald the end of innocence. But they must be strong. Their role is to witness it, to not break before it, and to offer redemption and refuge to all those broken by it.

No one, Lev says, is too broken for them.

But what are they? a voice calls from the crowd. *What are the signs?*

Lev's gaze seeks the member out until it settles on a man sitting just across from Bea.

Rob.

He's one of Lev's closest friends; he's been in The Project since the beginning. Bea isn't sure she understands why. Rob is constantly questioning Lev, questioning God, questioning the work. He cannot give his tithe without asking *why*. He can't accept his assignments without asking *why*. The self-lessness their work demands of them is absent in Rob, and even if he ultimately participates, Bea wonders how much his participation is truly worth if he can't seem to do it while keeping his disrespectful mouth shut. Lev studies Rob and then makes his way over, crouching to Rob's level before pressing his hands against the sides of Rob's face. He kisses Rob's forehead. Light dances across their skin. Despite the crackle and pop of the fire and how quietly and closely Lev speaks, they all hear his voice.

Faith, my brother, Lev says, *is not a question. It's the answer.*

Everyone around them is still, watching.

Do you have faith? Lev asks.

Yes, Bea thinks, though Lev isn't asking her. Rob swallows, his Adam's apple bobbing nervously up and down. Even the minutest hesitance, Bea feels, must be an answer.

The wrong one.

But if we knew what you know, Rob says, raising his chin, *we would be better prepared. We would be stronger for it.*

Faith is what prepares you in the face of the unknown. Faith is what enables you to stand before it and to stay standing when others fall. Lev rises. *God chooses what to reveal to us and when. If you were meant to know, don't you think I would have told you? How long have you walked with me, Rob? Do you walk with me still? Where is your faith?*

It's here, Bea calls out before she can stop herself. She shrinks when Lev finds her in the dark . . . but then other voices follow.

Here! It's here! And here!

Lev turns back to Rob and asks him again: *Where is your faith?*

Rob is frozen, his mouth hung open.

The world is being shaken, and what is not shaken will remain. Where. Is. Your. Faith?

Rob says nothing.

Lev tells him to stand.

After the meeting, Lev sends for Bea, and Casey leads her to his small cabin near the edge of the lake, tucked away from the house. Inside, it holds only a small kitchen, a bathroom, a desk, a bed. Lev doesn't need much more than that. He stands at the window, staring out at the moonlit night. Atara greets Casey and Bea at the door and Bea runs her hands over the husky's fluffy coat. She's nervous, worried she spoke out of turn at the meeting, that she's disappointed him somehow.

Thank you, Casey, Lev says.

Casey dismisses herself, shutting the door quietly behind her.

Lev faces Bea, regards her tenderly.

You did well at the protest, he tells her. *I knew you would. You brought Foster to us. That's why I sent you. And tonight—you rallied our people in the face of another's doubt.*

She nods.

Where is your faith, Bea?

She presses her hands against her heart.

He crosses the room to her, bringing his hand to her cheek. She feels warmth spread throughout her body from his palm.

How long have we known each other?

Six months. She can't believe it's only been six months.

And yet I can no longer imagine The Project before you, he says, his eyes on hers. *When I enter a room, the first face I look for is yours. God called me to you in a way He has called me to no other. You must feel that too.*

She nods, her eyes filling with tears.

From the very first moment he came to her, she felt it.

I was the question, she says, her voice trembling, her body trembling. *You were the answer.*

He rests his forehead against hers.

There is no flaw in you, he says.

He presses his mouth against hers.

"When did she stop being a member?" I ask faintly.

My body is numb in the way my body was numb when Bea told me, for the very first time, what had happened to our parents. On some level, I think I'd known; they were never there on my fleeting trips to the surface. I would open my eyes and the hospital would bloom around me, Bea hovering, Patty—though I didn't know who she was at the time—hovering, but never Mom or Dad. I would slip back under, feeling a bit unsettled, but half-convinced next time, next time they'd be there.

When I was finally, truly awake, I found I'd been left behind.

"September," Lev answers.

September. I try to hold myself to the numbness, to not give into the raw, furious pain I sense just beyond it. September.

I turn away from him.

"Casey—never said anything to me at the sermon."

After Bea told me they died, I was sedated. I remember vaguely, the seconds before that; the feeling that my heart was on the verge of total disintegration—

And then nothing.

When I woke up again, Bea was holding my hand so tightly, my fingers ached.

So tightly, I felt it long after she decided to leave me behind too.

The way Bea talked about this place to me, her eyes shining with it, her body trembling with the relief of its discovery and all it meant for her was nothing I knew how to reason with. She was a stranger to me then. *I've found God, Lo, I've found Him.* The Unity Project was so burned into her there was no other place for that stranger but here. And if that stranger isn't here, and my sister still isn't with me—

Who is she now?

"I stood right in front of you—"

"After arriving unannounced," Lev finishes. I face him. His arms are crossed and he's staring out the windows. He glances at me. "We can either talk about when we should have had the conversation, Lo, or we can have it now."

"Where is she?"

He turns to me. "We're not sure."

"I want to know everything."

My voice is shaking, my whole body, I realize, shaking, as numbness gives way to shock. I wrap my arms around myself, trying to keep still. Lev licks his lips, and I watch him think, try to guess what he's thinking, as he stares at me.

"Do you know the mere fact of you standing here in front of me is . . ." He gestures to me, his hand following the path of my body from my face down. "It's . . ." He trails off.

"What?"

"It's God's work."

"Bullshit."

"You're a miracle, Lo. It's sad you don't see it."

He seems lost in it for a moment, in me, and the longer he is, the tighter my skin feels around my bones. The wind outside makes itself known again, another rattle against the windows. The soft tapping of the dog's nails sound on the floor as she reenters the room.

"You won't like anything I'm about to say," he tells me.

"Why would that stop you?"

He hesitates, but when he speaks his voice is soft. "Bea was terrified of the possibility of losing you. And when it was certain you would live, it made it that much worse. She wanted to keep you in a place where she would never have to confront that again and that place was as far from her as she could make it. It was here. And she was happy here. She had purpose here."

I shake my head slowly over and over as he speaks, trying to reconcile with everything he's saying: my living was a greater burden to her than my death would have been.

"Three years ago, she was again confronted with another prospective, earth-shattering loss. It nearly killed her. And then Jeremy died and that was the final straw. If she was going to lose people, it would be on her own terms." He pauses. "So she did to us what she did to you: she ran. And I let her. Because I've never held anyone here who didn't want to be."

I bring my hand to my chest.

"You're telling me she loved me so much she let me go."

"Yes."

I remember the way Bea looked at me when I was hurt. How afraid she was of me. How that fear consumed her and pulled her away bit by bit. She was at my bedside, and then she wasn't, the chair next to my bed, and then she wasn't, standing tentatively in the doorway, until she wasn't, until she was gone . . .

I imagine my calls with Casey, but now Bea is at her side, relief smoothing her face every time Casey hung up on me and the day I gave up—

The day I finally gave up.

My heart on the verge of total disintegration.

"Lo," Lev says, moving toward me because it must be all over my face. I hold my hand out, keeping my eyes off him, and he stops in his tracks.

"What happened three years ago?" I ask.

"She almost lost Emmy."

I squeeze my eyes shut.

"Who is Emmy?"

Atara keeps pace with Lev as he leads me down the hall.

She's an elegant animal, eyes only for him. I watch her make minor adjustments to her gait as he does his. We pass a series of closed doors until he stops and points to the floor and Atara sits, her tongue hanging out. Lev rests against the frame, his eyes on me as he knocks lightly on the door with the back of his hand. After a moment, it opens and a pretty brunette steps out. She's tiny, her skin pale white. She wears a denim work shirt and black leggings. She smiles at Lev after briefly glancing at me.

"Jenny," Lev greets her. "I'd like a moment alone."

"Of course."

She slips back into the room, and after a moment, slips out again, Foster close behind. His eyes meet mine before flickering away. I turn, watching as they head toward the Great Room and when I turn back, Lev is looking at me expectantly.

"You go," I say shakily.

He nods and steps into the room. I wipe my palms on my thighs, my pulse thrumming in my ears and I feel a desperate urge to turn around, to head back to Morel, to bury myself in its familiarity, in everything I knew to be true there, and to stop holding so tightly to the things that brought me here. None of this would be happening if I could just let things go.

Why can't I let things go?

I look upward at the ceiling, at a small crack in the plaster branching out from the light fixture there, listening to Atara pant.

I take a deep breath and enter the room.

It's a child's room. Toys and books scattered all over the floor, tiny tables and chairs, a small bed next to a bookshelf. The windows in here overlook still more wilderness and I watch the pines sway back and forth for a long moment before facing them.

The little girl, the one I saw at the farm, stands next to Lev, her small hand wrapped around a cluster of his fingers. She stares up at me and then presses herself closer to him, pulling at Lev's hand until he gives her his attention, kneeling down so she can whisper in his ear. He regards her tenderly in response and then says, quietly:

"Emmy, this is Lo."

She eyes me warily, unsatisfied.

I move carefully toward her, like I could spook her if my actions were too hasty, but it's more for my own protection, as though I could let this moment unfold slowly enough to preserve a point of return. To walk away. I stop in front of her and I can tell my silence unnerves her but there are no words I can think to say.

She looks like Bea.

The shiny brown hair and rosy face, the too-close-together brown eyes. I can see beyond this moment, know with every passing year Emmy will become more and more my sister. I'm briefly overcome by a raw wave of anger that my body doesn't know what to do with. It wants to shake her on the impossible chance Bea might feel it too, wherever she is. I close my eyes until the urge disappears. When I open them, the Bea parts of Emmy fade away, and what's left is my mother and my father. That's my mother's button nose in the center of Emmy's face. The soft shape of her mouth, my father's.

I never thought I'd see them alive again.

Emmy stares back at me and I wonder what it is she sees, if she knows that my eyes are my father's and the line of my jaw, my mother's. That the color of my hair is Bea's. If there's a connection here she's making that she doesn't understand— but feels.

She brings her hand up to the side of her face and after a moment, I realize she's questioning the sight of my scar against her own soft and unmarred skin. A tear slips down my cheek. I lower my head as another falls and lands perfectly center in the open palm of my left hand.

We schedule our first interview for the New Year.

Emmy's existence takes hold of me like a virus.

I wake up in the middle of the night, sick with it, and then I stand in my bathroom, staring at my sweaty reflection in the mirror. I try and fail to let this part of Bea's life wash over me, but it lingers, then digs itself inside. She was born in 2014. In 2014, I was sixteen and Bea was two years older than I am now, a mother. In 2014, I was a year out from telling Patty I appreciated all she did for me, but I needed to go back to Morel. Life with her was her life, steady, quiet. Mine was in the distance, chaotic, a mess—but *mine*. All I wanted was to claw my way back to my sister, but the whole time she was so surrounded by new love, she buried her old family and built a new one on top of its bones.

Other things I know about Emmy:

She was premature, like me.

She nearly died. Like me.

"Where the hell have you been? I've been calling."

Paul's voice is the first to greet me when I fly through the door. He's standing next to the coffee carafe, and I very smartly stop myself from congratulating him for figuring out how to work it himself. I'm breathless, ran all the way here. I lean against the kitchen island, gasping, and manage an apology, telling him I overslept.

"Unbelievable," Paul says, as though he's never fucking done it himself. I stare at him, pissed, and he stares back at me, pissed, and points. "I'm paying you to work, not to waste my time. Hustle harder! You've got a lot of catching up to do."

My face burns as I make my way to my desk. I turn on my computer. There's an email from Paul (passive-aggressive subject line: *For Lo, wherever I may find her*) outlining several conflicts of interest across his schedule with the request that I un-fuck them, on top of every other menial task I'm paid to do. I get to work, dreaming of the moment I get to slap the Lev Warren profile on Paul's desk and the look on his face when it finally happens. An hour later, I've un-fucked exactly nothing and I'm uncomfortably hot because I'm still wearing my coat. I shrug it off at the same time the door swings open, drawing my eyes away from my screen.

Arthur.

He looks so different from the last time I saw him. Snow-dusted instead of rain-soaked, hair neat around his head, his eyes clear, not red, face flushed but not tearstained. He's sad, still, but his sadness has evolved past a stage of grief—it's just a part of him, indelible, now.

He glances around the office a little nervously, maybe a little curiously. The last time Arthur was at *SVO* was before the break-in. Paul finally had the slogan on the wall painted over, but the color wasn't an exact match and Arthur's eyes instantly seem to find the discrepancy. While he's distracted, I fire off a quick text to Paul, letting him know what's going on.

"Hey, Arthur," I say uncertainly.

"I was wondering if I could—if Paul wasn't busy, if I could—" He can't seem to complete the request because it lives too closely to what happened the last time he was here.

He clears his throat and gestures to the wall. "Feels really different in here since the . . ."

"Yeah."

"So is he busy?"

I pick up the phone and dial into Paul's office. It's still ringing when he steps into the room. His eyes land on Arthur and he frowns.

"Art," he says warily. "Hey."

He doesn't quite meet Paul's eyes. "Door still open for me?"

Paul's face softens. "It was never closed, Art. Come on in."

Arthur's face sags with relief, his mouth trembling a little as he rounds my desk and heads into Paul's office. Paul shuts the door behind them both. I whirl around until I'm facing Lauren, awaiting her verdict.

"It was about . . . I don't know, five minutes before they started screaming at each other the last time?" she says. I pick up my phone and set a timer. Now that she's got my attention, she leans forward. "You've never been late once since you started here. What happened?"

"Nothing happened. I overslept."

"Weird, because you don't look like somebody who's sleeping at all."

After five minutes, nobody's screaming. Another thirty pass before Arthur finally emerges from Paul's office, looking a little tired but otherwise—fine. He gives me a thin-lipped smile on his way out. When he's gone, I get up and knock on Paul's door.

"Yeah," he calls.

He doesn't look at all surprised to see me there. He gestures for me to close the door and sit down, but I stay where I am.

"What's up with Arthur?"

"Just wanted to talk."

"You get an olive branch or what?"

"I did." He leans back in his chair. "He needs a friend. Holidays are coming up and he hasn't had Jeremy for any in . . . a long, long time—but it's different when you know they're still around. I'm glad he reached out. I don't think he should be alone."

"Has he given up on The Project?"

"I was waiting for you to ask me that," Paul replies. He stretches. A few of the bones in his shoulders *pop* and we both grimace at the sound. "He's decidedly not giving up. I've agreed to keep an open mind and he's promised to temper his expectations. Anyway, he started a Facebook group, I guess, asking for people with similar stories, reaching out to the media, but Facebook shut it down. Too libelous. He said we got an invite. I didn't see one. Did we?"

"Maybe? We get lots of Facebook invites so I've got a filter set up. Probably sent it straight to trash, if we did."

Paul nods and turns back to his computer.

"He's moved it to Telegram."

"What's that?"

"It's a messaging app. Lots of journalists use it. It's got good encryption and self-destruct options, anyway . . ." He types a few things and then says, "Ah, here we are." Nods at his screen. "He started a channel. It's like a noticeboard . . ."

I round Paul's desk to take a look.

THE TRUTH ABOUT THE UNITY PROJECT. Arthur's plea to the public is much less grief-stricken and much more composed than his last attempt.

MY NAME IS ARTHUR LEWIS. I AM SEEKING
ANSWERS REGARDING THE DEATH OF MY SON,
JEREMY LEWIS, A TWENTY-THREE-YEAR-OLD
WITH HIS WHOLE LIFE AHEAD OF HIM. JEREMY
WAS A MEMBER OF THE UNITY PROJECT AND

DIED CUT OFF FROM HIS FAMILY AND FRIENDS,
WITH NO SAVINGS, NO PROPERTY, NO HOPE. THE
UNITY PROJECT HAS RAILROADED ANY ATTEMPTS
AT GETTING MORE INFORMATION ABOUT THE
CIRCUMSTANCES SURROUNDING, AND LEADING
UP TO THE END OF JEREMY'S LIFE. THEIR LACK
OF TRANSPARENCY LEADS ME TO BELIEVE THERE
IS MORE TO THE UNITY PROJECT, AND JEREMY'S
DEATH, THAN MEETS THE EYE. I WILL NOT REST
UNTIL I FIND OUT WHAT IT IS. I KNOW THERE ARE
PEOPLE OUT THERE WITH STORIES OF THEIR OWN,
WHO MIGHT FEAR REPRISAL FROM THE PROJECT
OR ITS SUPPORTERS. IF YOU ARE ONE OF THEM, I
INVITE YOU TO COME TO MEET ME AT MY HOUSE
ON 43 DAUD AVENUE, SATURDAY, JANUARY 13, 2018
AT 2 P.M. SO THAT WE MAY DISCUSS THIS SAFELY,
AND SECURELY, IN PERSON.

"Is that his house?" I ask, making a mental note of it all.
There's no way I'm going to miss staking that out. "He's just
putting it all out there?"

"He's desperate," Paul says.

"What a way to ring in 2018."

"Tell me about it." He points to the little eye icon at the
bottom of the post. It's been viewed over five hundred times.
"Look at that. I bet The Unity Project's watching it."

"Did you tell him about the break-in?"

"Why, did you?" Paul turns to me, his tone clearly im-
plying I shouldn't have. I shake my head. He relaxes. "No, I
didn't, and I'd like to keep it that way. I love the guy like he's
my brother, but I think he'd enjoy that turn of events a little
too much."

I somehow manage to keep the sinking feeling in my gut from showing on my face.

Lev's voice in my head.

We didn't break into your office.

Arthur knew. He more than knew. The way he looked around *SVO*, his eyes skimming across the exact points of destruction. His destruction . . .

Paul looks up at my sudden silence. "What?" and I can see this small reconciliation with Arthur has made him lighter in a way I don't want to ruin. I know what it feels like when what you think you know about someone has left you so far behind the reality. It feels impossible to find your way back into a narrative when it's left you the world's fool.

So I don't tell Paul.

I get back to work.

The phone on my desk rings.

I don't want to pick it up.

It's snowing by the time I leave for the night, the large flakes disappearing when they touch down, but in a few more hours, the street will be covered. Morel holds its snow—not like the city—and some parts of it stay perfectly clean a few days after, even. For that brief period when everything ugly is covered under the sparkle of something so new, the world almost feels like it's living up to its potential.

On the way to my apartment, I pass a flyer stuck to a telephone pole.

DO YOU NEED SOMEWHERE TO STAY TONIGHT?
*HOT MEALS * BEDS * SHOWERS * CONNECTION*
YOU HAVE A SAFE SPACE AT THE UNITY CENTER

2012

When Bea wakes, Lev's legs are tangled in hers, his body pressed against hers, his arm tucked firmly around her, holding her close. She's never been so held in her life. She reaches up carefully, tracing her fingers along his arm, gentle enough not to disturb his sleep, but enough for her to indulge in him a little more before the day, and the work, begins.

Atara sleeps on the floor at the end of their bed.

Their bed.

She loves these quiet moments after waking up and, especially, those minutes before falling asleep, when they're spent and sweaty beside each other, full of one another. She thinks—a little sheepishly—that it's one thing to be Chosen by God and another entirely to be Chosen by Lev. It's as perfect as she's ever felt.

Lev shifts, waking. He presses his face against the curve of her neck, his fingers tickling across her stomach. She laughs, squirming away from him as he pulls her back, pushing himself even closer. She can feel his smile against her skin. He whispers *Good morning* across it.

She feels his want against her and opens herself to it.

There is no flaw in her.

When she leaves the bedroom, Casey is there. There are no barriers between Casey and Lev. She is an extension of him and it doesn't bother Bea because there is no part of Lev

Bea does not accept. She loves Casey as Lev does, and Casey loves Bea, as Lev does.

The first time Casey found Bea and Lev together, Bea was worried. She'd often wondered if Casey's devotion to Lev bordered on other, more unrequited feelings, but Casey took Bea aside and pressed her palms lovingly against Bea's face. Their eyes met and Bea knew, at once, that it would all be okay.

You're my sister, Casey whispered in her ear.

Bea moves quietly down the hall and when she rounds the corner, she pauses at the window overlooking the property, listening to the sounds of Chapman House coming alive, the waking and welcoming of a beautiful new day. She bows her head.

I give thanks to you, God. You are good. Your loving kindness is forever. May Lev bless us and keep us and give us your peace.

Foster shares a two-bedroom apartment with six other members and when Bea comes to collect him, he tiptoes past one of his roommates sleeping on the living room floor. His eyes are bright; he's always so ready for everything; he moved out of NYC within a month of being offered a placement just outside of Morel. Bea is humbled by Foster's belief and Lev is proud of her for it. Her greatest accomplishment in The Unity Project, so far, might be him.

After Foster quietly closes the door, he folds her into a hug. There's something about his gratitude that makes Bea feel so powerful. He's older than her, more educated, more accomplished, has saved actual lives as an ER physician—yet *he* calls *her* at night to thank her for saving his. His faith radiates from him now, a stark contrast to the brokenhearted man she found in the chapel; a child had died due to an intake error, the aftermath a desperate, ugly scramble to assign blame. He still has nightmares of that tiny body seizing, the small heart it held, stopping. She'd brought him to Lev, days later, who pressed his hands to Foster's shell-shocked, gray face, and whispered in his ear.

I know what the world has brought you to and all that you have had to endure. I want you to know the path to redemption will ask less of you than you have already been forced to give, and give more than you have ever received. Do you accept your atonement?

Bea got to witness Foster's baptism. She stood on the shore of the lake, tears rolling down her cheeks, as Lev put Foster under the water. He reemerged dazed, blissful, redeemed. It was so . . . affirming to see her journey reflected in his eyes. She'll never forget those seconds when the water was everywhere, air nowhere, the sun glittering past the surface, a new world. For one brief moment, she thought she would die.

Then her head broke water and God was everywhere.

They step outside and into The Project's truck, giddy with the day's work ahead. She lets Foster drive. He pulls out of the parking lot while Bea clutches her bag to her chest and they make their way to Bob Denbrough's house on the opposite side of Morel. The Unity Project is in a very specific phase of development that Lev calls *sewing.* Half of their efforts are devoted to expansion, the other half is now devoted to sewing themselves into the fabric of the communities The Unity Project has established themselves in, to give themselves every possible advantage to succeed in bringing salvation to the world.

You are, Lev told them the other day, *our doctors, our social*

workers, our members of the PTA, our secretaries, our counselors . . .
Make use of these talents. Spread our Word.

Foster has already proven himself worthy in this regard.
Without his contacts in the hospital, they would have never
learned of Bob Denbrough's wife's overdose. The burden
of her husband's infidelities finally got to be too much. She's
going to be discharged today. It's not public knowledge and
could never be, but The Unity Project can't be idle in the face
of someone else's suffering and so they've created a care package for the couple to find when they get home. There are
fresh-made baked goods inside, some Project literature and
a note of support.

Forgive and comfort him, lest he be swallowed up by excessive
sorrow. Confirm your love to him.—The Unity Project

On their way back, Foster asks Bea what it would take to
end up in Chapman House. He wants, he says, to be close
to Lev. Bea understands that feeling. She *is* close to Lev but
there's always a part of her that wants to be closer than that.
She feels some distance, a space reserved only for God, and
she wonders if the longer they belong to each other, the less
discernible the distance will be.

Come when he calls, Bea tells him. The natural progression
is from Morel, to Bellwood to Chapman, once you've proven
yourself.

She wasn't the natural progression, he points out.

What Lev and I went through, she tells him, *was different.*

It's the opening he's seemingly been waiting for. He's
heard the story, but never directly from her, and some things
about Lev and The Project should never be posed as a question. He makes sure it's not a question now:

I believe everything—but I'd like to hear you say it.

And Bea tells him.

Lev Warren brought her sister back from the dead.

She lives in the memory as she walks Foster through it, and the miracle lights on his face as though he is there, witnessing it in real time.

He wishes he could have witnessed it.

Where is she now? Foster asks of Lo.

Lev's seen her in The Project, Bea says, and she has held onto that vision every day since joining because every day, there's something beautiful happening in The Project and she finds herself so eager to share it with Lo. *But when is not for me to know.*

They pull up to his apartment. Before Foster leaves the truck, he tells her to wait a moment. He has something he needs to say to her, something he needs her to hear.

He wants her to know how empty his life was before her. He wants her to know how he'd get up every morning feeling his purpose as a healer, but day by day, it was slowly ripped away from him, buried under bureaucracy, until he had none. He wants her to know he never thought he would be able to live in the aftermath of that dead child, and all those fingers pointed at him, but she arrived with God's forgiveness in her open hand and gave him the will to continue. He tells her that he read in the Bible to *take hold of hope* and that *hope is an anchor of the soul.*

She gave him hope, she anchors his soul, Foster tells her, reaching into his pocket to produce a small jewelry box.

He wants her to know how grateful he is.

JANUARY 2018

"We're family," Casey explains. "You take care of your family."

I'm sitting in her office. My recorder sits on her desk, capturing every word between us. I've brought everything I thought I'd need for an interview and everything Google told me I would. An audio recorder, my phone to play backup for it, and a legal pad playing backup for them if they should somehow both decide to fail me. A pack of pens. A small Moleskine with all of my notes and the questions I'll ask Lev when I'm in front of him. It shouldn't seem like I'd need more than that but it wasn't like I could ask Paul for advice.

Casey gave me a tour of Chapman House. I saw bedrooms, offices, recreation spaces for adults and children alike, the kitchen. Now she's breaking down how The Unity Project's work is possible. There's a reason Casey plays spokesperson for the cause. She's incredibly polished, poised. She speaks in a tone of voice that would sound perfect on TV, in the same way her sermon voice sounded perfect for the sermon, and the way it sounded so perfectly cold when she was telling me my sister wanted nothing to do with me anymore—and to please stop calling.

"Project members are housed together in residencies across Morel, Bellwood and Chapman," she says. "We've invested in multiple properties in those areas and some members have donated their own homes to invite their brothers and sisters in. We have a system in place that ensures the care of our membership."

"Walk me through it."

"All right." She clasps her hands together. "Let's say you work full-time for The Unity Project. You'll live in Project housing and we'll assume all the financials—living expenses, groceries, utilities, medicine. Whatever ensures your personal well-being, we handle. There's nothing you need to worry about. If you work part-time for The Unity Project, we'll offset certain expenses to make it easier for you to contribute to the cause. We arrange travel, childcare, things like that." She pauses. "What it's really highlighted for me is how many people want for the opportunity to be a part of something this meaningful and important—but they just can't afford to. The red tape of living gets in the way. We want to remove that, to get rid of all burdens or obstacles—financial, physical, emotional, whatever—so they can. Not only do we care for our members, we *invest* in them. We sponsor members—"

"Sponsor?"

"We'll pay for their education or professional courses if they pursue or are on a career track that can give back to The Project's work. For example, we have some members who are pursuing employment in the healthcare field. We'll assist them, and in turn, they'll volunteer their services at The Unity Centers and avail themselves to members in need."

"Where do you get the capital to do this?"

"Donations, tithes, fundraisers, we have several benefactors—"

"Your father?"

"This is completely off the record, but yes. He's made significant contributions to our work over the years." She moves the conversation along before I can pursue this. "On the record, what I'm most proud of is the way we all come through for one another. The Project represents a wide-ranging group of people with varying skill sets and talents. Their assets help us determine their placement—full-time members are assigned to communities that can most benefit from their expertise, whatever it may be—but what they offer others, they also offer to each other. Like I said, we're family. That's what family does."

"You think everyone here truly believes in God and Warren's New Theory, or do you think there's a chance they're just in it for the perks?" I ask. She stares at me and I shrug. "I could pretend to be a believer for a lot of what you're offering."

"But everything we offer is to facilitate God's work," Casey says. "And answering that call isn't easy. Becoming a member means exercising total selflessness and giving up everything to give your life to God through acts of service to others. To exemplify the way the world can—and will be—if we all make the same choice. It's not a free ride. It never has been." She pauses. "Speaking of family, Emmy's here."

"Speaking of family, how come nobody knows Lev Warren has a kid?"

Casey pauses, as though she wasn't quite anticipating that going on the record. "Lev is no stranger to threats on his life. People want to hurt him. And sometimes the easiest way to hurt someone is to hurt what they love the most. We all agreed that Emmy be invisible to the public eye until she was old enough to make that choice herself. We'll have to talk about how you approach this in your profile . . ."

"Does The Unity Project have a lot of enemies?" I ask.

"We've made a lot of people unhappy with us over the years. Right-wingers think we're plotting some kind of socialist takeover. Liberals consider us too close to God . . . the Catholic Church might be one of our most vocal opponents—"

"Really."

She nods and then digs through some papers on her desk, tossing a few Bible Tracts, some church bulletins and flyers my way. They all seem to be renouncing false prophets. I recognize one of them; that blue-sky Bible Tract I found in Jeremy's wallet.

That same verse on the front.

But the Lord is faithful, He will lend you strength and guard you from the evil one.—2 Thessalonians 3:3.

"Subtle, isn't it?" Casey asks. "Most churches don't really love Lev's anti-church rhetoric, as I'm sure you can imagine. They flood us with their propaganda, trying to convert members back . . . we get them at the house, at the farm, at all of the centers . . ."

Her phone chimes. She glances at it.

"He's ready to see you now."

She didn't tell me I'd be interviewing Lev in a cabin on the other side of the property.

She gives me directions—down the path through the pine trees to the lake, head right, keep to the outside of the woods edging the shore; eventually the cabin will reveal itself—and says it should only be a fifteen-minute walk, but it's a trek I didn't quite plan for. She lets me out the back door, eyeing my boots as I trek into the trees. Snow has accumulated in spite of their cover and I end up ankle-deep in it, trying to ignore the way it seeps into my socks. My toes are numb by the time I clear the path but I have to admit, the view almost makes it worth it; the lake stretched out endlessly before me, the water half-sheeted by ice, beautiful in its stillness and the way it reflects the sun. I admire it until an uneasy feeling settles over me. I glance behind me. The path is in shadow from this side of it.

There's nothing there.

I head right, keeping to the outside of the woods like Casey told me to, unnerved by the quiet. Smoke drifts lazily into the sky, and I know I'm getting close. Finally, a small log cabin with a forest-green roof and a forest-green door reveals itself. I'm halfway to it when a rustling sounds behind me. I stop and turn, and there's still nothing there—at least nothing I can see.

When I turn back to the cabin, the door is open.

———

It's small inside, an intimate space with a kitchenette, a table for two, a desk by the window, and a couch in front of the fire. A door leads to what I assume is the bathroom. There's a bed in the far corner, blankets rumpled, unmade.

Lev leans against the sink counter, watching me. He's wearing a white T-shirt and black jeans, a pair of thick worker's socks. I bring my bag to the table and empty its contents there, setting the recorder up, placing my phone beside it. When I'm finished, I turn to him and speak for the first time since stepping inside.

"Whenever you're ready."

We sit across from each other at the table, his hands wrapped around a mug of coffee while I flip my Moleskine open to my notes and questions. My gut twists nervously and I try to keep my voice steady when I ask him how the *Vice* interview went so wrong.

"They told me it would be about potential game changers," he says. "But that wasn't as interesting an angle as potential cult leaders. So much of your profession hinges on likes, shares, retweets, click-bait. How do you maintain integrity in the face of that?"

"You're not interviewing me and I'm going to push record now."

He nods and I state the date and time, my name and who I'm sitting across from. I ask Lev to state these same things, to say that I'm recording this conversation with his consent and for what purpose. Listening to him say it—*I am allowing Lo Denham to interview me as part of* SVO's *profile on The Unity Project*—overwhelms me, everything I've ever wanted made more real by the sound of his voice. I get lost in it.

"Whenever you're ready," he says, lightly mocking, bringing me back.

I flush and clear my throat. "I want to start at the beginning."

"Which one? I've had many."

I look at what I've written in my notebook. "Why don't we just go from when and where you were born, what your upbringing was like."

"1980, Indiana. Small town called Almer."

"Your mother abused you."

I look up from my notes. His expression is neutral, but the silence between us serves as punctuation enough for what he really thinks of my opening.

"She did," he finally says.

"Describe your childhood."

His eyes drift away from me, to the ceiling. "I lived in an apartment above a launderette with my mother until I was about eight, then we rented a house far outside of town, no neighbors. I had to walk a couple miles just to get to the bus to go to school."

"What's your earliest memory?"

"Standing at the window of the apartment. I was watching people walk by . . . I was waiting for her. I was watching for her. She wasn't there with me. I don't remember where she was, but later, I'd look back on that memory and realize two things: the first was that I was too young to be left alone—and the second was that I wasn't fearful of her return. I was anticipating it, I *wanted* for it, even. That's the only time I ever remember not being afraid of my mother."

"When did the abuse start?"

"I was four, maybe a little older." He smiles a small, bitter smile. "I remember the first instance vividly. Not the *why* of it. She'd hit me in the face. My nose bled all over my favorite *Thundercats* shirt and I was devastated when the stain ruined it. It's amazing the details you retain . . . that was the beginning. When we moved to the house, it got much worse. There was nowhere to go. I was constantly afraid, all of the time." He pauses. "And that's how I'd describe my childhood."

He watches as I absorb the information and this is the part I was unprepared for—the expectation of response. How do you respond to information like this? There's nothing in my notes for something like this. I finally settle on a question I don't think anyone could answer:

"Why was she like that?"

"Because of me. Or so she liked to say."

"Can I talk to her?"

"She passed away a few years ago."

"So there's nothing you can offer to corroborate what you're telling me?"

He presses his lips together and stares down at himself, and then he rises from his seat and moves to mine, standing very close, waist-level, in front of me. His long fingers grasp the edges of his shirt, and he pulls it slowly up, revealing his abdomen, a stretch of what should be perfect, untouched muscle and skin but instead hosts a smattering of scars, puckered circles like the ends of cigarettes, deep lines that begin above his pelvic bone and disappear below his jeans. One scar looks like a very large landmass on his left side; a burn. Part of me wants to reach out and touch them to make sure they're real. The rest of me is left speechless and nauseous.

These happened to him when he was a child.

I try not to show my relief when he lets his shirt back down.

"What were you like, as a child?" I ask weakly.

"I was prone to outbursts, periods of depression. Fits of rage," he says as he returns to his seat. "But I never hurt anyone the way I'd been hurt. I did, oftentimes, hurt myself."

"Do you think the abuse you endured made you desperate for the approval and love and adulation of others?"

"Yes." He leans forward, resting his arms on the table. "And that's why I started a cult."

I blink, glancing at the recorder, making sure I got that on tape.

"You—"

"I'm taking your uninspired line of questioning to its most reductive conclusion," he replies, a hint of contempt in his eyes. "Do you feel defined by your trauma, Lo? Or that other people define you by your trauma?"

"This isn't about me."

"Your scar tells a story whether you want it to or not."

I bring my hand to my face as soon as he says it, ashamed of myself for doing it. He finishes his coffee and stands, setting the empty mug on the counter before facing me.

"Do you define yourself by your trauma?" he asks.

I hesitate, then look to my notebook, trying to figure out how to redirect the interview back to where it needs to be— not what he wants it to be.

"You're not interviewing me," I tell him for the second time.

"What if we were having a conversation?" he asks. "If you want this profile to be worth anything, you have to give something of yourself to it."

"Then no," I say flatly. "I don't."

"Really? How much of what you do or say or want is filtered through what you've been through?" He moves to me, putting his finger beneath my chin, tilting my scar toward the light. "And how much of what you've been through determines what you do or say, whether or not it's what you truly want?"

I swallow, aware that he must feel it.

"I do or say whatever I want."

He lowers his hand.

"You don't drive."

"I can drive."

"But you don't," he says. "Casey noticed something interesting about you."

"And what was that?"

"You rarely look at the road. You keep your eyes on your hands or you track the journey on your phone—you might look up now and then, but only if you can bring yourself to do it."

He searches for the truth of this on my face and I can feel it there, in spite of myself, hating that everything he said is real.

I keep my mouth closed.

"There was so much I cut myself off from for fear of my mother's reprisal. I was constantly anticipating her abuse, thinking I could prevent it. I used to—" He pauses, his eyes suddenly distant. "I'd walk by a church, in town, and I felt this . . . *pull*. I wanted so desperately to step inside. And I knew nothing would make my mother—who felt so abandoned by God, and left to rot by the universe—angrier. I was weak. I yielded to her wrath instead of His Word. So I kept walking past until one day—I couldn't. God chose me, but I also had to make a choice. I had to let go of all I knew I was at that moment. I had to accept my trauma to release myself from it and as soon as I did that, there was space enough inside for me to receive God's grace and set me on my path.

And now I am beyond that pain, Lo. But you—you live inside yours. You live inside your accident . . . and you are so afraid of the next."

I stare down at my notes, furious, the lines of my handwriting blurring into nothingness.

"I'd like you to ask me more interesting questions," he says.

The one that ends up coming out of my mouth is one I don't have written down.

"If The Unity Project is for everyone, why did it refuse me?"

"Beyond the fact Bea didn't want you here?"

I flinch and reach forward, turning off the recorder.

"You can't join for anybody but God and you can't join without faith," he tells me. "Your sister, for example—as much as she was running from all she'd gone through with you, she was also running *to* God. She had faith."

I lean back, a bitter taste in my mouth. I stare at the recorder and I can't believe I've already let this get away from me, that I let that wounded little girl take over this entire interview. That I let her howl.

"Do you believe in God, Lo?" he asks after a moment.

"I only believe in things I can see."

He points behind me.

"Look."

I turn and find my reflection in a mirror at the other side of the room. Even from here, my scar is visible, a streak of white lightning cutting across my face.

"Denham," Paul says, stopping at my desk. "Got a minute?"

I glance up from my computer. "What's up?"

"I'm about to ruin your life."

"I got news for you, Paul."

"Funny. Look, everything I've got on my calendar this week," he says, "I need you to cancel and reschedule for two weeks from now." I stare at him. "Well, most things. Anything involving ads or sponsorships, offer Lauren in my place. If they're not willing to talk to her, tell them it has to be two weeks from now."

"If they're not willing to talk to me, tell them we don't want their money," Lauren calls from her desk and Paul grins.

"What's going on?" I ask.

"If you needed to know, you'd know."

He slips into the office and when I look to Lauren, she's smiling at her screen because whatever it is, she's been told. It's clearly above my pay grade.

"You know," she says lightly, without looking at me, "while Paul's doing his thing, you're going to have to make *my* coffee."

At lunch, my phone rings. Ripley's Auto Repair. My car is ready; all I have to do is drive it out of there. It was Patty's. A ten-year-old Buick she put in storage as soon as the doctors told her she shouldn't be on the road anymore. She handed it over to me and told me I'd be a fool not to make use of it and I guess I was; I paid the storage fees and let it rot. It wouldn't start when I tested it this weekend. An expensive mistake, but now it's fixed.

I use my lunch break to pick it up, handing over the cash in exchange for the keys. I stand at the driver's side so long, someone asks me if there's a problem.

"No problem," I say faintly.

I press my lips together and reach for the door handle, noticing the tremor in my hand. I fumble it open and get inside, adjusting the seat, putting the keys in the ignition. The sound of the engine coming to life, the feel of it—is terrifying. I close my eyes and take a deep breath. I open them and push on the gas. I forget to put the car in reverse, slamming the brakes before I can crash into the garage wall and take Ripley out with it. It earns me some disgusted looks. I turn the radio on and try to focus on the music as I back out, onto the road.

The first car that pulls up behind me makes me want to stop completely and abandon the Buick at the intersection. I fight the instinct to close my eyes. My knuckles ache from their death grip on the wheel. By the time I've made it to my apartment, my body is wound so tight, I can barely get out of the car and when I'm finally able, I stand in front of it, staring at my warped reflection in its body, one hand clutching the keys, the other against my cheek, my scar, my heart fluttering weakly in my chest like I just did some brave and wild thing.

I wake up in the middle of the night gasping and soaked in sweat, a nightmare slowly receding to the corners of my mind. I grasp at its edges until I can conjure what shocked me back into consciousness: a shape at the end of my bed, slowly taking form, a man.

His hands reaching to me in the darkness.

I haven't dreamt of him in a long time.

2013

Bea wakes alone, moonlight spread across her unclothed skin.

Goose bumps prickle over her body, she feels the air against her back, the absence of Lev, and she knows that something is wrong. It isn't just that he's not with her. It's something else, something more, and she's afraid of it. Her eyes flutter open slowly. She rolls over in their bed. It takes a moment for her eyes to adjust to the darkness and when they do, she finds him sitting at the window seat, facing her.

Lev, she whispers and he doesn't respond.

His silence is powerful, intimidating at the best of times, but this . . . this reminds her of coming home two years ago to a quiet, dark house, to the swing in the front yard unmoving, and knowing deep in her bones that something had changed in her world and there would be no going back from the moment it revealed itself to her.

She moves out of bed carefully, naked, and kneels at his feet.

What? she asks, grasping his hands, pressing his knuckles to her lips. He stares down at her, his expression unreadable and it scares her so much she pulls herself closer to him, resting her head on his lap. Now the accident is in her head, a thought takes hold, and she can't help but ask: *Is it Lo?*

The question shakes Lev from his reverie and he presses his palm against her cheek and while the tenderness of his touch soothes her, the slight tremble in his hand worries her more.

Rob has left The Project.

She doesn't understand. How could anyone leave them? Even Rob. She'd thought he was getting better—they had worked so hard to correct him, to show him the path—but now, Lev tells her, he's fled.

He left a note.

Lev reaches into his pocket and hands it to her. She rises, reading by moonlight, and while she reads, Lev pulls her between his legs and buries his face against her. She presses her free hand against the back of his curls as every single one of Rob's words burns into her. Rob came to The Project to help people, to help this shit-infested world shine, but he only feels he's traded one cesspit for another.

We started out so promising. I could feel God through you, but now I believe you have claimed yourself as God and I believe this has corrupted you. I do not feel God anymore.

Bea shakes her head slowly, her anger rising; she has never seen a more abiding servant to the Lord than Lev. She skims the rest of Rob's grievances. They have taken from him, he says, the last five years of his life and he wants all he has given in the name of God returned to him.

Lev stares at her expectantly when she's done.

He had no faith, she says.

No, Lev agrees quietly. *He didn't.*

JANUARY 2018

Arthur lives at the edge of Morel. The clean, unadorned lines of his property strike me as lonely in the same way my apartment sometimes strikes me as lonely, a space its inhabitant doesn't quite know how to occupy. Sometimes, when I step inside my place, it feels like a language I've forgotten how to speak and the days I feel that way are the days I most remember what it was like to have a home and a family—and what it means to not have those things anymore.

His house is across from a small park, empty this time of year. I sit on a bench, facing the street, watching his front door, waiting to see what, if any, Project detractors will find themselves in front of it. It's cold out, the metal of the bench numbing the backs of my thighs, my eyes watering from the bitter air as much as the deep, thrumming ache it causes in my bones. I could have driven the Buick out but an idling car parked close enough to Arthur's house for a good view struck me as a little conspicuous.

I check my watch. It's almost time. When I glance up, there's a fluttering behind the curtain covering Arthur's front window. I imagine him pacing anxiously behind it, hopeful.

I'm hopeful too; there have to be more stories like mine and his.

A man walks down the street toward Arthur's house. He's young, early twenties. As soon as he reaches the path to the door—he keeps walking.

I exhale and wait as Arthur waits.

A half hour passes.

I can't feel my hands, they're so cold, and I'm about to call it when a black sedan pulls up just shy of the house. It lingers there so long, I think it must be a coincidence but something about it makes me stand and move closer for a better look.

The car stops idling, the engine cuts. A tall, white man steps out of the driver's side looking about as old as Lev. His red hair is curly around his head and he pulls at the bottom of his coat before digging his hand into his pocket, producing his phone. He glances at the screen and then the house, as though checking the address, then moves to the door. There's no question he's here for Arthur's meetup.

"What are you doing here?"

The voice sounds from down the street, sharp and familiar, sending a shockwave through me. At first, I think it's directed at me, but it's not. The redheaded man looks up and I follow his gaze to—Casey. I step back quickly as Casey marches toward him, furious. Even when I was pushing my luck with The Unity Project, trying to make my way to Bea, I'd never seen her this mad. Her face is blotchy red, her hair flying wildly around her head as her black trench flares behind her. She asks it again:

"What do you think you're doing?"

As soon as she's close enough, he says her name and grabs at her arm. She jerks away and their voices blur together, indistinguishable. She gets as close to him as she can seem to stand it, and he, for his part, seems to be doing his best to remain calm. The whole moment crescendos; Casey pushes him hard in the chest and then, to my astonishment, turns on her heel and climbs into the sedan.

He stands there for a long moment, his jaw set, and then

gets into the driver's side. I watch her as he starts the car. Her face is completely contorted with rage. She snaps something at him and turns her face to the window and her rage gives way to surprise as her eyes meet mine. Shit.

The sedan pulls away from the curb.

When I look to Arthur's house, he's watching from his window and I duck out of view before he sees me too. I make my way back to my apartment, thoughts whirling.

She calls me hours later, long after I've googled who the man might be and discovered who he is: her brother, Daniel. I stare at her name as it lights up my phone and when I answer, she doesn't wait for my greeting. She tells me we need to talk. Off the record. In person. She's still in town, she says. When I ask her to name the place, she picks The Unity Center.

The Unity Center is near the heart of Morel, just slightly tucked away from the sinus rhythm of the town, offering a level of privacy for those who might want to seek assistance away from prying eyes. It's a large building, three stories tall, designed to do several things at once. The first story is where the action is: at the front of the building, past intake, is the dining room, which is adjacent to the kitchen. It serves breakfast and dinner and light snacks and drinks throughout the day. A recreation room neighbors the dining area where people can relax, breathe, socialize; anything that's not disruptive or destructive. At the very, very back are showers and bunks, room to sleep fifty. Per its website, once you've made use of all of those services—or regardless of whether or not you do—you can avail yourself of The Unity Connection, which runs on the second floor. The third, presumably, is for staff facilities.

I've never been inside The Unity Center before.

I've never actually seen the work.

It's clean, well-lit. Tonight the place seems busy; I'd estimate about a hundred people in the dining area, enjoying dinner. The din is friendly-sounding, loud. Calligraphic script is painted across the wall at the far side of the room.

GIVE AND IT WILL BE GIVEN TO YOU.
—LUKE 6:38

My eyes travel over the faces here. As with the sermon, all walks of life seem represented in Project space. A girl who looks around my age with a small plate of food. She eats like a bird as her gaze flits nervously around the room. A raucous group of boys in their twenties take up a table. A pair of old women sit side by side, their free hands clasped tightly together. A man in a wheelchair. A woman holding her baby to her breast. What appears to be a family huddles together, talking happily.

"Hi," a soft voice says beside me. "Is this your first time here?"

A young Asian woman gives me a kind smile. She's wearing a bright pink shirt with The Unity Project's logo subtly displayed over its pocket. Her hair is cut into a sleek bob, perfectly complemented by the delicate, kitten flick eyeliner at the corner of her eyes.

"Yeah, but I'm not—" I'm not quite sure how to finish the sentence. I clear my throat. "I'm here to meet Casey."

"You're Lo?" she asks. I nod and her smile widens. "Wow. Lo Denham."

"That's me."

"I'm Mei. It's so great to finally meet you," she says,

extending her hand. Finally? My surprise delays me enough to make it awkward. "Casey just touched base, she'll be here shortly. She got a little held up, but please, sit down, grab a snack if you're hungry, coffee, water." I nod my thanks and she gives me a lingering smile as she returns to her duties, whatever they are.

I fade into the background, circling the room. Members move around the adjoining kitchen, preparing food. I notice counselors at every corner, eyeing the crowd. I watch as Mei takes notice of the nervous young girl. She makes her way over, her expression warm and inviting, and sits in the empty seat across from her.

I move a little closer.

"Are you safe?" Mei is asking by the time I'm near enough to hear and the girl frowns, asks her what she means. "Typically, when someone as young as yourself comes to The Unity Center, they're in a crisis state. Maybe you extricated yourself from a potentially life-threatening circumstance . . . such as abuse or—"

"I'm not in that kind of trouble. I'm—fine." The girl studies everyone around her and then looks down at the small plate of food she's acquired. "I don't think I need that kind of help." She swallows. "Maybe I don't have a good enough reason to be here . . ."

She moves to leave but Mei reaches across the table to stop her and the girl does stop.

From here, I can see her trembling.

"The Unity Project—that's the group who's behind The Unity Center, in case you didn't know—believes one of the greatest problems we have societally is our collective misconception of what it is to be in need and what it is to need help," Mei explains. "The world wants to see people hit rock bottom before they make use of our resources to get back on their feet. It's very rare people come when they feel control over their life beginning to slip. They always come *after*, when so much of the damage has been done, if they come to us at all. You don't have to be our worst case to be a worthy case."

The girl's eyes fill with tears, and she swallows, trying so hard to maintain control. I recognize everything about the way she's holding herself, and it puts a knot in my throat.

Mei smiles at her.

"Would you like to talk to someone upstairs?"

The girl nods.

I exhale. I didn't even realize I'd been holding my breath.

"Lo."

I turn and Casey is here, looking even more harried than when I last saw her hours ago. She's striving for some semblance of togetherness; her hair is in a tight ponytail at the back of her head. But it's all in her eyes—I'm not seeing her at her best.

"We'll go up to the staff room," she says.

We have to walk through the second floor to get there. It's made up of offices but has the respectfully quiet vibe of a library. Some doors are open, members working on computers or taking phone calls, others are closed, whiteboards on those doors declaring CONNECTION IN SESSION. If you need help beyond what The Project can immediately provide, they will find it for you. A name on one of the doors catches my eye.

"Is Dana here?"

"It's not one of her days," Casey says without turning around, as she leads me farther down the hall and up a short staircase. "She often works with vets, though, connecting them to peer support and financial programs, that sort of thing. When she came back from her tour, she just got thrown into the deep end. It traumatized her. She vowed to be there for others the way no one was for her." She pauses. "I hope that's the kind of thing you'll put in your profile. There's a lot more to us than meets the eye."

"And even more to you than that," I say, as we reach the third floor.

There's a lounge here for Project members. A couch in front of a television, a small kitchenette, a few tables and chairs, and a room at the back with a row of beds for people working late. Casey nods in greeting to the few members here. They're sipping coffee, taking a moment to themselves or talking to one another. She leads me to a small room around a corner, sectioned off from everything else.

"This is the quiet room," Casey says, opening the door. "It's hard, working here. To care for so many, to take on so many burdens . . . we wanted to make sure members had a place to steal away, to reconnect with themselves, pray—even if just for a moment."

I step inside. It's slightly claustrophobic, but could maybe be a refuge in the context Casey presents. There are no windows here. The walls have been painted a sky blue to compensate and there are plants at all corners of the room. A table sits neatly in its center. I don't feel much like sitting, and neither does Casey. I lean against the wall while she smooths her hand over her head, taming flyaways that aren't there.

"Why were you at Arthur's?" she asks.

"Why was your brother?" I ask back. She clenches her jaw. "And I wasn't *at* Arthur's, I was keeping an eye out. When Lev offered me the profile, he said I could do it my way, on my terms. That's what I was doing." I study her. "What's

Daniel's problem with The Unity Project? Between your dad and you, is he feeling left out?"

"My brother was there for my father—or at least that's what he'd tell you."

I stare at her.

"I thought your dad was a huge proponent of The Project's work."

I can see her thinking, her eyes moving back and forth, tracking nothing, lost. This is so far out of bounds of normal Project business, clearly so personal she doesn't know how to speak about it. She finally sits in the chair at the table, and I can't remember ever seeing her so small.

"Have you ever . . ." She trails off. "You saw my speech at the sermon, didn't you?"

"I was escorted out after that."

"I give the same speech every time," she tells me. "Having everything, wanting for nothing, feeling empty, hoping for death." Her eyes slowly meet mine. "And that's not even the half of it. If I took you through what I'd been through before Lev found me, you would . . ." She slowly shakes her head. "I . . ."

"Tell me."

"You shouldn't ask me that. You wouldn't, if you knew what you were asking." She closes her eyes and keeps them closed. A tear slips past her and she brushes it away hastily, opening her eyes. "I'll just tell you this: my father is a sick man. And the things I know about him would put him in the ground."

Her tone offers no space for further questions, and there's an eerie distance in it that makes my stomach turn. "If he's done something that bad, maybe you should."

"He's more useful this way."

I pause. "Are you saying what I think you're saying?"

"What do you think I'm saying?"

"He's funding Project initiatives in exchange for your silence?"

"He bought this building. And the other two." She leans forward. "It would have taken years for us to get the money we needed to make The Unity Centers happen. Do you know how many hungry mouths we feed in a single day? Beds are ninety percent claimed tonight. It's going to be so cold out. It's inhumane to leave people on the streets, in the cold. Do you know how many connections we make that can mean the difference between life and death for so many?"

"The end justifies the means, is that it?"

"My father might not accept atonement for his sins," Casey says, "but that doesn't mean he can't still pay for them. If this is the result, I'm fine with that."

"And Lev is too?"

"It's my business. He leaves it to me. My father accepts this arrangement because he has no other choice, but every so often, my brother interferes. That's what Daniel was doing today. He was hopeful he'd walk into some kind of uprising but nobody else showed up, did they, Lo?"

I shift, uncomfortable. "Not that I saw."

"What do you think that means?"

She smiles faintly, briefly—sadly—and then stares down at her hands. Casey has always been a mystery to me, less a person than a specific function of whatever the moment required of her. The face of The Unity Project. An obstacle between me and Bea. This makes her feel real and I'm not sure I like it.

"If Arthur had held that meeting six months ago, I would've been at it," I tell her. "Because of Bea and because of you."

She regards me thoughtfully.

"I think anything I say to you about that would feel hollow."

"I'll take anything, Casey."

"Do you remember the last time we saw each other?"

I know she means before the sermon.

And there's no way I could forget.

The Project was holding a fundraiser at the Morel Community Center. I can't even remember what for. I didn't know if Bea would be there, but I knew Casey would, and by then, I was so frantic with a need for answers, real answers, that I didn't care who I met that day.

I was seventeen and I got as far as the door.

Casey stopped me from getting through it.

I can still feel it, the way the world fell around me, turned me suddenly thirteen again. It was like I had a sense of the ending before it happened. I sobbed, screamed for my sister. I remember Casey's grip on my arm as she pulled me away. I don't remember what she told me, but I remember that hard, final look in her eyes and all my want left me. I went home and woke up the next morning in the absence of the one last part of me that was holding so tightly to my past.

It was like I had died.

"I'll do anything to protect this work," she says, "and Lev's vision. You felt like a threat to both, because you couldn't accept that Bea—"

"You said she didn't want me—"

"And I was telling you the truth," Casey says, and I cross my arms and look away from her. "And now you know that I was telling you the truth."

"But you never ever told me *why*." My voice cracks. "What do you think I'd—how else could I take it? It only ever looked like you were keeping her from me."

"I didn't always handle it as well as I could have," she admits. "You tried my patience like very, *very* few people have."

I laugh a little. "Small consolation."

"I think we would have always ended up here, Lo. Lev often told me to be careful with you because you were—" She stops abruptly, and there's something in her face that tells me it would be useless to ask her to finish the sentence, but I want more than anything for her to finish that sentence. Because I was what? "But he'd never seen you in person after, didn't know how willful and reckless and determined you were. I was a little in awe of it . . ."

"Awe," I echo.

"Yes," Casey says. "And I didn't know how to honor Bea's wishes and tread as carefully as the situation warranted. I was often reacting to you instead of thinking it through. I could have finessed my approach. Knowing what I knew, I could have—and should have—at least tried . . ." She shrugs, helplessly. "Regardless, I knew nothing would stop you. Whatever you might think of me, Lo, I never underestimated you."

It's the closest thing I might ever get to an apology from Casey Byers. The only thing I can manage to offer in response is to nod. There's no forgiveness in me, I don't think. Just a brutal acceptance of all that has been lost and a resigned march forward in the face of no other options. She might have done it differently but what does it matter, if it's already been done?

"My father's favorite pastime was underestimating me,"

Casey says. "He wanted me empty. I was just a body and then Lev, he comes along, and he sees more than that. He saw my *soul*." She looks up at me and her eyes are full of fire. "Do you know what that's like, Lo? To be really, truly seen?"

My next interview with Lev is at the Garrett Farm, over the weekend.

Between this and *SVO*, it feels like I never get a day off.

I listen to his famous 2014 sermon—the one that supposedly predicted the 2016 election and its fallout—on the way, the sound of his voice whispering in my ear as the road disappears under the Buick. It's better in the car today but only a little. The long stretch of highway is desolate, the absence of others keeping my anxiety to a dull roar.

I've received revelation.

The recording is muffled, as though made through someone's coat pocket.

In two years, a darkness will settle over our nation, brought by a man who wears no masks. He is who he claims to be. He will call for a wall built on the promise of greatness, but the foundation is rot. The first brick laid will be fear. The second: ignorance. The third: hate. Your neighbors are no longer your neighbors. Their masks will come off, and they will spread the darkness. They will rally in hate. Innocents will die. Children will suffer.

No matter how many Project-related Reddit rabbit holes I've fallen down, I can't find any offering proof that this recording is fake or tampered with. Lev said these words. They meant something to people then, they mean even more to them now.

History will be made in this dark time, but remember: whatever is born of God overcomes the world.

My phone rings, cutting through the audio, startling me. I grab it from the passenger's seat and hit speaker, cutting off Lev's voice.

"Hello?" Silence. "Goddammit, who *is* this?"

The call disconnects.

The recording resumes.

Stand with me in faith and our faith will overcome the world.

I tighten my grip on the wheel.

The farmhouse seems empty when I pull up. I get out of the car and take it in, wondering how life plays out inside its walls without me there to witness it. There's an unavoidable performance that attaches itself to anyone who knows they're being observed and I want to know what the day-to-day really looks like—if every breath in and out is prayer and gratitude, serenity, if you wake up constantly feeling a part of something.

What it's like to wake up feeling like that.

No one comes out to meet me. I watch the door to the house a long moment, just to be sure of it, and then I grab my bag and make my way to the barn down the road in the opposite direction. This is where Lev first held Project meetings before it became a space for the annual sermons, before the crowds overwhelmed them and forced them to get the tent.

The door is half-open and I step inside, taking it in. I was expecting something more . . . rustic; Lev preaching next to the pigs. But this barn has been renovated—it's the kind you rent out for weddings. Clean. Shiny hardwood flooring. Old farm equipment displayed artistically on the walls. Hay bales accent the overall aesthetic. Their smell tickles my nose.

Foster stands in the middle of the barn. I'm quiet enough that I get a glimpse of him in those few revealing seconds before he realizes he's not alone. His head is tilted upward and I follow his sad gaze to the nothing he's staring at.

"I think Lev's in the house," he says when he notices me. "Waiting for you."

"I know." I study him. He's in blue jeans, a tactical winter jacket, black gloves. If I'd never seen him doing pat-downs at the sermon, I'd assume his work here was something along those lines. His reddish blond hair rests nearer to his shoulders now, beard still neatly kept.

"So are you Lev's official bodyguard or what?"

He chafes a little at the word *bodyguard*. "I'm Lev's security detail, primarily his and Emmy's." He pauses. "This isn't part of an interview, is it?"

"Off the record. For now."

He scrubs a hand through his hair, flushing. "I don't know that I could say something anyone else here couldn't say better . . ."

"I'd love a range of perspectives." I cross my arms. "You recognized me at the sermon, didn't you? You tipped Casey off."

"Yeah," he says. "I did."

"How did you know me?"

"I've always known about you, Lo."

"Because of Bea?"

He nods. And then, "Everyone here does. Not everyone would know you to look at you but . . . but everyone's at least heard about her little sister."

It settles over me and it feels bad when it does. She had everyone on alert for me. Pulled out all stops just to keep me away. I bite back every bitter response I want to give Foster and ask how well he and Bea knew each other instead.

"She got me into all this." He opens his hands wide, trying to encompass *this*. "The Project changed my life. Wasn't much of one before."

"What's it like, being a member?"

"It's hard to describe . . . you can't put a definition on this kind of . . ." He contemplates it for a moment. "The Project found me. I think if you ask any member, that's what they'll tell you . . . you meet these people and it's like there's this light just shining out of them . . . enough that you can't help but want to find the source. And then you find the source."

"Lev."

"Yeah." He glances at me. "You haven't spent time with Emmy, have you?"

"It's not really what I'm here for."

It feels cruel coming out of my mouth, but somehow better than admitting the truth; I didn't open this door. I have no say over how long it might stay open, who closes it and when. The most control I can have over this is whether or not I step through it.

I need that control.

"She's a great kid. I hope you get to know her. She's kind of shy around strangers—" I wince at the sting of it; to be closer to Emmy by blood than Foster is, and be the one who is the stranger. "Once she gets past it, she's a fireball. I can barely keep up. She's a lot like Bea. Busy-Bea."

I've never heard anyone outside our family call her that.

"Must've really hurt Emmy when Bea left."

Foster smiles sadly at the ground.

"She'll come back."

He sounds so sure, it gives me pause.

"How do you know that?"

His eyes catch something—someone—behind me.

"Should we talk out here?"

I turn. Lev stands at the barn's entrance but I'm not sure how long he's been there. He's in an olive-green winter army coat, black jeans and boots. He leans against the doorframe.

"Makes no difference to me."

Lev's eyes flicker from me to Foster.

"Foster," he says. "Go on up to the house."

Foster does as he's told. Lev and I watch him cross the barn and slip outside.

"I was just admiring your car," Lev says. "You drove here."

"It's a thing I do."

"It seems I misread you."

I dig into my bag to pull out the recorder. I hold it up, make sure Lev sees it. I don't want to miss a moment of this. He nods his consent.

"If I had my way," he tells me, as soon as it's recording, "I'd live on the farm."

"Why don't you?"

"People would come here between sermons seeking my counsel and I could never refuse them. I was stretching myself too thin. Casey noticed and she made some executive decisions to protect my energy." He smiles slightly. "The Unity Project runs on faith—and her."

"What happened to the Garretts?"

"They live in town now. They prefer it."

He steps farther into the barn, nostalgia lacing his voice as he continues to talk. "You should have seen it then. I imagine the sermon in the tent came across as a bit of a spectacle to you."

"If it doesn't have to be a spectacle, why make it one?"

"I didn't say it *was* a spectacle, I said it was a spectacle to you. Faith is an expression and some people find certain types of expressions more resonant than others."

"People who attend your sermons—some of them believe you can see the future," I say, and Lev inclines his head. "That you predicted the outcome of the election. Is that true?"

"I'm not interested in indulging that kind of speculation because—"

"Because it detracts from the work," I finish. "But this question has dogged The Project for years and I think the public deserves an answer: did you see the future or didn't you?"

"I spoke what God told me to speak. Some of his messages are easier to discern than others." He pauses. "The 2014 sermon was a mirror. We see in a mirror dimly, and then face-to-face. That's what happened."

"Do you consider yourself a prophet?"

"A prophet is only a messenger."

"That's not an answer."

"It's the one you get."

"You *do* consider yourself God's redeemer."

"Yes."

"Or do you just have a really healthy ego?"

He pauses. "I was long ago stripped of my ego."

"Did you bring a girl back from the dead?"

He smiles at the rapid-firing of questions, immediately understands I'm trying to trip him up. My fingers ache from holding the recorder so tightly. It's chilly in the barn, but I don't want to go up to the house because when I think of writing this moment as it happened, it reads better here; dust motes floating in the air, Lev's face tinged with the cold. The way our voices echo slightly as they play off each other. The sound of his boots as he paces the floor.

"In God, anything is possible," he tells me.

"That's not an answer either."

"It's still the one you get." He pauses. "I was going to be a priest."

"I know."

"I thought that was what God meant for me. Well, it *was*, actually. I hadn't correctly discerned His calling. God connected me with the church not to bring me *to* it, but to bring me *through* it. To walk me through its corruption, to bring me lower than I'd ever been in my life so he could show me a better way, so I, in turn, could show others."

"How low?"

He comes to a gentle halt in front of me, contemplating.

"When I walked into church the first time, a boy, God's love was everywhere," Lev says. "And I had never known love. And when I knew His love, I stopped knowing fear because God's perfect love casts out fear. Are you afraid, Lo?"

"Of what?" I ask.

"Anything." His eyes search my face when I don't answer him. "When I felt God's love, I was no longer afraid of anything but when I got to seminary, I no longer felt God's love. I was more alone, and more afraid, than I'd ever been. It was a test."

"What do you mean?"

"God took His love from me to see if I would prove myself worthy of its return. I left seminary and I went home to

Indiana, to my mother. Her anger was as alive as it ever was. I was made a boy again and she put her hate in me."

I swallow, too afraid to ask him exactly what he endured, which one of those scars on his abdomen speaks to this moment of his life.

"What did you do?"

"I suffered my way back."

"What does that mean?"

"I kneeled and I prayed to God for thirty hours."

"What did—" My voice catches. "What did you pray for?"

"My mother," he says, and it's the last thing I expect to hear. "I asked God to bless and keep her safe. I told God I would serve Him in the name of her forgiveness and God knew He could trust His vision of The Project with me. He restored me. He made me His redeemer."

"And what makes you so special?" I ask.

"I'm not special. There's nothing special about me. Or maybe—" He steps toward me and he is very, very close. "Or maybe it's that we're all special . . . because everyone has been Chosen by God. Everyone has been Called by Him."

"Even me."

"Even you." He pauses at the small, derisive smile this puts on my face. "You think that's worthy of scorn?"

"If God's calling me, how come I don't hear anything?"

He brings his mouth to my ear. "You're not listening."

"Maybe he's just not loud enough."

"But how would you even know God to hear him? Your faithlessness is all over you. You believe so much of your anger, your need, your hurt, and your loneliness stems from what you've been denied, but you need to know this: if we deny God, he will also deny us."

I step back from him.

"There is so much waiting for you beyond your want and your pain and your loneliness, Lo." His gaze trails over my body in a way that makes me feel small, as though he can see all that lies beyond flesh and bone. "Aren't you tired of denying yourself?"

I watch Lev return to the house through the windshield of my car.

It's dark out, raining a little, the kind of rain that's quick to turn to sleet. I want to get ahead of it as much as I can. I start the car, the rumble of the engine reverberating through my body. I shake my hands out, clearing my throat a few times, like I could expel the tight feeling in my chest, then I pull away from the house and drive the long stretch of road back to the highway, chewing on my lip, Lev's voice in my head, trying not to imagine that there is a God calling out to me right now and the only thing standing between us is—

Me.

My phone rings from its place on the dashboard. I glance at it quickly—UNKNOWN NUMBER—before glancing back at the road. I'm nearing the intersection at the same time as a semi. The sight of it breaks a cold sweat out on the back of my neck. My phone continues ringing and I push on the gas when I don't mean to, then try to correct with the brake.

Nothing happens.

"God," I whisper.

I push the brake pedal again and nothing happens.

I turn the wheel hard, and in that moment between the road disappearing out from under me and the sudden stop that lies ahead, I listen.

2013

No one has ever left The Unity Project before.

He calls a meeting at Chapman House, in the Great Room.

There's a low murmur of confusion as everyone arrives and settles in; no one but the three of them—Lev, Bea and Casey—knows what this is about. Bea sits dutifully at Lev's feet, Atara seated next to her, as Lev stands before them. Casey stays to one side, keeping careful watch of everyone. Lev wants a full report of reactions later. Bea spots Foster, sitting near the back, and he gives her a questioning look. She shakes her head imperceptibly. His questions are not hers to answer.

Finally, Lev wordlessly calls them to order, raising his hands.

The room falls silent and Lev's eyes fall on each of them, taking them all in. Bea wonders what he sees when he looks at them. If he's as sure of them as he ever was or if he now only sees a vast new potential for betrayal. From here, Bea recognizes the deep hurt in his eyes—to have given so much, to have had it thrown back in his face.

I want to speak to you of paradise, Lev says.

Bea closes her eyes.

Paradise, he says, his voice flowing over her, *is not a place you go, it's the place that I carry within me. God has entrusted me with this gift. And for as long as you are in my presence, for as long as you live in my faith, you shall have the keys to the Kingdom. Its walls will protect you. Your faith fortifies its walls.*

She opens her eyes.

Betrayal of that faith, Lev says, moving carefully through them, *weakens its walls. The world outside of The Unity Project is corrupt. Isn't that right, Foster?*

Yes, Foster calls.

The world outside is so sick with sin, sin is more inborn to us than God's grace. But you—all of you—have been returned to it. You accepted the gift of your Atonement. He opens his arms to them. *You were Redeemed.*

Amen, Bea says.

Amen, they all say.

We are here to offer salvation to those brave enough to seek it, Lev continues. *When no more will claim their place among us, we will close our doors. Remember your vows: the world will fall around us, but we will remain untouched, for no harm shall happen upon those under my wings. And when the world has undone itself, when the nonbelievers have burned themselves away, all that will remain is our paradise. This has always been my promise to you.*

Sometimes, Bea thinks heaven is here and now but when Lev talks like this, she knows she's wrong. If today is ecstasy, tomorrow will be a greater bliss.

Lev will lead them into that tomorrow.

But the path from redemption is as open to you as the path toward it, Lev says. *And just because you are here, in The Project, does not mean you are impervious to the temptation of sin, of vice, of materialism, of ego and greed and doubt. You must be—* have to be—*stronger than that because your weakness becomes our weakness, and your corruption corrupts us, and it jeopardizes our paradise. I can't accept this, especially when I'm doing all I can to take you with me. I have something to tell you: Rob Ellis was weak and his weakness was corrupting us. I saw this in him. I recognized his threat to our work and our future together, and I asked him to leave. He is no longer a member of The Unity Project. You are all safe with me once more.*

The shock of it ripples through them, that Rob is gone, that his very existence was sabotaging them. How close they came to losing all they had built. Bea watches their stricken faces reflect each other, their betrayal, deep. Their anger, fresh.

The relief, palpable.

Thank you, Foster says from his side of the room, and Bea is quick to echo him, and they are quick to echo her, and soon, the room is filled with their song of gratitude and Lev swallows, visibly moved by the way they've rallied around him.

I have to confess something to you, he says, once they've settled down. *I didn't want to believe that I could lose faith inside these walls. I thought that if God had commanded your presence here, you would always stay the course. But I was naïve to think the task set before me would be so straightforward. We are all here of our own free will and because of this, at any time, we could lose sight of our destiny. I believe God sent Rob to make sure I had not become complacent. He was a reminder to be vigilant. I will never be complacent again. I can never—and I will never—lose any of you again. If I can save you, I will always choose to save you.*

He closes his eyes for a long moment, and then opens them.

He tells them to stand.

PART THREE

JANUARY 2018

That sudden *crunch,* the whine of metal forced in on itself.

The impact earthquakes over my skin and buries itself into my bones. My head hits the steering wheel. The car horn blares into the early evening.

I sit up slowly, bringing a shaking hand to my forehead.

My fingertips come back red.

My hand drops limply to my lap.

The crunch and the whine of metal.

The car horn, still blaring.

"Mm." I make the sound through my closed lips and then I grasp at my chest until my hands find the seat belt and I pull at the seat belt and I keep making that sound, not quite a word, not quite a cry for help. Patty's busted-up Buick. I lost control.

How did I lose control?

I remember the sickening feeling in the pit of my gut when the road left me.

The *crunch* and the whine of metal.

My head launching itself against the steering wheel.

The horn blaring.

The horn, still blaring.

I squint through the cracked windshield.

The front of Patty's Buick is crumpled against a tree at the bottom of a ditch.

I was coming up on the intersection before the highway.

A semi was coming.

The brakes . . . was it the brakes?

Or was it me?

The horn stops suddenly. My door opens.

I turn my head to it.

"Lo? Lo, what happened? . . . God, you're bleeding. Lo, can you hear me?"

Lev bends down, his necklace glinting in the light and I find myself reaching for it. I grasp at it, my focus in and out.

It's so quiet now.

"Mm."

"Lo."

I open my eyes. I don't remember closing them. Lev brings his hand to my forehead, inspecting the cut. Whatever he finds seems to satisfy him enough to move his hands from there to my chin, trying to force me to meet his eyes.

"Lo, look at me," he says. I am doing everything but looking at him. "Are you hurt? Does anything hurt?" I bring my hand to my forehead, but he's seen that. "Anything else?" He glances behind him. "Foster, I want you to take a look at her."

"What happened?" I whisper. I can't seem to organize my thoughts or catch my breath. I pull at the seat belt, tight across me, and more than anything I want this crushing thing off of me. "I don't know what happened . . ."

"You were in a wreck. You're—"

Lo. You're my sister. You're thirteen years old.

My heart crawls all the way up my throat and I can't—I can't breathe. Hands reach past me, unbuckling my seat belt and as soon as I'm free of its stranglehold, I scramble out of the car, but I only make it a few steps before my legs give out. I collapse to the snow-covered ground, the aftermath of two accidents, gasping for air. I can't breathe. I was in a wreck.

"Who am I?" I ask, but I don't know why I ask it.

You're—

"Lo—"

You're my sister. You're thirteen years old.

"Lo," Lev says again.

"Everyone's—dead—"

Lev kneels in front of me and I watch the knees of his jeans grow dark, soaked through from the snow, and I know that I'm kneeling on the same ground, that my clothes must be wet and cold and clinging uncomfortably to my skin but I can't feel anything.

"Who am I?" I ask again.

"Lo," Lev says and I shake my head over and over and then his voice, again, firmer this time: "Lo, look at me. Now."

He puts his palms against my cheeks, my tears pooling at the edges of his hands. He presses his thumb gently into my scar and suddenly, I'm there again; I'm in the hospital with its grim white lights, a girl on a bed, the IV lines, the ventilator, the man standing over the bed, the sudden shock of being forced back into that body.

Who am I?

"Lo."

I take a shuddering, coughing breath out and force the air back into my lungs, and then I gag on it. I scramble away from Lev, digging my hands into the ground, my hair clinging to my face, my face slick with sweat, cold.

I remember being helped to my feet, then being suddenly in the farmhouse.

But nothing in between.

I'm ushered into a small bedroom by Project members

who then disappear. I sit on the edge of a small bed, staring at my hands. Each time I come back to myself, I'm in a different place or position than I was before. The gaps terrify me, as does the strange, stunned complacency of my responses to anything they ask or ask me to do, my body just along for the ride like those early days after waking up in the hospital. I kept waiting for the moment I would return to myself, become the girl I was before.

It never happened.

"Who am I?" I ask stupidly, before I can stop myself. I know it's wrong. I know who I am. Foster frowns. "No, sorry. I know. I . . ." I exhale, rubbing my hands together. I don't know how to explain to them that I am in one place, my body is in another.

Foster turns to Lev. "Urgent Care."

"No," Lev says. Then, to me, "Lo, you're in the Garrett Farmhouse. You were in an accident." He pauses. "Just not one you think."

Foster looks me over, asks questions with a certain kind of authority that must speak to a certain former life. When Lev finally explains Foster used to work in a hospital, it makes too much sense. I feel like I'm in the hospital.

I bring my hand to my forehead. Dried blood flakes beneath my nails. I squint at the ceiling. The light fixture there is old, the glow of the bulb is cold.

"The Garrett Farmhouse," I say.

The hospital was cold.

"Yes," Lev says.

"I don't feel right," I whisper.

"I'm going to get her some water," Foster says.

He disappears and I close my eyes. I imagine standing outside of my body and then stepping into my body and when

I open my eyes again, Foster is holding out a glass of water to me. I take it, not realizing until this exact moment how thirsty I am, and I down half of it in one go before my throat seizes and I choke. I cough, my eyes watering, and hand the empty glass back. I don't remember finishing it.

Lev watches from the doorway, his arms crossed.

"Will it scar, do you think?"

Scar. I bring one hand up to my face, to my cheek, expecting my finger to slip into the open space, the wound, but they meet that ugly gathering of skin. They'd stitched it up so hastily the first time, they had to open it up just to close it again, properly, making the damage worse.

"Shouldn't. It's shallow. Head just bleeds a lot. Steri-Strips should take care of it."

"Bring me the kit. And then start making calls about the car . . ."

I close my eyes and inhale through my teeth, listening to the sounds of Foster leaving the room. I think about the Buick out there in the ditch, crushed.

How? How did I . . . ?

Foster comes back and disappears again. Then the sound of Lev's quiet footfalls as he moves closer to me. I open my eyes slowly and he's pulled a chair from the writing desk in the corner of the room. He sits, a first aid kit in his hands, and digs into it, frowning slightly as he decides what he needs and what he doesn't.

"What happened?" I need someone to tell me.

"I heard the horn," Lev says, setting certain things aside, bandages, alcohol. "I'm going to get a little closer to you now."

He skirts the chair forward and then reaches for the bottle of alcohol, opening it, shaking it into a cotton ball. He dabs the cotton against my head with such care, I barely feel it. My gaze drifts to his necklace. My brow furrows. I reach for it again, letting it sit in my palm. It's small, round and cold, silver. I can finally make out the etching on it: an anchor.

"What does that mean?" I ask him.

Lev gently removes it from my grip and lets it fall back against his throat.

"Bea gave it to me."

"Why?"

"For when Emmy was born."

It quiets me. Lev takes a couple of Steri-Strips and presses them against the cut, and only after it's done do I realize that I just let him do it.

I stare at my hands.

"How do you feel?" he asks, and then, "Not good, I'm sure."

"I don't know what happened," I say.

I close my eyes and I see it all, the semi, the intersection, my phone—I open my eyes.

"Where's my bag? My phone—"

"We have it. Don't worry."

"And the car—"

"We have people on it."

"I need to go back to Morel."

I don't know that this is true.

"You should stay."

"I need to go."

I stand and my stomach turns. Lev grasps my arms and forces me to sit back down before I'm entirely vertical.

"Lo," he says. He lets me go, carefully, and then reaches down and begins to untie my bootlaces. He slips my right foot, then my left foot from them. The roiling in my gut reminds me of that moment when everything wasn't where it was supposed to be. The road gone, falling into the ditch, the tree. The semi. I don't remember the accident, but I imagine I do; my parents in the front seat, Dad briefly smiling at Mom when the truck twists into our lane.

You live inside your accident . . . and you are so afraid of the next.

"Did you see this?" I whisper. "Did you know?"

He looks up at me. "What?"

I press my lips together.

"You're shaking," he says. I stare down at my hands and it's true. They weren't shaking a moment ago, though, I swear. I swallow, my mouth dry, suddenly thirsty again. I glance around the room for the water, but it's gone because I finished it. I forgot.

"I don't want to be here. I want to go home."

After a long moment, he asks, "Is there anyone waiting for you there?"

"What do you mean?"

"You shouldn't be alone,'" he says. "And the only way I could let you leave here like this is if there was someone in Morel waiting for you, to take care of you."

But there's no one.

I reach for my forehead absently and scratch at my freshly-tended-to skin. Lev pulls my hand from my face. All of this registers somewhere past the surface, everything I'm doing wrong after I've done it. Some part of me still not connected.

"I can take care of myself."

I feel the blood drain from my face. Nausea washes over me. Lev says, "Lay back, lay back, lay back . . ." pressing against my shoulders until my head meets the pillow beneath me.

"In the hospital," I manage, "every time I woke up, I was alone."

I stare at the ceiling and then I reach for my forehead. I can't seem to leave it alone. Lev grasps my hand and holds it tightly between both of his own. I slowly return my gaze to his. Once he's sure I won't worry at the bandage, he rests my hand gently on the mattress and moves to leave. I reach for him.

"I take care of myself," I say again.

But I've reached for him.

He hesitates, then sits down beside me.

"I am so sorry," he says, "that no one has taken care of you."

2013

She finds Lev naked, studying himself in their bedroom mirror.

She follows his gaze as it roams over his body.

His hair, his beautiful curls. She loves the feel of them through her fingers, loves lying with him, pushing them back from his face while he looks at her. His eyes are a deep, rich brown and there is no end to their intensity. She had to train herself to keep eye contact with him those first few months in The Project because it felt like he was seeing more than she had agreed upon and she wasn't sure anyone could withstand such scrutiny. He told her sometime later, when she confessed this to him, that he often felt the same way, in his own way. He saw with God's eyes—and that was often more than any man could take.

Their gaze trails past his broad chest, his strong arms, the skin tight across his muscles, both of them arriving at his mother's abuses at the same moment. She cried the first time she saw the constellations and continents of burns on his body, the cuts across his hip bones. Who would do something so ugly to a child?

Don't you understand? he'd whispered, wiping her tears. *She made me what I am.*

She's a terrible woman, calls Lev asking for money and complains bitterly about the way he's spoken of her to the public. Her health is failing and Bea relishes in this.

Lev forgave her but Bea doesn't have to.

She crosses the room and wraps her arms around him, pressing herself against him from behind. He leans back against her, breathes her in.

If anyone doesn't provide for his own, he says quietly, *he has denied the faith—*

No, Bea says, bringing her lips to his shoulder. *No . . .*

And is worse than an unbeliever, he finishes, staring at himself in the mirror. She closes her eyes, resting her head into the crook of his neck and continues to refuse his words.

I have failed to keep one of God's chosen, he says.

Rob's departure has weighed heavily on Lev in ways that no one but she, and Casey, can see. He doesn't sleep well, paces at night murmuring to himself, trying to understand when and where he lost his hold. Rob had been one of the very first to express faith in Lev and to trust so completely in his vision, and that faith strengthened Lev's resolve to carve out a path like no man before him. Lev doesn't understand where things soured. Everything Lev does for them is what he has been asked to do by God, and if he is failing to convey the Word, if his followers now run from it, there can only be one reason: *I've failed God.*

Bea doesn't agree. No one knows what it takes from Lev to answer to God and then to answer to His Chosen. To be all things to all of them. It's not so much to ask they meet him in all they do and no consequence should surprise them when they don't. If you serve God in all things, if you are dutiful and obedient as you promise to be, there is no consequence.

Lev's hand drifts to his scars. He presses against them with his fingertips, wincing as though they're still as raw and painful as the day his mother made them.

I have to go to Indiana, he tells her, *to seek revelation.*

She can't stop Lev from sacrificing himself on his mother's altar, but Bea is not ready to accept any of this as his failure.

When Casey accompanies Lev to the airport, Bea heads into Chapman. They all know where Rob lives; they've kept a close eye on him since his defection. A one-bedroom basement apartment on the bad side of town. He didn't leave with much in his pockets.

He couldn't have expected to.

She knocks on his door, tries to imagine trading the safe and sturdy walls of Chapman House for what she sees here. Flaking plaster, mold on the walls, water damage on the ceiling, a crack in the door. She raps her knuckles against it and waits for Rob to answer.

After a moment, he does.

He makes no case for leaving. He's drawn, shrunk in on himself, his skin sickly pale. He doesn't look like he's sleeping or eating well.

He looked whole in The Project.

I never thought Lev would send you, he says.

He didn't. I'm here on my own.

He eyes her skeptically, but he opens the door. She steps inside and it's worse inside. There's nothing to it, no furniture. A rolled-up yoga mat on the floor and some blankets— from where, she wonders. There's a card table and two folding chairs in the center of the room. As they make their way to it, Bea's eyes linger on the mess of the kitchen counter. She spots a Bible Tract with a ringed coffee stain on it. She picks it up. St. Andrew's. She knows this church. Her parents are buried in its cemetery. She eyes Rob, holding up the tract, a question in her eyes.

He knows how Lev feels about church.

Rob has no patience for the things she's not willing to say.

What do you want, Bea?

She sits across from him at the card table. He is too big for it and she is just small enough. She reaches for his hands, wrapping them in her own.

Come home.

His lip trembles and he closes his eyes and Bea holds her breath. It can't be that easy but part of her believes that it should be. After a long moment, he opens his eyes and says: *No.*

Your family misses you, Rob. Lev misses you. I miss you.

I—He chokes, presses his lips together, and shakes his head. A flush of anger wells up inside her; she doesn't understand. He says, *I want everything back. I want everything back that I gave to him in the name of the Word. I want my things, I want my money, I want my*—He can't seem to finish the sentence, the things he wants becoming less easy to define, impossible to return. But The Project does not take what one is not willing to give.

You would betray Lev like this? He did everything for you—

Lev betrayed me.

Lev loves *you.*

Rob stands abruptly, ripping his hands from hers.

That's not love.

Then what is it?

He opens and closes his mouth several times before clenching his teeth and moaning through them. He presses his knuckles against his head, then his fingers drift through his hair, pulling at it, her question at the forefront of the war he's waging against himself.

It scares Bea.

She keeps herself very still.

He lets out a sob.

It's not love, he finally whispers. *It's not love.* In one swift movement he's in front of her, his hands on the arms of her chair. *Look at me and tell me it's love.* He leans closer, his breath sour on her face. *Tell me it's love, Bea.*

It has only ever been Lev's love. And how badly and how far Rob has fallen in such a short amount of time is proof of this.

This is what life looks like without it.

What else could it be? she asks.

Rob moves away from her, disgusted, shaking his head.

He tells her to leave.

Three days later, Lev calls her from Indiana. His mother is dead.

He sounds so relieved.

JANUARY 2018

There's still time, someone yells.

There's still time. Maybe he just had to get this close to the other side to realize it was there all along because sometimes that's the moment life brings you to. But more often than not, it feels like it's this one: you lie down on the tracks.

You lie down on the tracks and the train is coming.

The boy, trembling, lifts his head to be sure.

I turn away, my heart pounding, forcing myself back through the bodies until I'm free of the crowd, only to be trapped by another, greater swell of onlookers.

One of them whispers in my ear: *Don't do it.*

Do what? I think hazily, staring at the sky, the world shaking underneath me.

I'm on the tracks.

I raise my head, trembling.

A semi is coming.

I roll off the tracks just before impact, falling through the sky. I hit the ground, gasping, and Bea's face hovers above mine, worried and full of love. She's so much younger, some-how, than she should be—and so am I; when I reach for her, my hands are small.

I'm so afraid of all the things I don't know could happen to you, she whispers. She fades slowly out as the hospital fades in and I feel the itchy tug of tape on my skin, the scratchy blankets against my skin. This is not a state of being, it's a halfway place between awake and not quite asleep. And then he comes into view: the man at the end of my bed.

He reaches for me.

My eyes fly open, my chest rising and falling violently as I bolt upright, feeling the strange pull of tubes attached to me, in me. The first word out of my mouth is, "Bea," and then, realizing my mistake: "Patty."

Then, realizing it again, the room comes sharply into focus.

The Garrett Farmhouse.

I roll over slowly, my body aching in the way I imagine a body is meant to ache after a minor car accident—a novel experience for me. Sunlight creeps along the outside edges of the window blind and I can't tell if it's the end of a day or the start of one.

I slowly take in the room, registering the things I couldn't manage to before. It's small, doesn't really feel like it belongs to anyone; a guest room for strays. The twin bed I'm currently occupying is wedged in a corner, a nightstand at the head of it—a glass of water and a lamp atop it—a desk in the opposite corner. I exhale when I see my bag rested neatly on it.

The bedroom door is partway open.

I touch my forehead and it bites back. I hiss. My shoes are off and there's a blanket covering me. I don't remember either of these things happening and I hate, so much, that I can't. It was one of the worst parts of my hospital experience, to be so beyond my own control, and so wholly at the mercy of anyone or anything else.

I get out of bed gingerly, ignoring the protestations of my bones, and make my way to my bag. I find my phone in the front pocket, still intact.

9:30 a.m.

I replay the previous night in my head.

I was in the car.

I'd left the road to the farmhouse . . . I was headed toward the intersection.

There was a semi.

I sit back down on the edge of the bed with my arms draped over my knees, my head bowed, trying to remember the drive *to* the farm. The car was fine. The car was fine, I know this. I made it in one piece—but I also didn't see a single semi. I curl my fingers into fists and bite my lip, trying to ignore the burn of shame across my skin, of Lev's voice in my head. *You live inside your accident . . . and you are so afraid of the next.*

And it happened.

But it wouldn't have, if I just . . .

If I wasn't so *weak*.

After a long moment, I feel eyes on me. I raise my head and turn to the door, and there, peering at me through its narrow opening, is Emmy.

I stop breathing, seeing her.

She'll never not be a perfect vision of Bea. Maybe she's even more perfect because she's free of all her mother's mistakes and still young enough to grow up halfway decent in spite of the damage that's already been done.

It is still so painful to look at her.

"Hi," I manage, my voice raspy. "Emmy." She brings her hand up to her cheek, like she did when she first met me. My scar, forever fascinating. "You remember me?"

For some reason, the question spooks her. She races down the hall.

I can't stay in this room forever, so I shove my things into my bag and shrug it over my shoulder, using the camera on my phone to do a quick self-assessment because there's no mirror in here. My clothes are rumpled, dried bloodstains on my collar.

No wonder Emmy ran away from me.

I smooth my shirt as much as I can. I run my fingers through my tangled hair, wincing when they catch. I knot it into a sloppy bun and then I open the door and face the hall. I make my way to the kitchen, where I find Lev at the stove, working two frying pans. He glances at me out the corner of his eye.

"What would you like?" he asks.

"Coffee. Please."

He reaches overhead for a mug resting on a shelf above the stove, hands it to me and gestures to the carafe on the kitchen table. I pour myself a cup, ignoring the nervous tremor in my hands, and notice Emmy's little body camped out under the table, not quite hiding, but not quite participating either. She's playing with a puzzle, fitting big wooden numbers into their spaces on the board. I take a sip of my coffee. There seemed to be more people here last night, but maybe it was just the same two, my brain refusing to track . . .

"It's quiet."

"I asked for privacy. Foster is around. He took care of your car—"

"Took care of my car?"

"We've got a mechanic in town, a member. He towed it last night."

"What's the damage?"

He turns off the burners and faces me. "It's totaled."

I set my coffee on the table, closing my eyes briefly.

"I hit that hard?"

"You don't have to hit hard, you just have to hit right."

He grabs a small plate and spoons some scrambled eggs and hash browns onto it. He opens up the fridge and grabs a bottle of ketchup, dousing the breakfast with an ungodly amount of it, grabbing a kiddie fork from a drawer. He crouches down to set it in front of Emmy. It's so sweet, it makes me sad.

"How much do I owe you for . . . ?"

"Nothing," he says, straightening. "What happened yesterday, Lo?"

The question hangs between us.

"I saw a semi and I . . . I panicked."

He crosses his arms, leaning against the counter thoughtfully. "You don't remember the first accident, do you?" I shake my head. "I think some part of you must. Deeply. Because that's where you were last night. You had a thousand-yard stare."

I look away from him.

"But there was also a part of you that was trying so hard not to be there anymore, to be present," he adds. "You *can* live outside of it, Lo. You clearly want to . . ."

I ask him how in spite of myself.

Before he can respond, Emmy pushes her plate out from under the table. Most of the egg and half the hash browns remain, but the ketchup is gone. After a moment, she crawls out. She's so small. Her clothes seem hand-me-down: a sweater with a faded picture of Rainbow Brite on it and brown corduroy pants, threadbare. Her sneakers are faded gray.

She makes a point not to look at me as she walks over to Lev, who scoops her up into his arms. She presses her head against him, her face fitting neatly into the curve of his neck. He rubs her back, kisses the top of her head.

"Who's that, Daddy?"

It's the first time I've heard her voice and the sound of it is startling. Its sweetness ripples through me. The words marble in her mouth the way a toddler's words tend to. She can't quite get the *th* sound out, turning *that* into *dat*.

"I'm your mother's sister," I say, before Lev can answer for me. Emmy doesn't acknowledge my contribution, just stares at him expectantly until he answers because the answer can only mean something to her so long as it comes from him.

She asks it again: "Who's that?"

Lev seems to hesitate. He kisses Emmy's head once more, pressing his cheek to her forehead, and then murmurs quietly: "This is Lo. She's Bea's sister."

Emmy's eyes light at this in a way that takes me a moment to understand, and when I do it makes me feel sicker than anything else that's happened in the last twenty-four hours.

When Foster comes back, Lev leaves Emmy with him.

He sits with me on the porch outside, while I wait for a taxi to come. Lev offered a ride, but I refused, desperate for time and space from him to think. My hands are shoved in my pockets, my eyes watering from the cold.

I ask him to explain it to me.

"Who is Bea to Emmy?"

How do the words *mother* and *Bea* live so separately in that little girl's head.

"She's just Bea." He pauses. "She loved her daughter, Lo."

"That's not love. It's cowardice."

"No." He shakes his head slowly. "I can't let that stand. Bea may have been afraid, but she was no coward. I had a mother who never recognized her limitations and her failure to do that resulted in so much pain. Bea made sure Emmy was surrounded by people who loved her and Emmy has never wanted from Bea what Bea was unable to give her. She made sure of that."

Unlike me, I guess.

I bite my lip, trying to keep from crying.

"How are you okay with this?"

"I have to be. I choose to be." I feel his eyes on me. "Don't misunderstand me. What Bea did hurt me badly, and I was angry at her . . . for some time, I was so angry. But there has to be something after the hurt and the anger. These things cannot sustain you. I look at you, Lo, and I see how tired you are. Last night, I saw it." He pauses. "I don't know how you do it."

I swallow hard. It's a relief to see the taxi pull onto the road. I get to my feet and make my way down the steps.

"I wasn't passing judgment," he says at my back. "I was expressing admiration."

I turn back to him, but I don't know what to say.

2013

Lev comes back from Indiana with renewed purpose.

He tells Casey to prepare a meeting for the moment he returns and steps into Chapman House, from the airport, to the sight of his family waiting for him. Atara bounds to him from Bea's side, her tail wagging frantically as she paws at Lev's legs. He sets his suitcase down and cups her face in his hands, his fingers drifting into the bulk of her coat, settling her almost instantly. He looks from her to the room, his eyes locking on every single member as he does, not only accounting for their presence, but deeply acknowledging it.

When his eyes finally meet Bea's, she feels complete. She missed him, as they all did, but it's different for her than it is for the rest of them. She does not live while he is gone.

She only exists.

He looks tired in a way she rarely sees, the familiar strain of Rob's defection on him still, and now, with it, the pain of his mother's death. If they were alone, she would pull him into her arms, offer herself as an anchor.

He closes his eyes.

I love you, he says.

And they him.

He opens his eyes. They stay seated as he winds his way through the room. When he reaches the center of it, he stares upward in that way of his, like he's seeing something so far beyond what any of them can see. Something divine.

She can't describe what it feels like to witness that, to be made certain by his certainty. It is so much better, having him here.

How I have suffered for loving you.

His disappointment hangs over them, she can feel their collective discomfort under its shadow. He forces them to sit with it for a long time, leaves them wondering what it is they've done and when the weight of it becomes almost too much, he speaks again: *My mother's death was not a gift, it was my punishment and your warning.*

What Indiana taught Lev was to hold tight to God's Chosen or they will fall to sin as his mother did, who rejected his divinity in all the days of her life. He had hoped there would be time, eventually, to Redeem her, but God made her an example to all those who turn their back on the faith, to all those who would undermine their commitment to Him—and as punishment to Lev, for losing a member of their flock. This is what will happen to them if they stray: they will burn and Lev will suffer for them just as Christ suffered. There will be no Paradise, only ash.

And is that what they want?

Tonight, he says, *I ask for your recommitment.*

He tells them to stand.

He demands a Spiritual Audit.

Casey implements it; it takes the form of a simple questionnaire and members fill it out over the course of the week. Bea and Casey are the only ones Lev trusts with the outcomes, and so they spend nights together poring over the answers, looking for the kind of spiritual distress that demands intervention and restoration of faith. It is an extension of Attestation, Lev tells them, and he requires members to dig deeper into themselves to satisfy it.

He wants them to look inward at their fears, their jealousies, their insecurities, their petty grudges. Did they feel their strengths were best utilized within The Project? Did they harbor anger or resentment or inappropriate feelings toward Lev? He knew that some members still retained loose ties to their previous lives, that certain familial contacts were unavoidable in the world beyond The Project's gates. He wanted a list of any and all potential contacts so they could be assessed. This part of the questionnaire could not, under any circumstances, be left blank.

Bea was not exempt; she put Lo's name down on her own.

She thinks of her sister often, thinks that at some point, the distance between her and Lo will become less pronounced as Lo ages. That one day, she'll be able to type her sister's name into Google and an Instagram account or a Facebook page will appear. But Lo never materializes in this way and so Bea finds herself constantly wondering, trying to imagine these new years on Lo's body and what they might look like. The difference between thirteen and fifteen can be astonishing. Bea didn't fully appreciate it until she was gathering photos for her parents' funeral and caught herself at both points in time. Still painfully a child in one, and still painfully a child in the other with the soft curves of a woman's body making their first tentative announcements. It terrified her then and to see the contrast so plainly was almost nauseating.

But Lo is nowhere online that she can find.

Bea realizes she doesn't even know if Patty has a computer.

Her tired eyes drift over member answers.

Name your closest friends within The Unity Project.

This is when her name, in Foster's messy script—truly a doctor's handwriting—catches her attention and what she reads makes her feel more than she can put to words.

Bea Denham is my closest friend in The Unity Project. I consider all members my brothers and my sisters, but she is the one who means the most to me. She delivered me from hell and has brought me the closest I have ever felt to heaven. I have never seen a greater embodiment of God, and the work, than I have in Bea—other than Lev himself. I owe her everything for bringing me to him. I consider them my anchors.

She thumbs at the necklace he gave her.

She tells Lev about visiting Rob.

She thinks he'll be pleased with her for fighting so hard for him, for their family, but she can tell, as soon as she's finished, that she's done something wrong.

He goes so still, studies her for the longest time.

I told you he's a stain. He weakened our walls. Why would you attempt to reason with sin? He presses his hand against her face. *Why, Bea?*

She thought it would make him happy, she says.

The face of God is against those who do evil. He cuts off their memory from the earth. And then, *Did he try to tempt you? Did he try to tempt you away from me?*

He could never, she whispers but that is not what he asked her.

He did. And he did not even have to call for you to go to him.

He lowers his hand and she feels it gone.

Where is your faith? he asks.

She kneels in front of him, her heart in her throat, and he pushes her hair from her face. He asks her to tell him the story of when she was in the hospital, the day that Lo was born. It fascinates him, and every now and then he wants to hear it: how Bea was so comforted in and by her mother's arms. He'd never known anything like it and she tries so hard to let him know it through her. Bea tells him of the promise. *Having a sister is a promise no one but the two of you can make— and no one but the two of you can break.*

When she's finished, he says, softly, *Those who promise are faithful.*

He asks her to make a promise to him.

Afterward, the two of them lie in bed, limbs entwined. Bea's eyes are watering, her flesh blistered and smarting from the blessing burned on the inside of her thigh. She's never felt a more perfect pain in her life. Lev has sealed the weaknesses in her faith with the strength of his own. He kisses her between her legs. When he asks her what it feels like, she says *love.*

FEBRUARY 2018

Paul storms into *SVO* Monday afternoon with murder in his eyes. The door slams against the wall and everyone watches, silent, as he stands before us, scrubbing his hand over his mouth, assessing the room.

"Somebody fucked up," Lauren says under her breath.

"Denham, my office. Now."

His tone makes my body go rigid, makes my heart rate rocket. I've heard him use it before—but always at other people. Never me. I stare at him a moment too long, can't quite process being on the receiving end of it. It has to be a mistake.

"Now."

I end up in his office, alone, with the door closed, waiting on him. I missed the whole high school experience: calls to the principal's office—though I was such a timid kid, I doubt I would have ever found myself there—but I wasn't looking to find it here.

The low murmurs of him and Lauren talking filter in and knowing that she's getting briefed on whatever I fucked up before I do makes me hate him and by the time he finally enters the room, the only thing that's kept me from leaving it is the dread anchoring me to my seat, and the question of what I could have possibly done to have earned this.

"You're really putting me through it," he says as he rounds his desk. "Jesus, Denham. You double booked my entire morning—"

"What? No, I didn't—"

"*Don't,*" he snaps, "argue with me." He sits down and logs into his computer, then, after a few minutes, turns his monitor, putting the proof right in front of my eyes. In a month full of impeccably scheduled interviews, phone calls, conferences, appearances . . . today is a mess.

"Great job," he says. "Explain it to me."

"I don't know how that happened."

"Make an educated guess."

I bite my tongue for three seconds, then swallow what I really want to say.

"It was an honest mistake, Paul."

"An honest mistake is still a mistake and I've been doing damage control all morning. And once I had that off my plate, I went over the schedule and I found—and this is at a glance—about four other conflicts scattered through the month . . ."

I fade out while he lists them all, forcing myself to maintain eye contact because I don't think Paul would respect anything less. When he asks me, again, how something like this could happen, I tell him I don't know, but I do.

"This is unacceptable, do you understand?"

"Yes. I'm sorry."

"Don't be sorry. Fix this. Make sure there aren't any other errors you might have missed. And don't let it happen again." He shakes his head. "I mean, what is with you, Denham? I don't even know where to start—"

"Are you serious?" My face turns red. "I've been working here for over a *year* and I slip up for what—the first time ever? And you're reading me the riot act."

"Don't cop attitude with your boss when you're in the wrong," he says. "And it's not just this. This is the result of a few things I've noticed lately, namely a lack of focus, engagement and participation. It's like you just . . . I don't know, you used to act like you had a stake in this and now you don't anymore. Ever since I told you I couldn't put you on staff. It's a privilege to work here. A lot of people would kill to be in your place."

"Funny, last time you told it to me, you were desperate for an assistant."

"Thin ice." He pinches the bridge of his nose. "You are on thin ice right now. You know, it's great that you can do your job well when everything is going well. If you want to prove something to me, prove you can show up when it really matters. Because that'll make a huge difference for you in the long run."

"I'm at the bottom of a ladder that only has one rung," I snap. "Somehow I doubt that."

When I leave his office, I close the door a little too hard behind me. Something just shy of a slam, but nothing that doesn't suggest I'm not pissed at him.

"He's working something big right now," Lauren tells me. "Like, really big."

"I know that."

"Whatever you think you know, think again," she says. "Paul's got a lot invested in *SVO*. There are no small mistakes. The smoother things are running here, the better."

"You know, I literally *just* got this lecture, Lauren," I say. "So save it."

2013

I want you to listen to something, Lev tells Bea.

He leads her to a quiet room, away from the rest of the house, his ThinkPad tucked under his arm. They sit together at a small table where he opens the laptop up. After a moment, a voice sounds from its speakers. Foster. She almost doesn't recognize it at first, it's so unlike anything she's heard come from him—so small and sad and uncertain.

I have been . . . I have not strayed. I am still a believer. I have faith in Lev and The Unity Project, and the work but I am . . . I am losing faith in myself. I'm plagued by thoughts that make me more and more convinced I'm not strong enough to be here. I do not want to corrupt a hope of future glory with my weakness . . . I don't know where my place is anymore . . .

Foster's voice breaks and her heart shatters. She brings a hand to her chest, swallowing, waiting for more, but there is no more. Foster's ragged breathing fills the room and the recording cuts off. She's seen him every time he's come to the house for Attestation and she has not once remembered him leaving the room looking as broken as he sounds on that recording.

He always found her afterward.

He was always so happy to see her.

When she looks up at Lev, there are tears in her eyes. He moves to her, crouches in front of her, reaches for the pendant at her neck. He runs his thumb over it, studying it.

She asks Lev if he's going to bring Foster to the floor. A lack of faith requires correction and if he is willing to say it at Attestation, some part of him must be seeking it. But she doesn't think she can bear to see Foster on the floor and she admits this to Lev. They will look at Foster, and they will know her faith was not enough.

Lev considers this.

Foster came to The Project a perfect soldier. His perfection is proof of your own. I will not assume the failure of his loss—but you will, if you don't save him.

As much as she was Foster's anchor, he was hers.

Those first six months in The Project, she felt unmoored, timid, a wreck of a girl. She clung to Lev like an accessory, trying desperately hard to get her feet under her and failing every single time. Recruiting Foster forced a steadiness in her that she never imagined herself capable of. She found total belonging in The Project's walls by becoming a space for Foster to belong.

And now she has to save him.

She has never been tasked with something so great. She goes to the farm, where she finds Foster working, cleaning out the barn. There'll be a public sermon soon. Casey says they'll have to think about getting a tent after this year. She expects after The Unity Center opens—they just closed the deal on a building in Morel—their numbers will continue to climb.

When Foster sees Bea, he stops what he's doing, bounds across the room and lifts her in his arms. She laughs, even as her brain tries to reconcile his joy with the utter despair she heard in his Attestation. To know this is bravado makes her ache.

He sets her down and asks her what she's doing there.

I'm here to help.

He smiles. *This work's too dirty for you.*

I just want to spend some time together.

His face turns red, the blush creeping from his neck to the tips of his ears. She takes a broom from the corner and begins to sweep. She doesn't know how to feel people out the way Lev does. Lev can look at anyone and know their trouble immediately and know exactly who he needs to be in response. She decides to borrow his words because there could be no better than his. After a long silence, she stops what she's doing and looks at Foster. His red hair catches the light coming in through the open door.

You came here a perfect soldier, she says softly. He stills and turns his head to her, curious. She swallows. *Your perfection is proof of my own.*

He exhales. She hears the quiver in his breath. He moves to her and presses his hands desperately, hungrily, against her face.

Then he presses his mouth to her mouth.

FEBRUARY 2018

The trip to Bellwood is especially gray today, the sky hung heavy with clouds threatening either rain or snow. I want rain, for the rain to melt the snow. I want the first signs of spring to make themselves known.

I want my bones to ache less.

Paul texts on my cab ride to the farm. *Could've handled myself better last week. Scheduled the apology I owe you for next time we're in the office.* I want it to satisfy me, but nothing will satisfy me until I've put Lev's profile on Paul's desk and he knows exactly what he's apologizing for. My fingers hover over my phone's keyboard, trying to think up the perfect reply. I leave him on read instead. I let my cabdriver get me close to the house and then I make my way up, shrugging my bag over my shoulders. Foster meets me at the door.

"Lev's upstairs, but he's resting."

I raise an eyebrow. "Resting?"

"He had a meeting last night," Foster replies. "Went late. He was supposed to be up by now, but if he's not, he needs it. I'll give it forty minutes."

I wonder what it's like to have people looking out for you like that, protecting your health, making sure you get enough sleep.

I glance up the stairs and listen for any sign of Lev, but there are none.

I hear Emmy humming to herself from the next room. I turn to it, but hesitate.

"You should talk to her," Foster says.

It's hard to imagine talking to her.

"I don't know what to say."

"Try to stay away from politics." His tone is halfway between amused and sympathetic. "Her favorite color is green. If she mentions a horsey, then she's talking about Atara." I raise my eyebrows and Foster laughs a little. "She heard someone say Atara was as big as a horse and that's . . . kids. She's afraid of 'grumbles,' which—I don't know if it's something you need to know—that's a thunderstorm. No clue where she got that from, though."

I swallow and nod.

"I'll give you some time alone," he says and I watch as he makes his way down the hall and slips outside. I follow Emmy's song to the living room, where she sits on the floor, drawing on a small whiteboard with markers. She stops when she sees me, stares with wide, wondering eyes—at my scar. Forever on my scar.

"Hi, Emmy."

"You're Lo," she says.

It sends a jolt through me, hearing my name in her voice. I can't remember the last time I heard a child say my name—if I've ever heard a child say my name. She's staring at me expectantly, like if I'm going to be in her presence, I better have a good reason.

"What are you drawing?" I ask.

"Circles," she says, the word somehow bigger than her mouth. I move closer to her and crouch down and I think she's made a generous assessment of her work, but I can appreciate the attempt. She forces a marker into my hand and asks me to draw more circles for her and I oblige, then she tells me, "Needs some hair."

"A circle with hair?"

She nods and draws clumsy lines in the circles, though I suspect she's aiming for the top. Her hands are so small, all five of her fingers curved around the body of the marker just to draw this unsteadily. There's something amazing about that to me—but I don't know why.

She looks at me and points to my cheek.

"What's that?"

It tumbles out so fast, eager and curious.

"It's a scar," I say, and she frowns. I can't tell if she understands or it's simply not the answer she wanted, so I try for a fumbling explanation.

"It's like . . . have you ever got hurt?"

She points triumphantly to her knee, which is perfectly fine.

"I got a green Band-Aid."

Her favorite color.

"Well, I got hurt but sometimes the hurt . . . it sticks around."

Her eyes widen. "It still hurts?"

Foster is still on the porch. I listen, and it's still quiet upstairs. I turn back to Emmy.

"Can I sit with you?"

She nods. "Draw me more circles, Lo!"

I draw her more circles in every color of marker that she has. Her eyes follow the motion of my hand, and then she tries, and fails, to mimic it.

"Do you remember how I'm Bea's sister?"

She thinks on it a minute and then shakes her head.

"You know Bea, though?"

She nods. Her tongue pokes out of her mouth as she gets to work decorating all the circles that I've drawn. I take my phone out of my pocket and swipe through the gallery until I find the picture I saved from Arthur's failed Facebook group. I tilt the screen to her, but she ends up ripping my phone from my hands.

"Jer'my."

She points to Jeremy. It shocks the hell out of me, that she'd recognize him. I clear my throat and I say, "Right, that's Jeremy. Where's Jeremy?"

"He's gone." She says this like it means nothing.

"Yeah . . ." I'm not about to ask her to elaborate, because the last thing I need to do is fuck up whatever understanding she has of death. I'd probably just end up traumatizing her with my luck. I point beside Jeremy. "Who's that?"

"Bea." She presses her pudgy finger against the screen.

The gallery disappears from the screen. I take the phone from her and pop it back open again, and Bea is there again, next to Jeremy. Living and dead. Both of them ghosts.

"Who's Bea?"

"My friend."

"Just your friend?"

"My friend," Emmy repeats.

I stare at Bea's picture.

I hate her for this.

I hate that she has a daughter who doesn't understand who her mother is—if she understands what a mother is at all—and I hate that I've spent the last six years of my life believing my sister was held hostage by people who took advantage of her pain. I hate that Bea made herself the author of all our narratives, twisting us into the characters that best served her purposes. I feel like a lie my sister told.

I don't want Emmy to be another.

I shove my phone back in my pocket.

"Can I tell you a secret, Emmy?"

Emmy scribbles across one of the circles. "Okay."

"Something just between you and me."

She stops coloring. "Okay."

"And you won't tell anyone? It's a big secret."

I glance toward the front of the room. I can make out Foster through a slit in the curtain covering the window. He doesn't seem like he's coming back in anytime soon. When I glance back at Emmy, I have her full attention. I guess four-year-olds know what secrets are.

"Bea is your mom." Emmy stares at me, and I don't know if she understands and I don't know what to reach for to make her understand. "Bea made you, Emmy. She's your mom. Do you know what a mom is?"

"Like Mommy Shark?" she asks.

"Uh . . ."

I don't know what the fuck that is.

"Emmy."

Her face brightens at the voice and my stomach crashes to my feet. I stand slowly and turn and Lev is in the hall, his arms crossed, watching us. I don't know how long he's been watching us. However much sleep he managed to get, it doesn't seem like it was enough. I've never seen him so unkempt: his clothes wrinkled, his face pinched with exhaustion.

"Emmy, go on into the kitchen for a minute."

She does as she's told, pausing at his side to give him a hug. He rests his hand lightly on her head and then she's gone. He stares at me for a long moment, and then asks in a voice I've never heard from him before: "What are you doing, Lo?"

"I thought she should know."

"You're just going to confuse her."

"She should know about Bea."

"She does."

"Yeah, Bea is her 'friend.'"

"I thought we talked about this," he says. "Emmy has everything she needs. She's never wanted for anything—"

"She doesn't know what's there *to* want," I interrupt. "And why does Bea get to decide that? Why do you? Why don't you look for Bea, why don't—"

"You think I just accepted this?" Lev steps into the room. "You think I wouldn't do everything in my power to make her see reason, to see the light, to come back and to embrace her daughter? Your sister was broken, Lo. Even God wasn't good enough for her—"

"Emmy still needs to know—"

"She needs to know what? Rejection? Absence? Wanting? Tell me how well those feelings have served you."

I flush. "That's not fair—"

"They've twisted you. You know they've twisted you."

"Maybe if someone had told me the fucking *truth*—"

"She's too young to understand that right now," Lev says sharply, and I suddenly realize he's seething and the only reason I didn't recognize it before was because he was working so hard to stay in control. "Why are you determined to inflict pain on a child?"

"I'm *not*—"

"Emmy is surrounded by love," Lev says over me. "I told you this. She has a father who loves her. She has countless members in The Project who all love her, who want her to be happy, who fill the gaps. I thought you understood and that it might inspire you to be brave enough to take this opportunity to fill those gaps in your own life . . . but now I see you just want to pull Emmy into your pain so you don't have to be so alone with it."

"Fuck you—"

"I won't let you poison my family."

"She's my family too!"

A small movement out of the corner of my eye: Emmy, clearly upset, cowering in the hall, the conversation itself so far beyond her years, but the anger driving it easy enough to parse at any age. She starts to cry and Lev goes to her, lifting her from the ground. Emmy buries her head into his shoulder and he rubs her back, soothing her from the nightmare that is me.

"I only ever asked you to write a profile," he tells me. "You need to leave."

The drive from the station back to Morel takes me past the cemetery. I watch it come up on my phone. I tell my cab-driver to stop, to let me out.

I stand outside the gate.

Bea buried our parents while I was unconscious. The consequence was an awful, unfinished feeling inside me; this faint belief that Mom and Dad could step through the door at any moment and tell me it was all a dream. Patty always tried to get me to visit, as though seeing the grave would help resolve the open-ended note Bea left me on, but I refused. Worse than the lingering expectation that my parents were still alive was the reality they were not.

I can't bring myself to step inside.

My phone rings, the sound awful, startling.

I dig into my pocket to answer it.

I want it to be Lev.

I want him to tell me he was wrong.

"Hello?"

The silence that greets me is crushing in its familiarity and the day has left me feeling so defeated, I can't even muster the will to disconnect. I just listen to the breathing on the other end of the line and then . . .

My grip tightens as a strange, sick thought takes hold of me.

". . . Bea?"

The breathing on the line pauses, electrifying me: confirmation. I close my eyes and tears immediately form, slipping down my face. I can sense her impending hang-up and I say, quickly, desperately, "Wait."

Silence.

"If it's you, stay on. Stay on the line. Please."

She doesn't hang up.

"Oh my God," I whisper.

I bring my free hand to my eyes, covering them.

"I miss you so much." As soon as the words leave my mouth, I'm crying in earnest, can't even hear her over the sounds of myself. I struggle to regain composure, quieting enough to be sure she's still on the line. For one terrifying second, there's nothing. "Bea?"

And then the relief of her breathing.

She's still there.

"Where are you?"

She doesn't respond. There's a small shuffle of sound; maybe she's holding her phone as tightly as I am mine, fingers going numb.

"Come back," I beg. "Please."

Still, nothing.

The absence of response is a weight I can barely breathe against. I believed—when I was younger, I always believed—once Bea was witness to my pain she would never be able to make herself the cause of it again. That I could finally be enough to make her stay.

"You told me . . . you told me Mom said being sisters was a promise no one but us could make and no one but us could break—remember? Do you remember that?" Still, nothing. I close my eyes. "So which is it, Bea?"

The breath on the line seems to hitch.

"Bea," I say again, desperate. "Which is it?"

And then, her voice.

For the first time in years—her voice.

"Good-bye . . ."

She hangs up.

2013

The first week after Lo regained consciousness, she would ask Bea the same question over and over:

Who am I?

Her voice was raspy and broken from the abuse of the ventilator, the lack of use, but the question was desperate and her eyes were wild, fearful, as she awaited Bea's answer.

Everything seemed to hinge on it.

You're Lo. You're my sister. You're thirteen years old. You've been in a wreck.

Lo would cry in response every single time.

It upset Bea. She wasn't comforted when the doctors told her Lo wasn't fully present yet, that it was unlikely she'd even remember asking the question. Bea suspected there was more to it than she could understand. Sometime after that, when Lo was much clearer, it happened again, but this time, her inquiry had changed slightly: *Who is this?*

Bea finally understands. As much as she didn't recognize Lo after the accident, it never occurred to her that Lo would not recognize herself. Other things about it dawn on her so far after the fact: how Lo would touch her fingers against her face, her scar, or look down at her body, perplexed. How, when Bea inevitably answered, *You're Lo,* it never seemed as if it was reaching her. Bea finally realizes that Lo couldn't—wouldn't—accept it. Eventually she stopped asking Bea the question, though Bea once overheard Lo quietly asking it to herself: *Who are you?*

Bea stands in the upstairs bathroom at the Garrett Farmhouse. She turns on the water, letting it run cold before splashing it over her face. She feels her skin tightening against the shock of it, feels her eyes open wide. She stares at her reflection in the mirror over the sink.

You're Bea, she says to it.

She can smell breakfast cooking in the kitchen. Bacon and eggs and slightly-burnt toast. She follows the scent downstairs and steps into the farmhouse's morning routine. Chapman House has a different sort of energy to it, it's more diffuse, free. At the Garrett Farm, there's less space and because of it, the way members move around and support each other in their daily tasks strikes her as something of a dance. It's so intimate, so personal, it takes her back to a time before the accident. Mom, Dad, her and Lo. The rituals they carved out in their small world.

How far they are from her now.

Good morning, Amalia greets her from the stove.

Bea moves to the kitchen window and looks outside. The ground is wet, muddy, the remains of last night's storm. It got so bad she couldn't drive home. The rain started moments after Foster kissed her. The sky opened up and she couldn't figure out whether or not it was God's command to her or a warning. She closes her eyes at the memory, how she could feel Foster realizing his mistake as soon as his lips met her own. How she could feel him slipping away from her for good. She had to make a choice.

Save him.

There was no choice.

When she opens her eyes, Foster has entered the room.

They sit at the table, ten of them in all, and hold hands ahead of the meal. Foster leads them in prayer. They bow their heads as he begins to speak. Bea keeps hers up and watches him. Halfway through, he senses her gaze, raising his head to meet her eyes.

We sacrifice ourselves in the name of spiritual service so that we may prove the perfect will of God, and blessed, he says to her, *are we, who endure temptation, for we will receive the crown of life, which Lev has promised to those who love the Lord.*

Who are you? Lev asks her that night, after she grasps him by the hand and leads him to their bedroom. She's on top of him. She wants to feel him. She wants to feel him against every part of her because he is God. She kisses him hard because she wants to taste God.

He asks, again, who she is.

She doesn't know how to respond. He likes it, he clarifies, but the woman who met him tonight is different than the girl who waited for him every night before; the one shyly seated on top of their bed, naked, her hair falling over her shoulders, tickling her collarbones, shivering with anticipation. Bea can't explain to him that she's more afraid now than she ever was when she was her. *Who were you?* suddenly feels like the more pertinent question.

Lev rests his hands against her hips and she runs her fingers up and down his arms, his strong arms, overwhelmed by how much his skin under her fingertips electrifies her, even still. He stares up at her. He sees no flaw in her. He quickly, carefully, puts her on her back and lets his hands roam her body, palming her breasts.

She thinks of Foster, his mouth grazing her neck, his skin

warm against her, yielding to his weight on top of her as the storm shook the world outside. It had been beautiful that morning, before Lev made her listen to Foster's Attestation, the sun a bright, burning star in the sky. She thinks of Foster, weeping against her, confessing his weakness, his love for her, his need to leave in the face of his love for her. He wanted to know her the way that Lev knew her and it was too painful for him to live in the shadow of that question. Losing Foster was not an option—losing anyone after Rob could not be an option—and so she asked him if he could know her like that for one night, would he stay? He said he couldn't do that to her but she'd gotten through to him in the end because what was it Lev said to them once?

Even the son of God did not come to be served, but to serve. He gave his life as ransom for many. Whatever you do for the least of my followers, you do for me.

She thought of that as she spread her legs.

Her body was ransom.

It was for Lev.

Weeks later, she volunteers to do the grocery shopping. She drives into town alone and moves through the aisles, filling the shopping cart robotically, methodically, distractedly, badly, forgetting the list, remembering the list, getting too much of some things and not enough of others. She stands at the checkout nervously, watching the cashier scanning and bagging every item and when she reaches the last, Bea says, *Wait, not this. I need this to be separate.*

She puts Casey's credit card away and pays with her own cash and says she doesn't want a receipt. After she loads up the van, she drives to the coffee shop two streets over and when she walks inside, she orders a hot chocolate and while they make it she goes into the bathroom with that one item she needed to be separate, that she paid for by herself.

She knows. She knows before she takes the test, before the faint pink line anchors her irrevocably to the present along with every other choice she made that brought her to it. She presses one hand against her womb, the other to her heart.

Who is this? she wonders.

FEBRUARY 2018

It starts raining on my way back to my apartment. I'm almost there when I realize I don't want to be there, that I don't want its silence, its emptiness, to be the culmination of everything I've been through today. I claim the busyness of the streets, pretending it's mine until I can't pretend anymore and then, when I pass *SVO,* I notice the lights in the office are on and I decide I'm going to cash in on Paul's apology now because if there's anything I need out of today, it's for someone to say they're sorry to me.

I cross the road and head up, shivering in the aftermath of the downpour, water trailing behind me. I stop outside the door, staring at the main floor through its window.

I don't see Paul.

I slip inside, tiptoeing my way across the room. Half-way to my desk, I hear the low murmur of voices from his open office, and it's only now I realize I could be walking in on something relating to whatever secret thing Paul's been working on. But if he didn't want anyone here to witness it, he would've sent out a memo. I round the edge of my desk and what remains of my world falls away from me.

Paul and Lauren.

Lauren, pressed against the wall of his office, Paul pressed against her. Her arms wrapped around him, her fingers death-gripping his back, dug into his shirt, his shirt loose around his waist, his belt open, her leg hitched around him as he thrusts into her, her eyes closed as they fuck. The view of the river, the pouring rain outside.

Witnessing this strips me of any sense of dignity I had or felt I had working here. The place and my place in it shifting before my eyes. What kind of fool was I, thinking my determination to be made real in this world by uncovering its truth would be more than Paul could ever deny. I don't even know if I'm relieved now, that all he ever saw when he looked at me was his assistant—or mortified that all he ever saw when he looked at me was his assistant.

My hand is on my scar without my realizing it.

I take a clumsy step back and Lauren's eyes fly open, meeting mine, and she exclaims, "Oh, *shit*," and starts extricating herself *from our boss* and when I see Paul fumble off of her, clearly knowing he's been caught, if not by who, I turn away. I head to my desk and start opening drawers. I don't keep a lot here, but I grab what I don't want to leave behind because I am more certain of this than I've been of anything lately: I am not coming back.

"Denham," Paul says as I'm shoving things into my bag, and hearing his voice turns my stomach. I can't make myself look him in the eyes. "Denham, it's not—" I slam one of the drawers shut, beyond words, shaking with rage. "Christ, Denham, will you look at me—"

I look at him and he stares at me, his shirt hanging around him, pants buttoned at least, belt still undone. Lauren is a blurry form in the background.

A little advice from a former assistant.

"I quit," I say and Lauren says, *Lo, come on.*

The shame permeating the room feels disproportionately

mine. I hate that I saw them like this. I hate them seeing me like this. I never want to see them again.

"Denham," Paul says at my back as I leave.

At my apartment, I take off my shoes and jacket, leaving them in a wet pile on the floor. I keep the light off, stripping out of my clothes as I make my way into the bathroom, where I study the silhouette in the mirror over the sink. The face and scar kept to shadow, the tangled outline of rain-soaked hair. If she's no sister, no daughter, no writer—no more than her accident—who is she? What's left? I press both of my palms flat against the glass and I wait and I wait, but she never tells me who she is.

2013

Bea misses her mother.

There are so many questions she never thought to ask her. Everything that's happening to her now was supposed to happen to her years from now, and in that vision of the future her mother was alive, the wisdom of two children behind her to assure Bea that, yes, *this is how it's supposed to feel. This is all how it's supposed to feel.*

There's nothing Bea has been through that compares to being pregnant. Time marches forward and she measures it in symptoms of life. The exhaustion that comes with the making of it. She sleeps and sleeps just to have enough energy to open her eyes in the morning. She crawls from her bed and moves through the day, awake, by sheer force of will alone. And then there's the morning sickness that doesn't just occur in the morning, and doesn't always end in the relief of vomiting, but follows her throughout the day, keeping her on the brink of tears because she can't remember what it feels like to feel well.

There's a grief she didn't expect and doesn't know how to put to words. She never got a chance to say good-bye to herself. She stares at her body, naked in the mirror, and she's sorry she never made note of it before it belonged to anyone else. She can feel all the ways this child has claimed her even if not all of it is visible yet. She knows it's there and that's enough. She wants to go back in time and really *see* herself before its conception. The flatness of her stomach, the soft curve of her breasts, all of her only, gloriously, her own. Her breasts hurt all the time and she finds herself obsessing over their future function.

She heard a heartbeat. Lev was there, his hand wrapped around hers. She thought that was the part that would make it real, but staring at the ultrasound screen, watching the soundwaves jump as the hectic rhythm filled the room—it sounded strange, like a message from some far-off planet, distorted by the space it had traveled through to reach her.

Lev comes in when she's studying herself in the mirror. As soon as she sees his reflection join hers, she moves to cover herself up.

Don't, he says, and she stands still as he walks to her and they witness her body and the miracle forming within it, together. She breathes slowly in and out, willing her heart to be calm. He reaches forward, putting his hands on her shoulders, then traces his fingertips over her collarbone. She shivers. He leans forward, bringing his mouth to her neck and he kisses her neck, whispers against her neck: *You're beautiful.*

He rounds her, lowering himself slowly to his knees and rests his head against her stomach and she brings her hands to his head, running her fingers through those curls that she loves so much, feeling a guilty knot in her throat.

Thank you, Lev whispers, *for what you have so fearfully and wonderfully made with me.*

Casey takes care of the details of Bea's pregnancy with such efficiency, Bea wonders if, in another life, she's been through this before. She schedules and drives Bea to all of her appointments—Lev only has time for the milestones, but

Bea thinks she prefers it that way—sits in the office with her, offers her hand when Bea needs something to hold. At some of her checkups, the doctors think the two of them are a couple. Bea doesn't bother to correct them.

She runs into Foster at Chapman once. He's leaving the Reflection Room at the same time she turns the corner, both stopping short at the sight of the other. He'd asked her, as soon as word was out, if the baby was his.

It can only be Lev's, was her answer and he'd accepted it.

He is the first to pass.

The next time she's at an appointment, she asks the doctor what the odd feeling she sometimes gets in her stomach is, tiny frantic wings. She doesn't think it's nerves, though she's nervous all the time. The doctor stares at her with some amusement and tells her that's the baby. *It's fluttering.* Bea is so struck by this, by these unexpected first movements—she had envisioned something much more obvious and at the hands and feet.stage—she asks to hear the heartbeat again, and this time, alone and without Lev, Casey in the waiting room, she cries. She thinks of what her mother told her all those years ago when Lo was born. She thinks that if being a sister is a promise you make, then being a mother must be a promise that you *are.* And for the first time since Bea found out she was pregnant, it's a promise she wants to be.

She wakes up to a damp bed.

Her body warms with embarrassment as she tries to figure out how she'll explain this to Lev, the first real indignity of her impending motherhood. She pushes the sheets back and is shocked when she sees all the red. She doesn't understand it at first and then, horrifyingly, she does: blood. It's blood.

She's aware of other things; the dull ache in her abdomen.

She slips out of bed carefully without disturbing Lev and tiptoes, covered in her own blood, to the shower. She strips out of her clothes. She can't look at her body in the mirror. She turns the water on as hot as it will go. Lev finds her there, curled up under the spray, sobbing. He steps inside with his clothes on to turn the water off and then wraps her in a towel. He helps her to dress because she is so overcome with grief, everything else feels too abstract to understand, let alone execute: the simple act of dressing. The simple act of walking out of the house. He leaves a note for Casey on the desk, the bloody sheets still on their bed, and drives Bea to the hospital. She watches him from the passenger's side. His face is pale and his jaw is set. She's still bleeding, can feel herself bleeding. She hates that she can feel it, this failure of her body, which up until this point did exactly what it was supposed to do.

God will keep this soul, Lev promises her.

This will be cold, the doctor warns her, smoothing the gel across her womb ahead of the ultrasound. She squeezes her eyes shut and wishes she could disappear.

But there's a heartbeat.

Lev holds her hand the whole ride home.

She can still feel herself bleeding. She's on pelvic rest. She should not lift heavy things. She presses her hand to her stomach and she thinks about the ultrasound. The small perfect shape of her baby, its heartbeat, and just there next to it—a stain.

FEBRUARY 2018

At the first hint of sunrise, I head to Chapman House.

I give them no warning, fumbling through the process of leaving the Poughkeepsie station on my own and then paying a stupid amount of money for the taxi that delivers me from civilization. The driver asks, doubtfully, if I'm allowed to be where I say I want to go. She lets me off at the road up, and I walk the rest of the way. The house seems even bigger, more impressive, meeting it on foot. When I reach the front door, I stand there, a dull whine in my head, wondering what will happen when Lev finds me on the other side. He may have told me to leave but he didn't tell me I couldn't come back.

I knock on the door.

No one meets me.

This possibility didn't occur to me. So many people live here, Casey works here—I thought there'd be someone. I round the house to the windows at the back and peer inside. The Great Room is empty, the lights off. Footsteps have been crushed through the freshly fallen snow leading from the door, interrupting the pristine landscape.

They ghost the path to the lake.

I decide to follow them.

The pines creak, rocking slowly in the wind, and the farther down the path I walk, the more I think about what Casey said about being alone with God out here, and I wonder if that means she experiences a deeper silence—or a richer one.

When the trees begin to thin, I hear voices ahead.

I slow my pace.

The lake comes into view, and I stay just inside the trees, cloaked in the cover they offer. There are two people near the water's edge and I don't know what to make of what I'm looking at, not at first. Lev. He's wearing a Henley, jeans, no coat. If I'm cold—and I am—he has to be freezing, but I'm too far from him to tell. There's another person next to him, a man, similarly underdressed. I spot Foster standing guard nearby. I inch forward, biting my lip. Lev and the man face the water with a certain kind of resolve, just enough to allow me to guess what might be about to happen.

And then it does.

My body seizes as they walk into the freezing lake. I flinch when the man yells as his body makes contact. I swear to God I can feel it, the awful, sickening burn of the water against my skin. Lev makes no sound. My pulse thrums in my ears at the sheer impossibility of that, of Lev's utter calm as he's enveloped by the lake, holding the man upright as he slowly collapses.

How does he not feel it?

Lev begins to speak. I can't make out the words from here but his voice is as steady as a single sustained note of a song before falling away and making space for the man to echo the note back to him, a pale, more fractured imitation.

And then Lev eases him bodily into the water.

I stop breathing as soon as the man goes under and I resolve not to take a breath until he resurfaces. My heart pounds in my chest, and then my head. Black dots pattern in front of my eyes. I exhale; I have to breathe. The man stays under. Fear presses down on me and I feel my hand slowly reach for my pocket, my phone.

What if this isn't a baptism?

And then Lev lets him up. It's violent, the sound of the man's choking coughs filling the air, but once he settles, he goes still beside Lev in the way Lev is still, as though he doesn't feel the cold now either. Maybe he's so shocked, he can't.

The man falls into Lev's arms and after a long moment of only holding him, the two make their way back to the shore, to Foster. When they reach Foster, they share the burden, supporting the man carefully between them as they continue forward.

The man sobs.

Their return to the house will put them directly in my path and I know I shouldn't be found. I assess my surroundings. I can't take the obvious route to Lev's cabin, but if I cut through the trees, keeping left, I should eventually come across it. I move as quietly as I can over the snow, have only just made it past the point of discovery when I hear Foster, Lev and the man in the space I just stood. The man is saying *thank you* over and over again.

I resist looking back, though all I want to do is look back, and continue pushing ahead until I'm finally rewarded with Lev's cabin.

Its front door opens for me. I let myself inside and take off my boots. It's halfway between warm and cool in here; Lev must have been in not so long ago with the fire lit. If he was in here working, there are no hints of that work left behind. I take off my coat and sit on the bed in the corner and lean forward, my head in my hands. I may not believe in God, but I don't move through the world with my eyes closed. I know what sacraments are and stripped of all the trappings and history and performance of church—Lev and the man, the water, the trees around them—made it all seem more real somehow. I think of Lev out there, in the water, perfectly still and untouched by the cold and it makes me wonder if that's what faith shields you from, if that's only one of the things that faith might make possible, and I'm suddenly, painfully aware of my own teeth chattering, my numb and aching joints, the shivers moving across my skin.

2014

The baby, a girl, comes too soon.

There's supposed to be more calendar pictures to go.

The birth happens so quickly, Bea can't even recall it in any specific detail. Her body is traumatized. She tore. She's stitched up and sore. The blurred sights and sounds of the delivery room could not take form over the roar of blood rushing in Bea's ears as it happened. Then that sudden, pronounced absence in her body and the flood of euphoria at what it signified: that she had brought something into being. Bea doesn't know if she'll ever feel so powerfully complete in her life again. She knew better than to wait for that first moment of skin-to-skin contact, but she waited for it anyway. All she wanted was her daughter pressed against her chest, to share heartbeats. She's still waiting.

She remembers Mom and Dad telling her the NICU was a special place when Lo was born; *It's because she couldn't wait to get here and see you.* But it's not a special place. It's a special kind of hell where the waxen, devastated faces of new parents stand over incubators to witness firsthand the fragility and unfairness of life. (She can't stand to think of the ones luckier than her.) To see a baby made more helpless by the universe than the universe has already made it is so profoundly wrong. The memories of Lo's birth drive home to Bea how far away her family truly is. No one in the waiting room shares her blood or her name. She thinks of her mother, thinks of herself tucked against her mother's breasts, her mother's arms around her, and she craves it so badly she has to find a bathroom to cry in. She wants her mother. She is a mother. Her milk hasn't come in.

Lev commands Foster to the hospital to help navigate the doctors and the nurses, the language they speak. Once Foster has talked to them, he privately pulls Bea aside and gives her his own diagnosis: the baby has to be his. No child of Lev Warren's would arrive in this world with so many complications. No child of Lev Warren's would enter life on the brink of death. What they did was poison, and it has poisoned the child. The baby needs to be cleansed of their sins or they will lose her forever.

Now that Bea has a daughter, she can't bear the thought of a world without her.

We have to tell him, Foster says.

But Bea can't bear the thought of that either.

What are you calling her? the nurse asks because no one should die without a name.

While Foster confesses to Lev, Bea goes to the hospital chapel where no one is, the journey comprised of one halting step in front of the other until it comes to an abrupt end. She collapses in front of the altar and the cross, pulled down by the weight of her grief, and she weeps. The last time she made an appeal to God, she was a child and now she is a mother. It's a mother's job to be strong for her child.

God, she begs with all the strength in her heart.

And then He appears.

When Bea raises her face, Lev's is in shadows. Her betrayal radiates off of him and it breaks her heart because she loves him, there is no man she loves more than him, and what she did with Foster was out of love for and devotion to him but she knows beyond any doubt that Lev will never see it that way.

And she knows now, that she would do it all over again just to be Emmy's mother.

Emmanuelle. French. God is with us.

Lust, Lev says moving to her, *when it has conceived, bears sin. And the sin, when it is grown, produces death.* He pauses, and he looks at her as though she is a stranger. *I upheld you like no other. You have betrayed me like no other.*

She bows her head.

I opened your eyes to glory, I brought your sister back from the dead, and in all that you have seen, in all that I have given you, you've still turned your back on me and now—now you have the audacity to ask me to sanctify this child that isn't mine?

He crouches in front of Bea, brings his hand to her chin, makes her look him in the eyes.

I'm sorry, she whispers.

God loves you. But for whom God loves, He corrects.

Tears spill down her face.

Will you suffer your way back to me, Bea? To save your daughter?

I'll do anything, she whispers.

He tells her to stand.

FEBRUARY 2018

There's still time, Bea whispers as she crawls into my hospital bed. She reaches her hand out, and wraps it tightly around mine. *I promise.*

I wake with a small gasp, a hummingbird's heart. I press my palm against my chest, trying to calm down. It takes me a moment to get my bearings.

Lev's cabin.

I'd curled up on his bed and closed my eyes, the clean scent of him against the pillow sending me to sleep. He's here in the room with me now, sitting at the desk, his hand against his chin as he works quietly on his laptop. It's one of those strangely dissonant moments where it almost feels like the life inside is real, yours, and before you can decide how you feel about that, it all fades away. Lev exhales and rubs his eyes, then turns his head in my direction, sees that I'm awake. Behind him, the window over the sink lets in no light; it's night. The fire crackles from the middle of the room.

It's warm in this room.

"You're very restless," he says, his eyes trailing over his blankets twisted around my legs. "I can't help but wonder if you ever wake up feeling like you slept at all."

I sit up slowly, untangling the blankets. I pull my knees toward myself, wrapping my arms around them. *No,* I want to tell him. *Never.* At least not in the last six years. But my voice is somewhere beyond me now, tired of asking questions my heart doesn't really want the answers to. I press my head against my legs, turning my face to him.

"Emmy's been asking for you. She said you drew good circles," he says. I close my eyes. So that was the only thing that stuck. Circles. He pauses. "I gave you no ground rules with her. That error was mine. I didn't handle myself well, Lo. I apologize." I open my eyes. "It's hard for me too. Emmy isn't the only one your sister left."

"Even God wasn't good enough for her," I say, my voice rough and worn at the edges from sleep. "Do you hate her?"

"I only feel gratitude."

"Gratitude."

"She gave me a daughter."

"Do you hate your mother?"

He shakes his head. "No. She made me what I am."

It puts a certain shame in me. That Lev, a brutalized child, could grow into a man who has any forgiveness in his heart and here I am, made so bitter by my own losses and their aftermath, I can't imagine what it would be like to offer forgiveness to anyone.

"How did she die?"

"She burned. A house fire. A lit cigarette."

I think about the smattering of dotted scars across his torso, how poetic it makes her end, and how hollow a victory that really is.

"Emmy *is* your family," he says. "And if you want to be here, as her family, to see her—your niece—I want you to know you're welcome."

I swallow hard, trying to maintain composure in the face of this offering. *Your niece.* This is the first time I've ever heard anyone claim Emmy as any part of me and I can feel the true extent of how much I craved it, and feared it, and how much I still fear it, but want it—now that it's been given. My heart can hardly make sense of finally being handed something I want and it's too much. I bury my head in my knees, my shoulders shaking. Lev crosses the room and rests his hand at the base of my neck. I almost curl away from it, from the shame it inspires, the weakness it reveals.

"I'm—"

"Don't," he says firmly, "apologize."

He lowers his hand and some part of me wishes it was still there. He moves away and some part of me wishes he was still close. He heads to the sink, reaching for a glass on the counter, and fills it with water and then returns it to me. I take a sip and then I set it on the floor. I sit up properly, my legs over the edge of the bed, keeping my eyes on my feet, his.

"Yesterday . . . I was going to ask you about the jumper on the Mills Bridge. I wanted to know what you said to her to keep her alive."

"I told her God saw her suffering and believed in her," he says.

"What's it like to hear God? What does it really feel like?"

"It's incredibly painful."

His answer takes the breath out of me. I can see it in his eyes, how much it hurts him.

"God has trusted me with his work," Lev continues, "and for all I do in the name of it, I will always fall short. I live in my failures more than you know."

"What are your failures?"

"I could not keep your sister. I could not keep Jeremy. The woman who stepped down from the Mills Bridge eventually found another. Every person who comes to a sermon and leaves and doesn't come back. God is perfect so these shortcomings can only be my own." He pauses. "Can I ask you something, Lo?"

"Yes."

"What's it like to not hear God?"

I think of the baptism, the man breaking past the surface of the water. The light that seemed to surround him. Before, I wouldn't have considered an absence of answer a lack of one, but now I'm not so sure.

"I've liked talking to you for the profile," he says, knowing that his question is one I'll never be able to give adequate response. "I feel the strength of my convictions when I talk to you. It's nice to be reminded of that. To have a space to share it."

"It won't be *SVO*."

Lev gives me a curious look, and there must be something in my eyes because he asks me, concerned, what's happened, what *could* have happened in the time since we saw each other last. Despite everything, I tell him. I tell him about what Paul did and more—how I was never actually working on something for *SVO* until Lev handed it to me and even then, it was never guaranteed—that I just thought I was good enough to make it happen.

Lev's quiet for a long time.

"The profile doesn't need *SVO*," he finally says. "*SVO* needed it. You could take it anywhere, Lo. *The Times, Time, The New Yorker* . . . Casey has many contacts. We can make this happen, you and me. Give it the audience we deserve." I look up at him and there's nothing in his face that tells me I shouldn't believe him. "Bea said you loved to write."

"She wasn't wrong."

"Why?"

The question overwhelms me, brings more tears to my eyes because the moment he asks it is the moment I realize no one has ever asked me before.

Not even Paul.

"After the accident, I realized if I'd died, it wouldn't have meant anything and I—" My voice cracks and he looks like he wants to argue, but I stop him because if I don't say this now, I might never. "And I haven't felt . . . anything since then." I swallow. "If you tell a story—something real, something *true*—you get to be alive in other people. And writing feels like the most . . . the greatest chance I'll ever have at being—alive."

He crouches in front of me and wraps his hands tightly around my own, pulling them close to his chest. The look in his eyes is as intense as it is tender, and I can't remember anyone ever looking at me this way before, and it makes me ache.

"What if I told you that you were already more alive in other people than you know?" he asks quietly. "Alive in more people than you ever thought you would be?"

"I don't know what you mean."

"Haven't you ever wondered why everyone here knows who you are?"

"I'm Bea's sister."

He shakes his head, his grip on my hands tightening.

"Who am I?" I whisper.

"You're my miracle."

"What?"

"The girl I brought back to life."

"What? No."

I twist my hands from his, my pulse frantic, and get to my feet. He moves aside as I cross the room to the door, but I don't know where I could go. There's nowhere else to go.

There's only here.

I press my forehead to the door as it hits me, dizzy. I close my eyes to keep the room still, and sense him moving closer, his voice soft, filling the space between us.

"I was there with you," he says. "Your sister brought me to you. You were at the edge of the world and death was all around you. God saw a greater purpose in you and told me to bring you back. And I put my hands to you and I did."

I turn from the door, opening my eyes, and he stands in front of me, as though—

As though he were only a man.

"All this time, I thought it was God's gift to Bea and I couldn't understand why she would reject it, but now I think I know. You weren't God's gift to her . . ."

He pushes my hair from my face so he can see all of me before bringing his palms to my cheeks, and my legs go weak, my head filling with sense memories, finally understanding what my body has been trying to tell me all along. The hospital, the darkness hovering at the edges. The man at the end of my bed . . . I can see it now, I can see him so clearly now I don't know how I ever mistook him as a nightmare.

I reach for his wrists, gripping them tight. He hesitates and then leans forward until his forehead is just shy of touching my own. His eyes pose a question that everything inside me, in this moment, wants to and is too afraid to answer.

"You were His gift to me," he finishes.

I let his wrists go and reach for him, letting my fingers trail the edge of his jaw before moving up, pausing at his lips before I open my palm and press it against the curve of his face. He turns to it, his mouth against my hand, a fever against my skin, and it sends a current all through me, makes the little distance between us suddenly so unbearable that I fix it in the only way I know how: I bring my hand to the base of his neck and I pull him close until my mouth is against his mouth. His lips are soft. I part them with my tongue. His breathing quickens, my own. He brings his fingers to the edge of my shirt and lifts it over my head, lets it drop to the floor. He exhales and steps back and everything that has ever been between us becomes nothing and everything else falls away. He presses himself against me, his mouth to my ear.

"There is no flaw in you," he whispers.

PART FOUR

2017

Her daughter doesn't know her name.

Emmy knows *Bea,* of course, knows the woman who makes the funny faces at her until she laughs so hard she's clutching her stomach and rolling around on the floor, the woman who makes her breakfast and introduced her to the untold wonders of ketchup, the woman who waves to her from every distance, near or far, upon the day's first sight and last, but Emmy does not know *mom, mother, mama.*

Sometimes Bea wakes up in the middle of the night, thinking she's heard the call, the response of her body so unconsciously primal—but she will never hear it. This is the cost of Lev laying his hands on Emmy, of bringing her from the edge of death to life.

This is the cost of Bea's sin.

Emmy has been alive for nearly three years. And in those years, she has grown into the most curious, vibrant beautiful little girl.

Those rare and precious nights Bea can steal away from Lev, those nights he's worked himself to the bone and the deepest part of sleep claims him, she creeps back to the house and stands over Emmy's bed, watching her breathe in and out. She whispers softly to her.

Mom . . . mother . . . mama . . .

It never seems to take.

It's such a small price to pay, Bea tries to tell herself. She would have died a hundred, thousand, million times for her daughter, if Lev had asked it of her. And he, in all his benevolence, did not ask it of her.

It's only lately that she wishes he had.

MARCH 2018

The absence of warmth, of Lev, against me.

I open my eyes. The bed is cold, blankets rumpled at the end of it. I roll over slowly and find him standing in the middle of the cabin. The early morning light cuts across his face, turning his skin beautifully golden as he stares at his phone.

I whisper his name and he doesn't respond.

His eyes stay on his phone. His silence is unsettling and I ease out of bed carefully, my bare feet cold against the cold floor. I stand in front of him, naked, soft shivers running over my skin. I want to be warm again; I want him warm against me again. I press my hand against his face, tilting it toward me.

Something is wrong.

He hands me his phone and abruptly walks out of the cabin, closing the door behind him. I turn to the screen and find *SVO*'s website there, its logo leading the latest headline.

I stop breathing.

INSIDE THE UNITY PROJECT: BRUTAL RITUALS, PHYSICAL AND EMOTIONAL ABUSE DEFINES LIFE INSIDE ONE OF UPSTATE NEW YORK'S MOST BELOVED ORGANIZATIONS.

My thumb scrolls the article, trying to make sense of the words.

SVO has a policy of the extremely judicious use of
anonymous sources . . .

The information we've presented to you has been
verified . . .

The op-ed you are about to read was written by
someone intimately familiar with the inner workings of
The Unity Project, who cannot be named . . .

I go to Lev. He turns to me, all of me unclothed, freezing in
the early morning air.

His eyes travel over my body while my eyes study his face
and I feel I'm seeing more of him than I ever have, the boy
he was, the one who stood at the mercy of his mother's anger,
who suffered it, who suffered every day of his life and still
managed to find a world worth saving in spite of it.

He was only a boy.

"You don't believe it," he says. "Do you."

I press my hands against his face, refusing to let the lies of
the op-ed fill what little space there is between us.

He tells us to stand.

I tell him I only believe in things I can see.

The last seventy-two hours have been a waking nightmare. *SVO*'s op-ed topped the national trending topics on Twitter for twenty-four hours. The public response has bordered on theatre of the absurd. The AP picked it up. *Vice* is having a field day. The NYC media has dug in, staking out all three Unity Centers, discouraging the cold and hungry from seeking food and shelter in hopes for a statement from any Project members who just want to get past them to help those who need it the most. Casey begins fielding calls from Project connections—counselors, doctors, mentors, educators and on and on—who are worried about guilt by association because no one has any strength of conviction anymore.

But Lev says this was always the world The Unity Project was up against.

I stand quietly outside of Casey's office, listening as they map the fallout, of their directives for members in terms of navigating the press (say nothing), what they'll do about the spring outreach initiatives they've planned, whether to wait for the worst of this to pass—*if* it will pass—or if those things are lost to them now.

Paul keeps texting me, asking me what I thought and congratulating me as though I had anything to do with it. He wants to meet with me, to talk. He has things to say he thinks I'll want to hear. I don't answer him.

Lev is choosing silence, more now than he ever has, and

maybe if this was another *Vice* piece, he could get away with it—but I've seen movements live and die on social media. Once it gets its hooks in like this, the window for recovery closes fast.

"You need to issue a press release," I say, letting myself into the room because I can't stand it anymore. They look at me. "A wholesale denial."

"It would only be seen as an admission of guilt," Casey replies. "The problem with the op-ed is there was just enough truth in it that we can't totally refute it. Yes, we have a Reflection Room. We don't record Attestations, we don't use them as collateral to prevent members from leaving—it's no different than Catholic confession. Yes, we have meetings where we hold each other accountable and work as a group to resolve conflict, but we don't *abuse* each other. Right now, the most frequently used search keywords alongside The Unity Project are *Peoples Temple, Jonestown, Dust and Stars, Haven* and *Branch Davidians*. This discourse leaves no room for nuance. We'd gain nothing from stepping into it now."

"Well, what if I still wrote my profile, like a counter-perspective? You need someone to be the voice of every bad thing everyone's thinking about The Unity Project—but who changed their mind. That's *me*. Like what Monica Lewinsky's *Vanity Fair* piece did for her or what *I, Tonya* did for Tonya Harding. You only need to redeem The Project in the public's eyes and—"

"*I* am the Redeemer." The sharpness of Lev's voice startles me, makes me flinch. He gives me an apologetic look, softening. "I won't seek redemption when I have done nothing wrong. I answer to God, Lo, and for that, God will keep us."

I stare out the window beyond Casey's desk, the pines

eerie silhouettes against the night sky and somewhere beyond them, the lake. I rub my forehead.

"I just don't understand why someone would do this to you."

"The op-ed was designed to stigmatize us enough to cease God's work. Without the work, there is no Project," Lev says. "This place is a Kingdom . . . it's only natural someone would want to claim it for themselves or, failing that, destroy what they cannot claim."

"We need a retraction," Casey says. "That's the only thing that could resolve this."

Her phone rings. We watch as she picks up and gives clipped answers to whoever is on the other end of the line, at whatever is being said, and then her face loses what little color it had left. She hangs up and stares blankly at nothing.

Lev moves to her. "Casey?"

"Arthur Lewis is suing us," she says.

Lev excuses himself and leaves her office, slamming the door behind him. I turn back to Casey, as much at a loss as she is. Her face crumples and she buries her head in her hands. She starts to cry. I feel the weight of her anxiety in the pit of my gut and no small amount of my own. Six months ago, I never thought this place could be something good for me, let alone the only good thing—and now . . .

She lowers her hands and takes a deep breath, reaching for any amount of composure she can grasp. After a long moment, she says, "It shouldn't surprise me."

"What do you mean?" I ask.

"That all this finally happened. Whenever there's anything good in the world, people just want to take it away. When there's something pure, they want to pervert it." She wipes at her eyes. "The Project holds up a mirror to the world's's failures and the world's response is to break the mirror. We exist in spite of the world, Lo, not because of it."

Certain things must remain untouched by this.

Emmy's bedtime is one of those things. I'm part of her ritual now, inserted myself by insisting I needed to say good night because *she* needed the promise of my being there in the morning—but maybe it's more that I want that promise from her.

We sit in the chair in the corner of her room and she stands on my lap, running her stubby little fingers along the spines of the picture books on the shelf behind me before picking one and settling in against me. I'm hoping she won't feel my tension. I hope she won't hear the waver in my voice as I read to her. I hope she won't notice my shaking hands.

At first, I was self-conscious about doing this, letting the stories die on my lips in all my awkwardness, but now I try to make them come alive for her the best I can and am rewarded with the funny, strange and unexpected questions each page inspires. She reminds me of me. I used to walk around as a kid brimming with questions my mouth was too afraid to ask. The difference, though, is Emmy isn't afraid to ask them. That, she gets from Bea. Sometimes I quiz her on what we're reading. *What character is this? What color is that?* And she answers and she gets all the answers right because she's listening to me and every time I stop to consider this, it's overwhelming. She loves when I tell her she's right. I love it too. I'm making memories with her, stitching myself into the fabric of her life.

I refuse to let a single shadow infringe on her light.

"Tomorrow," Emmy says, slipping off my lap, "I'm going to draw."

"Yeah?" I put the book back. "What are you going to draw?"

"CREEPY UNDERWEAR!"

She cackles, no doubt inspired by what we just read.

"What's this about creepy underwear?" Lev asks, stepping inside the room.

She starts telling him about their eerie green glow but he interrupts her, scooping her into his arms, airplaning her around—to her total delight—before crash-landing her among her pillows. He pulls the blankets out from under her and then tucks her in. She has a nightlight in the corner because, just like I was at her age, she's afraid of the dark.

"See you tomorrow?"

My voice cracks, in spite of myself. Lev notices. She doesn't.

"Tomorrow!" She nods.

"Settle down," Lev says, sitting at the edge of her bed. I make my way slowly out of the room, listening to his good night to her. I've memorized it. *Peace . . .*

"Peace I leave with you. Peace I give to you. So lay down and sleep . . ." There is no hint of the last few days in his voice. He keeps it from her, makes sure all the ugliness outside doesn't get in. I don't know how he does it. It's all I feel as I close the door behind me, just as he finishes the prayer: "You'll wake, for God sustains you."

He emerges from Emmy's room to find me crying, trying not to suffocate under the weight of all these future losses when I've barely survived the ones of my past. He looks at me, his face full of concern. I tell him I want to join The Project.

"Oh, Lo," he says, and pulls me to him.

Arthur is unlikely to win his wrongful death suit, but there's something deeply compelling about a devastated father showing up on TV, his tie askew, holding a photo of his dead son, lamenting their lack of reconciliation, the years that have been stolen from them, saying that he knew it all along, he knew we were bad. It's gasoline, thrown on the fire. Jeremy was pushed to the brink in The Unity Project, forced to witness and endure untold atrocities that put him in the path of an oncoming train. I know how compelling Arthur is because when he sat across from me in McCray's, I believed him.

It inspires a whole new series by *Vice*; anyone who has ever circled Project space—especially those who attended public sermons—has a story to tell.

The public thinks we are monsters.

The press asks Governor Cuomo his feelings about the "cult" operating out of upstate New York. One by one, The Unity Center's connections cut ties. MURDERERS is slashed across the center in Morel in crude red paint, and as the world continues to ask Lev to answer for his crimes, he holds fast to the fact he has committed none. He will offer no explanation and settle for no less than a retraction.

But to get the retraction, he needs the name.

My heart pounds as I slip into the Reflection Room. Atara tries to follow me in, and I *shoo* her down the hall before closing the door behind me. After a long afternoon of quietly roaming the halls, I discovered this is the only other place in the house my cell gets any bars. I stand near the window and I call Paul. He picks up on the third ring. The familiarity of his voice makes me sick. I can almost hear the victory in it and I can imagine how he looks right now, unkempt in the way he gets unkempt when everything good is happening and he can't quite keep up with himself. It wouldn't surprise me if he was sleeping in the office, trying to stay on top of the glow and basking in it as much as possible.

"Denham," he greets me and I almost don't know who that is anymore. "Thanks for calling back. I haven't seen you around town and I've kept my eye out . . . you hiding?"

"It doesn't matter where I've been."

My anger quiets him. I tighten my grip on the phone.

"You're right," he says after a moment. "Believe me, I'm well aware that any amount of time you're willing to give me is more than I deserve."

"Way more than you deserve." I pause. "How is it over there?"

"Intense." But he can't mask his satisfaction. This is Paul in his element, Paul with his hooks in, Paul with his teeth dug into the bone. "Incredible. I'm sure you saw it was the nationally trending topic on Twitter. Stayed in the top five for twenty-four hours. Crashed the website more than once. And now with Arthur . . . this thing's going strong. I'm connecting with CNN this afternoon. It's a big moment for *SVO* and every time I step into the office, I keep thinking you should've been a part of it."

I stare out the window, at the gray sky outside.

"And whose fault is that?"

"You didn't have to quit on the spot," he replies and it's the wrong thing to say. He exhales. "Look, I know how unprofessional it was. I don't do that. In fact, I've never done that before. I understand how it probably looked to you."

"Do you?"

"I do. It's serious with Lauren and it didn't start until after I promoted her . . . she thought if you'd want to know anything, it'd be that."

"She thinks so much of me."

"Actually, she does. And I do too." Bullshit. He adds more to the pile: "I consider you a loss, Denham. I want to make it right."

"What does that mean?"

"Come back to work for me."

I don't know what I was expecting Paul to say, but it wasn't that.

"I don't want to make your coffee anymore, Paul."

"I don't want you to either. I've actually gotten really good at making it for myself." He waits for me to play along, offer a retort, and when I don't, he clears his throat. "Look, here's how it is: you're smart, Denham. You have the passion, you have the ambition and I didn't know what to do with that, just like my bosses didn't know what to do with me. It was a very sobering realization—finding I'd evolved into the type of people who stood in my way. I don't want to squander new talent, I want to publish it. It's why I started *SVO*. So I want you to come back. I'd like to mentor you. I want to help you bridge gaps, climb the ladder . . ."

I dig the fingers of my free hand into my palm and focus on the sting. There's some last lingering part of me that tweaks to his offer because when a want burns itself into you that deep, it doesn't all go away at once, but everything that's replaced it is louder. Paul can fuck whoever he wants, it doesn't matter. But the truth does.

The truth is the only thing that does.

My silence has clearly surprised him, enough so he scrambles to fill it.

"You're a raw talent, Denham, and you've got a damn good instinct. You called The Unity Project before I did."

Finally, my opening.

"You told me The Project was clean."

"On paper it is, but it's dirty as hell."

"An anonymous op-ed, though? Shouldn't that be a last resort?"

"It was."

"And you just take it at face value? What's your proof?"

"Audio and video—among other things."

"Send it to me."

"*What?* I can't do that, Denham. It would reveal my source—"

"But how do you know they didn't fabricate the evidence or—"

"It was vetted. Give me some credit. I didn't build a career by printing things I *hoped* were true. I was neck-deep in this. Everything I published was real and I wish like hell it wasn't because it was a goddamn horror show. And if it keeps going the way it's going, Lev Warren will be forced to pay for it and that's fine by me."

"I'm giving you about as much credit as you gave me. You never took me seriously, Paul." He sputters in protest, but I keep going. "You *did* hire me because it made you feel good about yourself—'give the tragic little kid with the scar a job.'

I bet you thought it'd be a perfect line in your next *Times* profile, right? You steal a story right out from under me and now you're acting like you're doing me some big favor—"

"Steal a story? *What?* That's not true—"

"I can't work for somebody who doesn't respect me."

Rain begins to fall, hitting the window, streaking the pane.

When Paul finally speaks, he sounds bewildered, hurt.

"I think maybe you're overstating some things," he says, "but nonetheless, I'm sad to hear that you feel this way. What would it take to convince you otherwise?"

"Tell me who wrote the op-ed."

The door behind me creaks open at the same time the words come out of my mouth. My heart stutters. I turn around slowly, and Lev stands in the door while Paul laughs in my ear.

"I'm not going to do that," he says and at my silence, the laughter in his voice dies. "I would never and I mean *never* give up a source. No journalist worth their salt would."

"Then there's nothing more to say," I tell him and he says, *Denham, wait,* but I move away from the window, the weakening connection cutting across his pleas to keep me on the line, and then I end it: "Good-bye, Paul."

"What are you doing?" Lev asks. He's not happy.

"I wanted to see if I could get you a name."

He steps into the room. "And did you?"

I shake my head. "I'm sorry."

"Did you really think you would?"

"I knew I wouldn't if I didn't try."

"Lo, if you make the slightest misstep—"

"I was careful."

"If you make even the slightest misstep," he says, his tone

hardening, "it falls on me. If someone discovers you've been trying to collect information from our detractors, under false pretenses, to use to our advantage, do you think The Project could recover from that? This was an unnecessary risk—"

"Maybe it's worth risking if you're going to lose it all anyway!"

"Do you think I'm doing nothing?" he asks.

My eyes burn with tears. "I don't know. You won't release a statement. You won't defend yourself, you won't offer a counter-perspective and you won't—"

"Just because I won't answer for someone else's lies doesn't mean I won't make sure they're answered for."

"I just don't want to lose this." My voice breaks. "I can't lose this."

His expression softens and he exhales, disappearing the strange tension between us by wrapping me in his arms. He presses his lips to my forehead, speaking against it. "Do you still want to join The Project?"

"Yes," I whisper.

"To join, you must be baptized. To be baptized is to accept your atonement and be Redeemed. But first, you must let go of all you know you are."

"What does that mean?"

"You have to release yourself from the life you're bound to. The water will wash away all lingering ties and cleanse your soul. When you surface, you are made new and you step into faith—perfect. But first, you must begin the letting go."

"What do I have to do?"

He leans back to look at me, gently pushing a strand of hair away from my face. Then he repeats the motion over and over, as he tells me tomorrow, I will go back to Morel with Foster and I will pack up all of the things at my apartment and I will say good-bye to every part of my life that lives inside that town, and I will make my home with him, permanently, here. That I must let go of everything that defined me before I stepped into The Project's walls, all traumas, fears, desires . . .

"My writing?"

"You won't need it."

My pulse quiets as I try to imagine a world where I could live without that part of myself.

"You said writing the truth was the greatest chance you had of being alive," he tells me, "but in The Project, you'll *live* the truth; there's nowhere else you will be more alive."

2017

If their family knew what Bea and Foster had done to Lev, how they had betrayed him, the walls of their faith would weaken beyond repair. All would be lost. Lev could not even live in the glory of this new miracle, of bringing Emmy back to life, without threatening to destabilize the foundation of all they'd built together and their hope of a future paradise.

It had to be enough that *they* knew.

Give me the necklace, Lev ordered at the time.

Whenever Bea sees it against his throat, she's transported to that night in the farmhouse, Foster's body pressed against hers and his mouth everywhere. She's supposed to live in the shame of her sin when she sees it, but Bea cannot accept her sin, cannot accept shame, when the result was Emmy. She cannot regret creating something so pure. Emmy is the antithesis of all the darkness Lev has said lives inside Bea. Emmy is the closest thing to God that she knows.

Lev understands this about Bea—and he will not give up on her.

You are my greatest challenge. Your sin lives so deeply within you, you can't recognize it anymore, but I will make you see it, no matter how long it takes. I will save you.

Foster is saved. His redemption took a different shape and sometimes Bea suspects his absolution is an extension of her punishment. He was called to the floor and stood in front of their brothers and sisters, and though they were not told the details of his trespass, it was enough for Lev to say one had been committed. Foster offered his body to Lev, a living sacrifice, and Bea remembers his screams, remembers wishing it could have been that easy for her. After Foster recovered, he was moved to the base. He was made security. He sees Emmy all the time, enjoys the designation of *uncle*—less than father but still, a name, access to her love. Foster is blanketed by Lev's forgiveness.

It keeps the two of them separate from each other.

When Emmy celebrated her first birthday, they'd given her cake. Bea had delighted, from the far side of the room, as Emmy sat in her high chair and got it all over her face and hands in that perfect way babies mess. When Casey swooped in to clean Emmy's chubby little fingers and face with a damp cloth, Emmy reached for her. Wanted for her. It bore a hurt so visceral in Bea—her child, reaching for another woman— that she thought she would die. She slipped from the room and found a quiet corner of the house to cry in and that was where Foster found her. When she felt his hand on her shoulder, her heart thrummed wildly inside her.

Are you all right? he'd asked and she jerked away from him, wondering if Lev had sent him, if this was some kind of test. Then, taking in her tearstained and devastated face, he'd asked, *Is this the right thing? Have we done the right thing?*

And she was sure that it was.

Who are you to question Lev?

Foster had stepped back, stunned, and she was not rewarded for her obedience and now she no longer knows what the truth of that moment was.

She thinks of it now, on Emmy's third birthday, watching from the back of the room as everyone surrounds her and sings her the song. She blows out the candle and spits all over the cake. Tears well in Bea's eyes, but she stays because she doesn't want to lose another of Emmy's milestones to her pain; she's lost enough already. Her eyes meet Foster's across the room. Later, she stands in that same quiet corner he'd found her in two years before, hoping he'll find her this time, ask those same questions again. He doesn't.

MARCH 2018

When I wake Emmy in the morning, she reaches for me.

She buries her head in my neck, sleepy-eyed and content, as I carry her into the kitchen. I'm still not totally used to the full force of her need, her affection. I always reciprocate after a moment's wonder—the wonder of her small body in my arms, the feel of the fast beat of her tiny heart against my chest.

I can't understand Bea walking away from this.

I set her on the floor to play and get to work flexing culinary muscles I never saw much use for when the meals I was making were only for myself. Everything Emmy eats has to complement ketchup—her favorite "food"—so it's home fries and scrambled eggs. If I'm lucky, a few of those things will find their way into her belly after she's licked them clean.

"Where's Daddy?" she asks as the food sizzles in the pan. I move to pour myself a coffee, but Emmy is underfoot, and I narrowly avoid knocking her down and spilling hot coffee all over her head. *"Shit!"* I say, and she covers her mouth in shock, and then I tell her never to say that word. She smiles impishly. I've watched Foster do this a hundred times, navigating every part of the space she takes up without incident, and wonder if I could trust myself enough to get that good at just existing with her.

"Where's Daddy?" she asks again.

"He's talking to Casey and Uncle Foster about important things. After you eat, we can go see him." I put my hand on her shoulder and move her back when one of the potatoes crackles and spits grease. "Careful of the stove, Emmy."

She clasps her hands behind her in *who me?* fashion. It reminds me so much of Bea.

When breakfast is ready, I put her in her booster seat and then I plate up, dousing the food in Heinz before placing it in front of her. She says, *hmm!* as she inspects her meal. The tiny fork does not meet her approval and she decides her hands better suit her purposes. I pick at what's left in the pans while she eats and tells me a halting, mashed-up story of what I think might be a few different TV shows. I try to follow along as she struggles to eat and explain this fabulous world she's pieced together.

Soon, she's raising her ketchup-stained hands to be let out of her seat. She grudgingly accepts a cleanup first. She fits neatly on my hip as I lead us out of the kitchen, down the hall to the Great Room, where she's waylaid by her "horsey." Atara adores Emmy, treats her with such gentle care. Emmy can tug on her ears and pull her tail and inspire no aggression—only love. Atara licks at Emmy's face, no doubt scenting breakfast on her breath. Emmy breaks into hysterics. Beyond her giggling, I hear voices floating down the hall from the direction of Casey's office. I tell Emmy to stay with the dog, that I'll be right back.

Casey's door is open a sliver and as I approach it, I hear her ask, "What did the landlord say?" I slow my pace and listen, though if I was meant to hear any of this, I'd be in that room.

Foster answers. "He ditched the place early 2017—"

"What about other residents? Did you ask around?"

"Bad side of town. High turnover. Anyone who was around then isn't there anymore."

"He can't just have disappeared."

"But that's exactly what he did because he knew we'd seek him out," Lev says. I creep even closer. "Look: we can account for Rob from here . . ." Rob? I hear the shuffle of papers. "To here. And now he's gone."

"My dad has contacts who specialize in this," Casey says. "But he's not taking my calls."

The floor creaks under my feet and the conversation in the room comes to a sudden halt. I knock lightly on the door and push it open, pretending I heard none of that, my eyes finding Lev's, hoping they don't give anything away. I'll ask him about it—just not right now. I tell him Emmy's done with her breakfast, that she's asking for him.

"Thank you, Lo." He glances at Foster. "You two should head out."

"You ready?" Foster asks me.

I am.

I follow the journey back to Morel on my phone, only sometimes finding the courage to glance at the changing scenery outside. I wonder if, when I'm baptized, this is one of those parts of me the water will wash away. Every time I do manage a successful peek, I see hints of spring. That clean, green feeling is only just in the air.

Rob . . .

Foster's voice pulls me from my thoughts. "Can I ask you something?"

"Depends on what it is."

"Do you remember it?"

I turn to him. "Remember what?"

"Lev—bringing you back."

I can't read his expression, but I can hear the tentativeness in his tone. The question is important to him and it took something of himself to ask it. The answer is important to me, but I don't know if I could do it justice with words.

"I had ICU delirium," I say. He raises an eyebrow. "You've heard of that?"

"You think the nurses were going to kill you or something?"

"No." But I almost wish I had because it would have been less painful than the things I did hallucinate. "I'd see my mom . . ." She'd hold my hand and she was crying. But she was also supposed to be dead. If I tried hard enough, I could put myself back in that hospital bed and feel it, it was so real. "Even after they told me she was dead, I would've sworn on my life that it happened. Or sometimes, I thought I was in a forest—"

"A forest?"

I laugh a little, but it's not really funny. I can see it now, lush green surrounding my hospital bed. The air was thick like it is in the woods in the summertime, and I could feel it on my skin, in my lungs. And even though I was in a hospital bed in the forest—which should have been the first clue something wasn't quite right—it all made perfect fucking sense to me at the time. It was everything else that didn't.

"At some point, I thought there was a man at the end of my bed, reaching for me. I'd have nightmares because I didn't know who he was or what he wanted, but . . ."

"It was Lev," Foster finishes.

"Yeah. Why did you want to know?"

"I just wondered what it felt like to be a miracle . . ." He trails off. "You were a legend. One of the first things I ever heard about in here was you . . ."

"I wish someone had told me sooner."

"Yeah, well, there's something Lev says."

"What's that?"

"'Whoever will lose his life for my sake will find it.'"

I suck in a breath through my teeth. I never thought I'd hear anyone say those words again and I feel them pulling me from the present, dragging me into the past, and I wonder if I'll ever be as far from the worst things I've experienced as I pretend to be. I can smell the station, can feel Jeremy as though he's close, as though I could almost reach out and grab him, hold him back. I close my eyes and I see him there.

"What does that mean?"

"It's surrender," Foster answers. "Accepting your atonement is surrendering to God. You can't join The Project for selfish reasons or you wouldn't last a day, because what it requires of you is so much that it can only be powered by belief in something greater than yourself." He quiets for a moment. "So no one could tell you. Not even Bea. The moment had to reveal itself to you when you were ready."

I don't say anything. I don't know how to tell Foster that God isn't the reason I asked to be baptized into The Project.

I know who I'm surrendering to.

It doesn't take long to clear out my apartment.

Foster hauls what few boxes there are to the SUV, marveling over how little a life I've made for myself in the last few years and part of me does a little too. It's sobering to see my incompleteness as a person so undeniably in front of me, the lies I told myself to exist within its emptiness—as though it wasn't a reflection of my own. I never wanted to carry that with me and it's a relief to let it go.

I understand, now, why this part is important.

"Ready?" Foster asks. I cross my arms and look up at my old window, overlooking the street. I could leave now, and have that be the end of it. "Lo?"

But there are other things I don't want to carry anymore.

"I have to go to the cemetery."

"What?"

"My parents." I turn to him. "I want to pay my respects."

He nods. "Sure. Let's go."

"I need to do this alone."

I don't want to be strengthened by Foster's presence, to have it urge me, finally, past that gate. I want to prove I can do this on my own.

"I don't know . . ."

"Just meet me at St. Andrew's in about an hour."

"I'm not supposed to leave you alone."

"What does he think is going to happen to me?"

"Come on, Lo," he says. "Everyone's on edge."

"Forty-five minutes?"

After a long moment, he relents. "Fine."

"Thank you."

"Forty-five minutes," he repeats.

I pass *SVO* on the way, slowing as the building comes into view. The lights are on upstairs, the middle of the day. My feet almost lead me to the entrance, the muscle memory so ingrained. I remember my first day, feeling like it was going to be one open door after the other from that moment on. How wrong I was.

I let it go.

It takes me ten minutes to arrive at St. Andrew's. I stand in front of the gate, a knot forming in my chest. Patty used to lay flowers down on the anniversary of the accident. I'd wait in the car, refusing to join her. *It's not good for you*, she'd tell me, but she'd never managed to change my mind. Eventually, I stopped going altogether. I thought this was the way to keep the accident from touching me but it just bound my losses tighter to me.

Lev was right; I did live inside it.

I step through the gate.

I have a general idea of where I can find my parents' head-stone. I shove my hands in my pockets, my boots crunching across what remains of the snow, as I make my way to it.

I move through the rows of graves, wincing at the vestiges of holidays still adorning some—fake poinsettias, garland, strings of Christmas lights—and the decorations that tell stories of neglect; fake flowers with ragged and torn edges, bleached from the sun. But all that is better than the nothing I've always done.

Their grave, when I find it, is modest and unassuming, and the knot in my chest loosens, the anticipation proving worse than the thing itself. It feels as much mine as it is theirs, in some ways. The Lo they knew died with them. Their shy, sweet girl. I've lived in those opposites so long now, to the extent I don't even know if they'd like me to meet me or be proud to know me. But maybe after I'm baptized, that will become less of a question. I hope it will. I reach out my hand, my fingers tracing the etched lettering of their names. I close my eyes.

I let them go.

"Bea?"

I open my eyes.

Maybe I misheard.

But then it comes again.

". . . Bea?"

The voice is none I recognize but it sets my pulse alight.

I turn and find myself face-to-face with a priest. He looks slightly older than Paul, with brown skin and wavy black hair, a soft, round face. He realizes his mistake almost instantly, his brown eyes noting my scar.

He inclines his head in apology.

"I'm sorry. I thought you were—"

"Bea Denham?" I ask faintly.

He nods, looks at me more closely. "You must be her sister . . . Lo?" I step back, stunned, as he holds his hand out. "Forgive me—I'm Father Michael."

I stare at his hand, the wide-open space around us shrinking down to nothing. His voice is deep, soothing, but it doesn't make me feel any less unsettled. He lowers his hand uncertainly. I raise my eyes to his, trying to understand.

"How do you know Bea?"

"I met her last year." He gestures to the headstone. "She was visiting your parents, like you are now . . . we struck up a conversation . . ." I bring my hand to my chest, trying to calm its frantic rise and fall, imagining myself walking through the gate sooner, finding her here. He studies me. "I'm sorry . . . am I upsetting you?"

"And she told you about me?"

"Yes."

"What did—what did she say?"

"She mentioned your miraculous recovery after the accident . . ."

I take a clumsy step back, bringing my hand to my forehead. There's a rage bubbling inside me, threatening to take over. She was here. She told him about me.

But all she had for me was—

Good-bye . . .

"Did she tell you she turned her back on me?" I ask and

he blinks, taken aback. "Does she still come by? Do you see her?"

He opens and closes his mouth, seems to realize he's inadvertently walked into a minefield. After a moment, he gestures to the church. "Lo, would you like to go inside to talk? Maybe there's something I can offer you—"

"No." I shake my head. "I'm not—there's nothing you can tell me I don't already know. I'm tired of hearing about my sister from other people. But maybe—maybe you could tell her something for me."

He frowns. "I'll do my best."

"Tell her—" I pause. "Wait. Do you know she has a daughter?"

Father Michael nods. "Emmy."

I close my eyes briefly.

"Okay," I say, bitterness stretched across my voice. "Okay, well. Tell her me and Emmy and Lev—we're doing just fine without her. That's all."

"I think I can relay that." He sounds sad.

"Thank you, Father." I glance back at the road, see the SUV making its way toward us, and knowing that I'm not that far from being with Lev settles me down some, quiets some of my rage. But its absence leaves me mortified. I turn back to the priest. "I'm so sorry that I—"

"It's fine. I understand." He pauses. "Lo, if I tell Bea these things and she should want to reach out to you . . ."

"She won't. But thank you."

I turn, making my way to the road.

"But if she does," he says at my back, "can you tell me how she could do that?"

I stop at the question, pressing my lips together.

Don't, Lo.

Just let her go.

It's what you're supposed to do.

"If she really wants me," I finally say, "she can find me at Chapman House. She knows where that is."

The sky breaks open, the sound of the rain cacophonous against the cabin's roof. Lev is caught in the onslaught. The door flies open and he hurries through, soaked, his curls plastered to his forehead.

"You think Emmy's okay?" I ask, startling as a loud clap of thunder sounds above us, trying to fight the urge to go to her, just to be sure. I put her to bed earlier but now I imagine her terrified awake by the sound. I hate not being close enough to comfort her.

"Why wouldn't she be?" Lev asks, peeling out of his coat and boots.

"The grumbles," I reply. He gives me a blank look. "Foster said she's afraid of storms . . . she calls them grumbles—"

"Right." His shoulders sag. He palms his eyes. "Grumbles. She'll be fine." I can feel his exhaustion in my bones. I watch as he moves around the kitchenette, putting the coffee on, which is the last thing he needs. "How was Morel?"

I hesitate, wondering if I should tell him about the priest. I don't think Bea will reach out, no matter my message. And I know Lev would not condemn me for my weakness, but he would be disappointed in it. I don't want him to look at me and see someone who isn't ready for the final step. I won't let Bea take more from me than she already has.

"I feel lighter," I tell him. "I won't miss it."

"Good," he says and moves to me, pressing his damp palm against the outside of my face. I cover it with my own. His eyes are proud, and his pride warms me. He says it again, tenderly: "Good." After a moment, he lowers his hand. I miss his touch almost immediately. "I'm temporarily relocating staff to various residencies this week. It will just be me, Casey and Foster here—and you and Emmy, of course."

"Why?"

"I need to get an understanding of the op-ed's impact across the wider membership. It's shaken some of our people. Staff will be my ears and eyes. If there are any misgivings, doubts, fears, concerns . . . this is the most expedient way I can address them."

"Makes sense."

"Oh, and before I forget—" He digs into his pocket and holds something up. At first, I don't know what I'm looking at and then I slowly understand. My phone. Or what was my phone. The screen is completely cracked. I take it from him and try the power. It's dead.

"What the hell happened?"

"Your guess is as good as mine. We found it in Emmy's room," he says. I close my eyes. "I'm sorry, Lo. Casey will get you a new one."

"Okay," I say tiredly. "Thanks."

His eyes drift over my body in a way that I understand. I set the phone down and I turn away from him, slipping out of my pants and then unbuttoning my shirt, feeling his eyes on me as I undress. I like the feeling but when I turn to present myself to him, he's facing away, staring out the window, lost deep in thought. I can guess what he's thinking about.

"Who's Rob?" I ask. He stiffens. "I heard the name this

morning, when I was coming up the hall . . . you think he wrote the op-ed?"

He turns to me. "I told you I wasn't idle."

"I thought you said you needed the name—"

"I said I needed a retraction. I didn't say I didn't know who wrote it." He crosses his arms. "Faith is trusting in what you don't know with the understanding that it will prepare you for all the unknown asks of you. You need to trust in me, Lo."

"I'm sorry." My face burns. "I do."

He holds to the silence, lets me sit with the shame.

"Rob is a former member," Lev finally answers. His tone is careful, guarded. "And he is the only member I have ever asked to leave The Unity Project."

I process it slowly. It's hard to imagine Lev turning someone away from The Project, when all he's wanted was to offer people refuge inside it.

"Why?"

"Because he was dangerous. He was a threat to members. It was a last resort. I never wanted it to come to that."

"A threat?"

"The Project welcomes all, but many of the people who come to us have been hurt. Many of them find comfort in my story. Some relate to it on a deeply personal level. Rob and I shared similar pasts and he idolized me. He'd never seen someone go through something like what he had, until he met me. And he would have never imagined what was possible in his life until he met me. He developed—a fixation. It was unhealthy."

"What do you mean?"

Lev lifts the corner of his shirt just a little, revealing his scars. It makes my stomach hurt, to see them. I can't get used to the sight of them.

I never want to get used to the sight of them.

"He tried to make himself in my image."

I step back, hand to mouth. "My God . . ."

He lowers his shirt. "As his . . . devotion intensified, members had to be good enough in his eyes to be worthy of me. He acted on my behalf, without my knowledge, and he hurt them to keep them in line." Lev pauses. "I had to tell him to leave."

I wrap my arms around myself.

"He didn't take it well, I'm guessing."

"He felt if he wasn't good enough for me, no one was. He's threatened us multiple times over the years. He did promise me he would be the end of The Unity Project." He exhales and looks away from me, to the fire. "I wanted to help him so badly, Lo. I count him as one of my greatest failures."

"You know for sure he wrote the op-ed?"

"Yes."

I watch as he takes off his clothes, leaving them carefully on the coffee table, before heading into the shower. I pick up his shirt and press it against my face, breathing him in. When the shower turns off, he finds me waiting for him on the bed, naked, my hair falling over my shoulders. He pauses just to take me in. I rarely see Lev smile, I realize, but I can tell when something pleases him. It's in his eyes.

I see it now, in his eyes.

"So how do you get the retraction?"

"Everyone has a price."

"And then what?" I ask.

Lev makes his way to the bed and leans down, his lips achingly close to mine.

"I will forgive him," he says. "And I will love him as God loves him."

2017

Bea steals away to the far corners of Chapman House from time to time and searches for Lo on the Internet, but she never manages to find her sister anywhere. Lo steadfastly refuses to live any part of her life online and Bea, in a strange and unfair way, resents her little sister for not being a light in her darkness, especially given the risk she takes in borrowing Lev's laptop to check. When her latest attempt to find Lo leaves Bea empty-handed, she impulsively googles Patty's name instead. She's shocked to discover the obituary.

She thinks it must have only just happened, but when she sees a full year has come and gone with her great-aunt six feet underground, it feels like the world has dropped out from under her. She tries to imagine Lo, somewhere, alone in that aftermath and it's so unbearable to her she's sick to her stomach. She sneaks into Casey's office for the landline—because she's sure now, they've been monitoring her phone for as long as she's had it—and calls Patty's number but it doesn't work because Patty has been dead for a year and no one told her.

MARCH 2018

It's quiet in Chapman House since the other members left, but Emmy does her best to fill the silence. Her audience whittled down to four means most of her demands for attention fall on me. She's exhausting, but I don't mind and I wonder if the novelty of her will ever fade, could ever fade. I'm playing with her in the Great Room, papers scattered everywhere (the game: draw whatever Emmy says), Atara dozing in a sunbeam at the windows, when Lev and Casey walk in. I can tell by the looks on their faces something's happened.

"Rob has demanded an audience in Bellwood," Lev tells me. Casey looks at one of Emmy's drawings, quietly praising it as she puts on her coat. "We'll be back later today."

I straighten. "I want to go with—"

"You can't," Lev interrupts before I can make a case for my presence, though I'm not sure I have one. "He was very clear about the terms of this meeting." His eyes meet mine. "I told you everyone has a price."

"We need to go," Casey tells him.

Lev gives Emmy a kiss, then presses his forehead to mine, promising me, under his breath, that everything will be fine, and then he and Casey are gone. I watch the SUV pull away from the house, uneasy, until Emmy decides I have a greater purpose.

"Draw!" she commands.

But I can't focus. Emmy is losing patience with me and it's

a relief when Foster comes in and offers to put her down for her nap. He lifts her in his arms and blows a raspberry on the sliver of belly peeking out from her shirt. She shrieks happily.

"Foster?" I call when he's at the door. He turns. "Did you know Rob?" He hesitates, and then he nods. "What do you think of . . ." I hold out my arms, trying to find the words. I don't want Foster to think I'm asking if the op-ed is true; I'm not. "What he did?"

"There's a name for people like Rob," Foster replies. "False witness. I hate the idea of him getting anything from us for it, but . . . like Lev says: leave it to God. He'll sort it out."

He leaves with Emmy. Atara paws at the front door and I let her out. I wrap my arms around myself and pace the room, can't shake the bad feeling that's taken hold. I can't even text Lev or Casey to check on them; they still haven't replaced my phone.

After what feels like a long time, I realize Foster hasn't come back. I make my way to Emmy's room. The door is half-open and I poke my head inside and the scene that meets my eyes is achingly sweet. Foster is stretched out on Emmy's bed, Emmy resting in his arms, the two of them fast asleep. I watch the steady, near unison rise and fall of their chests, their faces perfectly at peace, before closing the door softly behind me.

When I step back into the Great Room, a new sound reaches my ears. Atara barking wildly outside. She gets frenzied whenever she so much as scents any wildlife whatsoever. I make my way over to the door and listen, waiting for her to settle. She doesn't.

It's something else.

I turn toward the hall, to get Foster, but change my mind.

I put my shoes and coat on and slip outside.

"Atara?" I call. She continues to bark. I follow the sound to the end of the road, where she stands, her hackles up, pointed toward the highway.

I slap my thigh. "Atara. Here, girl."

But I'm not Lev and she doesn't listen to me. She continues to bark, agitated, at whatever it is she's seeing. And she definitely sees something.

My stomach flutters.

I glance in the direction of the house.

I could go back or I could go forward.

I go forward.

There's an old station wagon parked at the side of the road, its lights on, running idle. The sight is eerie in how out of place it is. No one comes out here that doesn't already belong here. I reach for my pocket, for my phone, and then I remember, again, that I don't have one anymore and that's the moment I realize this was a mistake.

The car turns off.

After a moment, the driver's door opens.

Atara's ears are pinned back as she barks.

A man steps out.

"Father Michael?" I put my hand on Atara's head, trying to calm her, to make her realize this is no one she needs to guard me from—I don't think. "What are you doing here?"

"I'm sorry if I alarmed you," he says. "She's a beautiful dog . . ." I scratch Atara behind the ears, staying close beside her. "I'm here on Bea's behalf."

I told her to come to me, I'd said to him, as though it would have made a difference.

I was only ever going to get into this car.

It's only when we pull away from the shoulder, from the road leading to Chapman House, that I ask him where he's taking me. I should have asked that first. My eyes are away from the window, gaze downcast on my hands. I clutch them together. I can't hold a thought beyond the fact that I'm going to see my sister.

I'm finally going to see my sister.

He tells me we're headed to a rectory, and I ask him how far it is from the house. He breaks the route down; it's about fifteen minutes away.

"I can't be long," I tell him. "I have to—they don't know I left."

"I understand."

I study Father Michael. His jaw is tight. His grip on the steering wheel is tight—so tight the skin strains across his knuckles. I don't know why he should be so tense. It unnerves me. I look around. The station wagon is surprisingly messy: there are some fast-food wrappers between us, crumpled napkins. There are books on the floor at my feet, some of them theological—but I spot a James Patterson thriller. Something about it catches my eye. I pick it up, feeling Father

Michael's eyes on me as I do. There's a card stuck between the pages, acting as a bookmark, but the familiar blue of it is enough reason to investigate further. I flip the book open. A Bible Tract. A blue sky.

That verse.

But the Lord is faithful, He will lend you strength and guard you from the evil one.—2 Thessalonians 3:3. I turn it over, my hand shaking. *Unity in Christ. Protection in St. Andrew's.*

"Oh my God," I breathe.

"Pardon?"

"Let me out—"

"What?"

"Let me out of this car—"

"Lo—"

"You send these to The Project." I hold up the tract. "You hate them. That's what Casey told me . . . I want—I want out of this car." I pull at the door handle like an idiot, but the door is locked. I pound my fist against it. "Let me out of this fucking car!"

He eases the car onto the shoulder, lets it come to a rolling stop. The door unlocks. I open it—I can't believe I was stupid enough to get into it in the first place—and I have one foot on the ground when Father Michael says, "Lev went to my church."

It stops me cold.

I turn back. "In Indiana?"

"After Indiana. St. Andrew's. Very early 2009."

"You're lying. He'd renounced the church then."

"And he was looking to save people from it," Father Michael replies. I swallow. "He walked into St. Andrew's under the pretense of connecting with my congregants through the

Catholic faith. He deceived me to get to them. One day, I came for mass. Half my congregation was gone, Lev among them. I had no clue what precipitated this exodus . . . a few months later, I ran into a former member of my church. I asked if there was anything I did or if they were going through any difficulties, if there was a way St. Andrew's could offer any kind of assistance and support—but they had found someone new to follow."

"He poached your congregation? That's why you send the tracts?" This broken moment pieces itself back together in a way that makes my stomach turn. "You're trying to poach members back? Is that what you did to Bea? Fill her head with lies and that's why she won't—"

"I want Project members to know that there's something beyond Lev Warren's idea of faith."

"People make their own decisions," I snap. "And if your congregation *chose* to go with him, you can't hold Lev responsible for that."

Father Michael contemplates this and then asks, carefully, "How did you get involved with The Project, Lo?"

"I was looking for her and I found something better."

"It doesn't concern you at all, that she chose to leave? Even in light of *SVO*'s op-ed?"

"That op-ed was a *lie*. I know her reasons and they had nothing to do with what was in it—or she wouldn't have left Emmy with them."

His silence fills the car.

"Wouldn't she?" I finally ask in a small voice.

"I can't answer that question," Father Michael says, his voice gentle in a way that makes this all feel that much worse. "But I know who can."

The car comes to a stop.

I look out the window. We've pulled up to a small brick house next to a run-down church. Father Michael nods and I step out of the car, my heart racing, still not convinced I'm not doing something colossally stupid. Why should I believe that a man with a dog collar would mean me no harm? Why should I believe Bea wouldn't lead me into something I couldn't walk myself out of, just because she's my sister?

She left me, after all.

Father Michael gets out of the car, turning the keys in his hands nervously. I follow him up the concrete path to the house. The door opens as soon as we reach it, and I come to a halt.

It's not Bea.

A man steps out. He's tall, white, just slightly over six feet, with broad shoulders and short, sandy-blond hair. There are deep lines at the corners of his eyes. His gaze slowly comes to rest on my scar, as familiar to him as he is unfamiliar to me. After a moment, he says, in a voice that sends a chill down my spine, "Lo Denham. I never thought I'd ever actually meet you."

I turn to Father Michael, the breath leaving my lungs and the world slowly fading at its edges. This can't be. "You told me it would be Bea—"

"No, I didn't." He avoids my eyes. "I said I was here on her behalf."

"They've told you about me," the man says, and the question of who he is disappears. I turn back to him and dig in my pocket for my phone before remembering, once again, that it's not there. But Father Michael doesn't know that.

"Please don't," he says quickly. "Don't be afraid."

"Your sister wasn't," Rob tells me, and he heads back into the house.

The rectory is dated, old. It smells musty, long overdue for a cleaning. The orange carpet should have been torn up long ago and its faded yellow wallpaper, stripped. There are hints of religion here and there, but more than anything else, it reminds me of how Patty's house might have looked if she lived for another twenty years and hadn't kept it up. I follow Father Michael slowly down the hall, glancing over my shoulder just to make sure of the way out.

We find Rob in the kitchen, which is as out of time as the rest of the place, right down to the mint-green fridge with rusted edges and the moldy tiled floors. He's opening and closing cupboard doors until he finds a glass and fills it at the sink, downing the water in seconds.

He's as afraid as I am, I realize.

Father Michael sits heavily down at the Formica table, setting the car keys in front of him and resting his hands between his legs. He and Rob exchange a knowing glance.

"You wrote the op-ed," I say to Rob.

He leans against the sink, closes his eyes briefly.

"I had to."

"Why?"

"Because I couldn't take it anymore," he says. He swallows. "Because when Jeremy died he was on his way to see me and I knew someone had to say something."

"No," I say, shaking my head. "No . . ."

"I tried . . . hard to get Jeremy out." Rob doesn't look at me. He's staring at his hands now. "But he was so twisted up about it, he just checked out. That's how deep The Project gets in you and how much a mind fuck it all is . . . poor fucking bastard."

"Nothing got Jeremy. He was sick—"

"He was vulnerable."

"How did he even know to look for you?"

Father Michael clears his throat. "We assume he heard it from Bea."

"No way. Jeremy died before Bea left," I say, and Rob and Father Michael exchange a look; they clearly believe otherwise. "That's what Lev said . . ." I trail off weakly, hating the way they look at me when I say it. I turn to Rob. "I have *never* seen anything happen in The Unity Project like what you wrote for *SVO*—"

"That's because Lev hasn't shown it to you yet." He turns his head to the window over the sink and I follow his gaze to the gloomy gray sky outside. "And by the time he shows it to you . . . how long have you been in, Lo?" I don't answer him. I don't have to answer him. I cross my arms. "I was the first to leave. It wasn't easy then. It's only gotten harder."

"He asked you to go."

Rob's whole face turns to stone.

"Is that what he said?"

"Yes."

"What else did he tell you about me?"

"It doesn't matter. I'm not here to explain myself to you. You tell me what you think you know, and I'll weigh it against what I do." I gesture to them both. "How do you two know each other?"

Father Michael speaks: "Rob was part of my church."

"I was there when Lev came." Rob runs his hand through his short hair. "And Father Michael was there when I left Lev. Thank God."

"Was it your idea to send the Bible Tracts?"

"I started sending them after I saw the shape Rob was in when he got out," Father Michael says, and Rob shifts uncomfortably.

"And I *didn't* get kicked out," Rob says. "I left. I *ran*."

"Why did you join?"

Rob clenches his jaw, clenches his fists. There's some kind of fight happening inside him. I glance at Father Michael, who watches Rob with a tenderness that reminds me of parent and child, though Rob can't be that much younger than he is.

"Lev has a way of seeing people," Father Michael finally answers for him.

Rob laughs bitterly. "He sure as hell saw me." He pinches the bridge of his nose. "We had this . . . my dad beat on me when I was a kid. And when I say he beat on me, I mean bad. I couldn't—I put it so deep inside me, I couldn't—"

"You don't have to say it," Father Michael says.

"Lev saw it. Nobody else saw it. He told me—" Rob's voice cracks and he takes a shuddering breath in. "He was the first person in my life to tell me I was worth something. And the moment he did that"—Rob snaps his fingers—"he had me. He had us all."

"Right," I say. "I'm just amazed he finds the time to abuse everyone in between running The Unity Centers, the outreach programs, the fundraisers—"

"He doesn't do that. Casey does all that, but he's fucking got her too. I need to be clear with you, Lo: when I wrote about the stolen money, confession as collateral, all-night meetings and the—*fire*—" He closes his eyes. "I'm talking about Lev. The Unity Project was my family and they're beautiful people. They just wanted to do some good on this fuck of an earth."

"And if it was as bad as you say it is, why would they stay?"

He goes quiet, still, for such a long time. Finally, he turns from the window and crosses the room as though to leave and then turns back. He exhales.

He lifts his shirt.

Father Michael winces, though this can't be the first time he's seeing it. I fumble back against the counter, my hand flying to my mouth. Lev warned me, but I wasn't prepared. The scars across Rob's body are a crude imitation of Lev's, the cigarette burns, lines, the mass of puckered skin on the left side. The skin is so traumatized, so red. It's not fresh, but it's like it hasn't accepted the wounds, still grappling with their violation.

He tried to make himself in my image.

I stare up at Rob, my throat too tight to swallow.

"He cleanses with water. He punishes with fire and the moment you sin or waver, or make any mistake in his eyes, in The Project, you have to be corrected. If he decides you haven't learned, he makes you walk the path of his faith." He lowers his shirt, and there's no relief in it because the image is seared into my mind. "For whom God loves, he corrects."

"You did that to yourself—"

Before I can finish he's close to me, in my face, angry.

I flinch.

"Rob," Father Michael warns.

"No," Rob says, and it's all he says, before moving away.

"Nobody would—nobody would just stay there and *take* that—"

"Oh really?" He whirls around. "Because I did. I did it over and over again and I wasn't the only one. You come into The Project, this world, and it loves you, and God loves you and He'll keep loving you, in spite of yourself. And what's this"—he gestures to his abdomen—"in exchange for that love, Lo? It's nothing. And every time I'd start to doubt, I'd watch people be held down and burned and when it was over, you know what they'd say?"

"What?" I whisper.

"'Thank you, Lev.' And when you see your friends, your family, saying *thank you* like they mean it—maybe you're the broken one. Maybe you just weren't burned enough—"

He starts to cry then, burying his face in his hands. Father Michael stands and makes his way to Rob, grips his shoulder tight, grounding him. I feel like I'm going to be sick.

When Rob finally lowers his hands, his face is damp, flushed.

"And despite all that, you're changing people's lives, you're doing God's work and you're making this world a better place and you can *see* it becoming a better place—how can you argue with those results? And at the end of all of it, you know what he's promising? He's promising *paradise*. That the sinners of this world will burn themselves out and all that will be left is The Unity Project. I didn't want to be left behind. I've been left behind my whole life. And *that's* why I stayed. That's why they all stay."

"When did you know you wanted to leave?" My voice shakes.

"The first time he burned me, that's when I really saw him. And I know abusers. I know their true face. And he couldn't hide it in that moment. In that moment, I saw him . . . and even though I *knew* who he really was . . . I still stayed."

"I don't—" I press my hands against my face. "He wouldn't do that—Lev wouldn't *do* that, not after what his mother did to him—"

"Did she?" Rob asks and I lower my hands, horrified. "You know his mother died by fire? He just so happened to be in Indiana at the time."

I look to Father Michael, then back to Rob. "You have to be kidding me."

"Once one thing is in doubt," Father Michael says, "the whole thing is in doubt."

I turn back to Rob. "You know who I am. You heard of me."

"We all heard about you, Lo."

"Then you know he *saved* my *life*—"

"You don't think the doctors might've had something to do with that?" Rob asks. "You were in a *hospital,* that's what hospitals are supposed to do—"

"They said I was going to die and Lev came—"

"You were young, you fought your way back—"

"I was *chosen!*"

They both stare at me with pity, like I'm some tragic thing. I don't want their pity and I'm not tragic.

Only one person has ever looked at me like I'm not.

"I'm so sorry, Lo," Rob says. "I know how much it means to feel that way."

My head pounds. I want to ask a million questions and I'm afraid of them all, so my mouth stays shut. I sit down in Father Michael's empty chair.

"You can't go up against The Project. After I left, they kept tabs on me. They did everything they could to try to make my life miserable enough to get me to come back. I reached out to Father Michael. He gave me sanctuary and they lost track of me long enough I could get my feet back under me and I did . . . slowly, but surely, I rebuilt my life and then . . ." He looks at me. "Then one day, last year, Bea shows up."

2017

Her family doesn't question the way she is with Emmy. Lev tells them she was too fragile for the gift God put in her arms, that nearly losing Emmy, after the loss of her parents, left her undone. She does not know how to overcome her fear and be a mother. They must accept it of her. Her family doesn't see her yearning, her need, her anguish born of his denial. They don't see it because Lev told them not to.

But the priest sees it.

He finds her on her knees at her parents' grave with a picture of Emmy in her hands, whispering *this is my daughter,* over and over again because she needs someone to know. He shows her compassion. He shows her concern. She forgot what it felt like to receive such things and this reintroduction overwhelms her. She confesses to him.

He knows someone who might be able to help.

Rob meets her at Father Michael's rectory days later. She somehow manages to steal away; it's not always easy for Lev to find her in the house. She'll find out if she was successfully gone when she gets back.

When Rob opens the door, the breaking point finds her. She sees herself small and frail in his eyes. And he is so much better than when she saw him last, healthier, solid, sure. She falls into his arms. She's dying, she tells him. She will die in The Unity Project if he doesn't get her out.

When he pulls away, she lifts her shirt and shows him. It's the first time she sees the devastation of what she's gone through on someone else's face. He knows this all too well, has scars of his own. She lies on the couch in the living room, and Rob tends to her abdomen, his hands navigating the spiderweb stretchmarks and the sag of her stomach that never quite rebounded from the birth, to the territory of skin that Lev claimed for himself.

He looks like he wants to cry.

This is infected, Rob says.

She breathes in and out through her teeth.

Tell me everything, he says, and she does. She tells him of Foster, and the necklace, the bond they formed. The aftermath of Rob's leaving, Lev's tightening control. She tells him of her daughter. How Emmy came into this world, stained with her sin, barely holding onto life and how Lev saved her in spite of Bea's betrayal. When she gets to that part, she wonders if she's wrong. If what has happened since is no less than she deserves, if removing Emmy from The Project will put her in harm's way. If Lev's gift of life lasts only so long as she is near him. A cold panic seizes her and she says, *I shouldn't be doing this,* and tries to get up from the couch, but Rob eases her back and he holds her hand so, so tight.

It doesn't work like that, he says. *It has* never *worked like that.*

Her daughter doesn't know her name.

Mom, mama . . .

It's not love, she says, but it comes out a question.

It's not, he promises.

By the end of their visit, they have a plan.

Tonight.

Leave with Emmy tonight.

When Bea leaves Rob's, she tries not to see the doubt in Rob's eyes.

Lev seems to sense she's been somewhere she shouldn't be. He asks her questions in a low, dangerous voice. She's failing to explain herself when Jeremy Lewis stands at her side and offers himself up.

She was with me, he says and paints an afternoon of Project work that kept her with him and she can tell by the way Lev looks at Jeremy that Jeremy will answer for this later. When it's over, Jeremy looks at her for a moment, hesitates— but goes. As she watches him retreat, it feels like she's seeing him for the very first time. He used to love it here but it's not in his eyes anymore. She didn't see it in his eyes. How long has he wanted out? And how many more of them are in these walls, screaming on the inside, desperate for escape?

She goes to his room later and slips a Bible Tract under his door.

MARCH 2018

"She never showed," Rob says.

I lean over in the chair, my head buried in my hands, my fingers knotted in my hair, pulling, trying to reject everything he's told me, trying to make it untrue. But I can feel it in my blood, my guts, my bones—something here is real that can't be denied.

"I thought she'd changed her mind. She was so torn up about leaving, that . . . I just assumed she went back, stayed there with Emmy. But then Father Michael tells me he meets you and you're saying Emmy's still there, but Bea's not . . ."

"So?" I ask.

"So if Emmy is still in The Project and Bea isn't—" Rob doesn't finish the sentence. My stomach aches. "Something bad happened to her, Lo. Because I'm telling you . . . she would have never, *ever* left her kid behind."

"She *did*," I say, looking up at him. "She called me—she kept calling me—I talked to her! I talked to her, she said—she said good-bye. I heard her voice—she said good-bye."

Rob frowns and looks to Father Michael, whose brow crinkles.

"What else did she say?" Rob asks.

I swallow. "That was it."

Rob pauses.

"When I left, I'd get these calls . . . first it was just heavy breathing, all hours of the day and night. I'd change phones, get burner phones. I'd change my number and they'd find me. They did it just to let me know they could always find me. When I started asking for the money I put into The Project—I was starving, barely keeping a roof over my head—I threatened to go public with what they did and then, when I got the calls, there'd be this voice on the other end of the line." He looks at me. "It was mine. It was my voice, Lo."

"What?"

"They'd spliced together my Attestations—because they record you in the Reflection Room—and the shit they made it sound like I'd said . . . are you saying you talked to Bea? Or that you *heard* her?"

"She said good-bye." I squeeze my eyes shut. "You expect me to believe—"

"It's the *truth*. Oh man, they tried to end me in every way they could think to do it. I'd wake up in the morning and find the gas was on or . . . I get in the car, and I'm going ninety on the highway and the fucking thing won't *stop* . . ." He runs his hand over his mouth. "My scars are real. I didn't do that to myself. They held me down. Tied me up." He exhales. "And after I'm done here with you, Lo, you know what I'm doing? I'm leaving town because I won't make it out of this alive if I don't. I didn't want to stick my neck out like this at all, but if Bea wanted one thing, it was to get Emmy out of The Project and I know the *last* thing she'd want to see is both of you in it—"

"You think she's dead," I say suddenly.

They both look at me, silent.

"No," I say, shaking my head. "No . . . I don't believe you—"

"We need to talk to someone," Father Michael says without meeting my eyes. "Call the authorities in Morel, Chapman—"

"They got Bob Denbrough wrapped around their goddamn finger," Rob says, "and half the Chapman Sheriff's Department too—"

"If you think she's dead, say it," I whisper.

"We need to figure out a course of action—"

"I don't even know you!" I explode. They both shut up. I stare at them, trembling, my eyes filling with tears. "If you think she's dead. Say. It."

Finally, Rob speaks: "I'm sorry, Lo."

I grab Father Michael's car keys from the table and I'm at the door before they realize what's happening and I'm in the car by the time they're at the door, pulling out of the driveway and back on the road. The sheer effort of being behind the wheel pushes me toward the edge of a full-blown panic attack but I have to get back to the house. Emmy's at the house. I reach an intersection at the same time a semi comes down the highway. I slam the brakes and come to a screeching halt, my body forced forward by the momentum—but the car stops.

It stops.

I park the station wagon in a clearing down the road from the house, tossing the keys in the front seat and then I run back to the house. As soon as I'm within arm's length of the front door, it flies open and Foster is there, wide-eyed and wild.

"Where the hell have you been?"

"I went for a run," I gasp. "I just . . . I needed to get out."

He covers his face with his hands. "Jesus *Christ*, Lo—I got up and you weren't there. I looked *everywhere* for you. You should have left a text, something—"

"I don't have a phone," I remind him and I'm amazed at how effortlessly all of this is coming out of my mouth. He's looking at me and he doesn't see someone who is dying. I look past him, trying to see into the Great Room. "Is Lev back?"

"They're about ten minutes out."

Fuck. "Where's Emmy?"

"She's having a snack and watching TV."

"Okay." I nod, my throat is getting so tight, in a minute I won't be able to say another word. "Okay. I'm going to head to the cabin, shower . . ."

"All right." He studies me. "Are you okay?"

"I'm fine."

He doesn't look like he believes it. "Don't go anywhere else."

"I won't."

I stare at him for a moment too long, my head full of Rob's voice. Foster and Bea. Emmy. Foster's child. I'm terrified I can see it now, how there are parts of Emmy that don't belong to me or Bea, our mother and father. And what I thought might have belonged to Lev—the curve of her jaw, her frame, her square shoulders—so obviously, painfully, belong to someone else. He grows uncomfortable under my gaze.

"What?" he asks.

"You said Bea would come back. Do you really think that?"

"Of course I do."

"Why?"

"Because Lev saw it."

I slam the door to the cabin behind me, pacing the room.

She can't be dead.

She can't be.

"You can't be dead," I whisper.

He saved my life.

I sink to my knees and press my hands against the floor, too shocked, too numb to cry. *She can't be dead.* I reach for her, trying to conjure her from nothing to prove me right. You're not dead, Bea, you're just not here.

Come back.

The door to the cabin opens and Lev steps inside, finds me on the floor. He says my name and I don't answer him. He kneels in front of me, concerned.

"Lo? What is it?"

I look up at him.

"Did you see Rob?" I whisper.

He looks away. "It was fruitless, but this isn't over."

I can't stop myself; I start to cry.

"Lo." He's alarmed. "What is it?"

"I'm scared," I manage.

"Of what?" He presses his hand to my cheek and I squeeze my eyes shut and I see a semi coming down the road and my brakes don't work. The calls, the breathing on the other end of the line. *Good-bye* . . . "Is it the baptism?" He presses his lips to my forehead as the tears continue to stream down my face. "Trust in me with all your heart. Don't try to understand it, just trust in me, and I will show you the path."

"If Bea came back," I ask, "where would she fit?"

I open my eyes, and find myself face-to-face with the necklace. It's turned around, the anchor against his throat, and from here, I can see, for the first time, what's etched on the back, what Rob told me was on the back: B & F.

I slowly look up at him.

He brushes a tear from my cheek.

"Do you think she'll ever come back?"

"Forget the things which are behind you," he tells me, "and look forward."

Tonight.

Leave with Emmy tonight.

2017

Bea waits.

In the cabin, while Lev showers, she curls up on the couch and closes her eyes. By the time he's done, she's made her body still, parted her mouth, turned her breathing even and deep. The light shifts under her eyelids, his shadow falling over her body as he contemplates it. And she prays—to who, she doesn't know—that he will let her rest.

She's afraid of what she is about to do.

She is afraid of how easy it would be to stay.

Lev reaches across her for the afghan on the back of the couch, laying it over her. She listens as he moves around the small space, waiting for him to settle in for the night, taking the bed without her. Eventually, he does.

After six years, she knows him, knows the way he sleeps, knows when he has fallen far enough past the surface, she can safely make her move. She knows, too, how limited this window is, knows how easy it is for the world to call him back.

She slowly slips out from under the afghan, rising from the couch.

She tiptoes across the room and puts on her shoes, grabbing her coat from the rack; she'll put it on outside. She takes a deep breath and reaches for the door, taking one last look back. Six years ago, she couldn't have imagined this moment.

Now she is awake.

The door creaks as she pushes it open. She closes it

carefully behind her. She takes slow, careful steps away from the cabin and when she reaches the trees, she runs.

When she reaches the house, the lights are off.

Lev hasn't woken, he hasn't alerted Casey.

Her heart could burst with the relief of it; another sign things are going her way.

She looks into the windows, the Great Room. Atara stretched out on the floor. She lets herself inside. Atara raises her head and Bea runs her hand briefly over her coat, stilling her. She hurries down the hall to Emmy's room, opening the door and stepping inside.

Her daughter is asleep, bathed in the glow of her nightlight. Bea moves to her, careful not to disturb her before committing this image to memory: her small, perfect daughter that she made, so peaceful, about to meet her mother for the very first time.

Her eyes fill with tears.

This is love.

MARCH 2018

"Emmy," I whisper urgently. "Emmy, put your shoes on."

She stares up at me sleepily, confused. I sense a meltdown and move fast, throwing her coat around her shoulders then grabbing her arms, pulling them through the sleeves a little too roughly. It distracts her, temporarily; none of this makes sense.

"Wanna sleep," she says.

"You will, you will, honey. We're going on a . . ." I glance over my shoulder, at her closed bedroom door, and listen for any sounds in the hall. "We're going on an adventure and everyone's waiting for you. I just need you to get your shoes on—"

I grab them and try to force the rubber boots on her feet. She shrieks so loudly in response that my heart stops. Never mind the shoes. The coat is enough. I pull the hood over her head while she squirms and whines and then I lift her in my arms and she loses her mind, yelling, *NO! NO! NO!* Everything's out the window. I just have to hope I have enough of a head start. I open the door and step into the empty hall and the sudden change of scenery quiets her.

We make it to the front door when I hear my name.

"Lo?"

The light goes on. Casey is there. She stares at me and Emmy, a shadow crossing her face, looking, for all the world, like she's seen this before.

"Explain this to me," Lev says.

Foster rips Emmy from my arms, carrying her back to bed, murmuring assurances in her ears. *It's okay, baby, it was a fun game and now it's bedtime.* Casey stands at the front door, her arms crossed, blocking one way out. Lev has stationed himself in front of the other, the expanse of windows. I stare past him to the cold night outside. Casey called him from the house and I watched as he emerged from the trees, nothing in his eyes. Foster's footsteps sound his return. He steps inside the room, shutting the door softly behind him.

"Explain this to me, Lo," Lev says again.

"Where is Bea?"

He frowns, looking to Casey and Foster, before turning his attention back to me. He crosses the room and my heart beats harder, faster, the closer he gets.

"What's happened to you?" he asks.

He brings his hand to my chin, tilting my face left and right as though he could find the answer there. His touch sends a jolt of panic through me that I can barely breathe against.

My body trembles.

He feels it tremble.

"What happened to Bea?" I ask.

"What kind of question is that?"

I can't stand his touch anymore. I raise my arms, to push

him back but he catches my wrists in his hands and holds them tight. I wince, and in response to my pain, he tightens his hold.

"I see you," I say faintly.

His eyes never leave mine. "I don't understand what you mean."

"What did you do to her?"

Casey makes a soft, scoffing noise behind me.

"What's she talking about?" Foster asks.

"Is it Paul?" Lev asks. "Were you talking to Paul again?"

"Again?" Casey asks.

"She's weak," Lev says to them, his eyes still on me. "Many will come in my name and lead you astray, Lo. Who has led you away from me?"

"Bea," I say.

He lets go of me. I make a sprint for the front door.

"Foster," Lev says sharply, and then Foster's arms have me, holding me in place. His grip is impossible and I know better than to fight it; I go limp. He lets me sink to the ground, allowing my defeat—but not my freedom. Lev's boots cross the floor, coming to a halt in front of me.

"Where"—my voice breaks—"is my sister?"

"We walk by faith, Lo, not by sight," he tells me softly, disappointed, "and when I accepted you into The Project, I knew that yours was weak but I made the choice to trust in your path, that you should shut your eyes and walk it. But that didn't work." He crouches in front of me. "So now you must shut your eyes and walk mine."

He tells me to stand.

They put me in the Reflection Room.

They lay me on the floor, binding my arms and my hands, and I fight them, but it makes no difference in the end. They turn off the light and leave me in the dark. I stare out the window, watching the moon move across the sky, its light slowly crossing my body. I cry. The salty, sick taste of my tears in my mouth. I wait.

The door opens.

Lev's silhouette fills its frame. He's holding something in his hands, but I don't get a look at it before he closes the door gently behind him. Whatever it is, he sets it on the small table in the corner. He looks down at me before kneeling at the center of my body, then reaches forward and begins to unbutton my shirt.

"No," I moan.

"It's good that you're afraid," he says quietly. "Fear of God is the beginning of knowledge. The foolish despise wisdom and instruction . . ."

"You're not God," I tell him.

He stares at me for a long moment, then brushes my hair away from my face, as though to comfort me. I try to twist away, but the bindings limit me, making me feel like a writhing, dying animal.

"I need you to understand suffering, Lo," he tells me. "You think you know it, but you don't. Those who suffer faithlessly are perverted by it. They are consumed by it. Their hurt becomes a reason to hurt others and that leads them to sin. They turn their face from the glory of God. But if you are faithful, at suffering's end, God will strengthen you and settle you and make you whole. That's what happened to me. He won't leave you in pain, he'll walk you through it. When I went to Indiana and stood in front of my mother's hate for the last time, God walked me through it. And He made me perfect."

He reaches into the back of his jeans and pulls out what I first mistake as a marker, but it's larger, thicker. He uncaps it, and two small wires twist into a perfect point. He pushes a button and they glow. He lifts the edges of my shirt, pushing it up, and inspects the skin, where I have more scars from the accident, less pronounced than my face, but still there. Without warning, he presses the cautery pen to my abdomen and for one moment there is nothing and then—a hot, furious sear against my flesh that my body does everything to get away from. I twist and spasm; Lev pushes my shoulders down until I'm still so he can mark me again and again, and a dead, sweet scent fills the air. I don't understand, at first, that the smell is me.

I'm burning.

I'm panting by the time it stops, his mottled abdomen in my head.

Rob's mottled abdomen.

My own.

He sets the pen down.

Tears stream down my face. He wipes one away, his fingers tracing the line of my scar.

"I know it hurts, Lo, but I'm not asking you to endure more than I was made to endure."

I close my eyes, swallowing back bile, trying to get my breathing under control.

"Did you do this to Bea?"

He doesn't answer and I begin to cry again because the idea of her going through this is more unbearable than living through it myself because I know, now, she went through it thinking she was alone. She was so alone . . .

Lev reaches for the table, for the other thing he brought, and I see it now: a kettle.

He sets it on the floor next to him and I feel the heat of it reach for me.

"Oh God. Please, please . . . please don't—"

He brings his face close to mine, pressing his forehead to mine. "This is nothing I'm doing to you. It's something I'm doing for you. I'm laying your soul bare as mine was laid bare, and in the next thirty hours, God will reveal you. This was my path and it's my gift to you." He straightens and takes the kettle, contemplating it before raising it over me.

"No, no, no, no—"

He shushes me then says, over my body, "'Whoever desires to save his life will lose it and whoever will lose his life for my sake . . .'"

He tilts the spout forward. The world explodes around me, my body convulsing as the scalding hot water burns my skin, burns through it, turning the whole world white.

"Lo," he says.

"You killed her," I whisper.

He buttons my shirt back up, and the material clings to the raw mess of weeping flesh. The fire still blazes across my stomach. I can't stop shivering.

"Lo." My eyes roll from side to side, trying and failing to focus. His hands are on my face. "Lo, look at me." I'm making mewling noises, dying noises. I can't seem to stop.

"I saved her. What happened to her was a mercy."

He tells me the next thirty hours are mine.

He tells me to pray.

"Bea," I say; my only prayer.
   I dream of the past, but I can't find her there.
   Every time I wake, I'm alone.

"You're okay," a gentle voice tells me.

My eyes flutter open and I curl in on myself because consciousness is pain, and the burns across my body rage. A reassuring hand on my shoulder. I look at Foster as he lifts my shirt, inspecting the wounds. He winces and I wonder if the humanity of his response is something I can reason with. If he loves Bea as much as Rob told me he did, as much as Bea told Rob he did. But then he lifts his own shirt, shows me his own scars.

"It will be worth it. I promise."

I shake my head. "Bea is dead."

"I told you, Lo. She's coming back."

"He killed her."

"Don't say that. Come on."

"He killed her." I sob, as he pulls me up into a sitting position. The pain is so bad, it leaves me breathless.

"You're not thinking clearly," he says.

I stare up at him. "Emmy looks like you."

His face goes pale. "What?"

"I could only see Bea in her, but now I see you everywhere. Emmy's built like you, she . . ." I inhale sharply, trying to catch my breath. "She has your hands . . . the shape of her face . . ."

"Who told you about Emmy?" he asks.

"Rob."

"Rob? But who—"

"Bea told him."

Foster moves away from me, his hand over his mouth.

"She wanted out," I say, my voice raising, desperate. "Bea wanted out. She wanted to get out of this—"

"I know. I *know*," he hisses, quieting me. "I know that. But she's not—it's because she just couldn't handle . . . Lev said she couldn't handle looking at Emmy and seeing her sin . . ."

"She *wanted* her daughter. She wouldn't have left her here. She was going to leave with Emmy and she never made it. But she would have *never* left Emmy behind. Never." My throat hitches. "You know she'd never leave Emmy behind. She's dead."

Foster shakes his head. "It's not true."

Casey's familiar footsteps sound down the hall, getting closer.

"Now I'm going to die," I whisper.

"*No.* No. You're not going to die—you're going to be baptized. That's all. You'll feel better when this is all over, you'll see, you'll see . . ."

He pulls me to my feet and I grab at his face, digging my nails into his cheeks.

"I'm going to die," I tell him again and he shakes his head, refusing it. "No, Foster, listen to me. I'm not coming back. Bea is not coming back. So please, *please* . . . while I'm at the lake, you take Emmy and go." I force him to look at me, to see the truth, to hear it, to feel it so close to his bones it can't be denied. "Take your daughter and *go*."

Lev stands at the edge of the shore, his face to the water and the slow setting sun.

"Go to him," Casey says softly at my back.

I make the walk to him alone, my steps halting, pained. The burns across my skin feel like they're spreading, feel like they're wrapping themselves around my body whole, burrowing deep past its surface. Every time I breathe, I can feel the fire claiming more and more of me.

I almost want for the water now.

I meet Lev with my arms clutched around my stomach. He looks beyond me, to Casey, and nods, signaling her back to the house.

"God has revealed you," he says. "Tell me who you are."

I hope Emmy is in Foster's arms right now, that he's carried her through the house, through the front door, has stolen away with her in a car, the road stretched before them, a whole beautiful future stretched before them . . .

I try to make these images real in my mind, real enough to die with.

"Who are you?" he asks me, holding out his hand.

"Bea's sister," I say.

He lowers his hand.

"'Anyone who loves their father or mother more than me is not worthy of me,'" he says. "'Anyone who loves their sons or daughters more than me isn't worthy of me. And anyone who doesn't take their cross and follow after me isn't worthy of me.'"

"Is that why you killed her?"

"You came to me so broken, Lo. I could see your loneliness, your want and your need. You thought you moved through the world invisible, but it's not true. Your pain was so obvious, so obscene, no one could stand to look at you. But I saw you and I've loved you and I have given you all that you wanted." He tilts his head, studying me. "Have you ever considered that everything that has happened was by design? That you were meant to be here? That Bea's greatest purpose was to bring you to me?" I flinch. "I saved you once. I will save you again. Accept your atonement."

"No."

"Then we'll leave it to God."

"What does that mean?"

"'Whoever believes in Him will never die.'"

"And if they don't believe?"

He holds out his hand again.

I take it.

We face the lake together and he gently, silently, urges me in ahead of him. The freezing water cuts into my bones, but my scalded flesh reaches for it. Lev walks in beside me, the water lapping his clothes. He presses his body to my body, presses his mouth to the side of my face before moving it to the shell of my ear.

"Be a part of this," he whispers.

He cups the back of my neck with one hand, the other pressing gently against my chest as he eases me into the water. The lake envelops me, taking the burn from my abdomen and bringing it to my lungs. Pressure builds behind my eyes. My legs begin to thrash and my arms grab at his arms and his hands hold me under, keeping me under. My pulse thrums loudly in my head, my chest begins to ache, desperately, and my heart calls for her, only her.

Bea . . .

I take a breath and I listen.

2017

He prays over her.

She can't make out the words.

She only hears the strained, awful sound of her own breathing.

He carries her down the path. She sees the pine trees from nearly upside down, the branches crisscrossing, tangled together. He takes her to the lake and as the water covers her body, all she sees is the sky and then, suddenly, she's a child again, on the swing outside her house again, pumping her legs hard, picking up speed, fast and faster still, taking herself higher and higher, higher than she's ever been. She thinks, faintly, she hears her name, but it's coming from too far below her and the sky is all around her now, stretching out before her, infinite.

PART FIVE

SEPTEMBER 2018

By the time I get to the train station, it's raining.

Raindrops streak the windshield as I pull into a parking spot down the street. I get out of my car and feed the meter, hurrying toward the station, but the low roll of thunder overhead seems like it might be an empty promise. It's going to pass us by, I think. When I get inside, I check the noticeboard against the wall. The train coming in from Bellwood is right on time. I make my way to its platform, cutting a path through the passengers, and wait. For one moment, I think I see a boy. I close my eyes and when I open them, he's gone. The train makes its slow pull up and I watch stranger after stranger detrain until my eyes land on a face I recognize.

"LO!" Emmy yells. People step out of her way—gentle amusement all over their faces—as she charges toward me, launching herself in my arms, Foster close behind.

I hold her. I just hold her.

We don't know where we'll talk at first.

We gauge the weather. It feels dangerous to take Emmy to a sit-down place, she has so much energy to burn, but then the clouds part and the sun comes out, and we decide on a park not far from the station.

Foster and I sit at a picnic table together. Children surround us, playing happily with one another. I watch as Emmy finds a group of girls, effortlessly inserting herself in a way I never would have been able to at that age. I watch them claim the swings, watch Emmy pump her legs with steely determination while Foster watches me. Every time I meet with him, he looks a little more whole and a little less complete and I feel it of myself, think he must be looking at me and seeing it too. I reach into my bag for my recorder and set it between us.

"Ready?" I ask him and he nods.

I push the record button and neither of us speaks at first. This is how it usually goes. There are a million questions; finding our way into the first almost always proves nearly impossible. Foster toys with the pendant around his neck. The anchor.

"You been following Casey?" he asks after a minute.

"Yeah. Money's amazing."

He snorts. There was nothing Casey didn't know that was happening within the walls of The Unity Project. As Lev's right hand, she was exposed to everything and helped make sure the worst of it happened, including, I'm sure, Bea's death. She spent a minute locked up before her dad bailed her out. Lev Warren estranged her from her family, she says, filled her head with lies, invented a history of trauma for her so the two of them could be close. They're fighting for a very lenient sentence.

I'm doing everything I can to make sure that doesn't happen.

"I've been thinking," Foster tells me after a little while, as kids shriek around us. I move the recorder closer to him, hoping it picks everything up. "I've been thinking that it was God. That it was God who brought you back when you were going to die, and it was God that saved Emmy when she was going to die. Lev took credit, but I feel God was working all these things because He knew you had to be Lev's end. That all these things had to come together for you to . . . for you to stop him."

"It amazes me," I say, "that you still believe in God."

"It amazes me you don't."

I shrug. "I only believe in things—"

"In things you can see," he finishes. He leans forward. "How'd you get out of that water, huh? How much more of a miracle can you be?"

I stare at my hands, my open palms, and then I look at Foster wordlessly.

"Something happened out there on the lake," he says. "Two people went in and only one came out. I saw you, Lo. There's no goddamn way you should've . . ."

They found me on the shore, my face pressed against the dirt, and I was still, like I wasn't breathing, but I was, while Lev drifted in the water behind me, his lungs full of it.

"If this was some divine plan wouldn't that mean God killed Bea?"

"No." He doesn't elaborate, but I can tell the question disturbs him.

I don't tell him I've been going to church more since it happened. But only after the service, sitting between Father Michael and Rob, the recorder in my hands. I listen as they talk about the aftermath, of the shuttered Unity Centers, of its brokenhearted members sharing their scars with one another. There are so many stories and I see myself in some, less in others—yet we all ended up under the hold of the same man. How does that happen?

I don't know how that happens.

I'm afraid it makes us weak, but Father Michael doesn't

think it does. He thinks The Unity Project was born of the world's failures, of its weaknesses. That it took strength to answer the call. That the good members did was as undeniable as the evil they fell prey to, and the necessity of that good, in this world, remains. He hopes we don't give up on it.

"Can I ask you something?" I ask Foster.

"That's what we're here for, isn't it?"

"When I brought up the op-ed to you in Chapman . . . you said it was a lie."

"I said Rob was a false witness."

"How could you say that, if everything he said was true?"

"Because—" He stops. "Because in that moment, it wasn't. He said it was abuse. I didn't think I was being abused."

"Do you miss it?"

He closes his eyes for a long moment, pain sharp across his features.

"I miss it so much," he says, his voice rough. He opens his eyes. "Do you?"

I reach my hand out to the recorder, to stop it, and then I stop myself. I swallow, hard, and open my mouth and then I close it again.

"I was barely there," I finally manage.

"Do you miss it?" he asks again.

My face crumples. He reaches across the picnic table and squeezes my hand. I exhale shakily and straighten, moving away from his touch. I can't stand it, anymore, when people touch me and I find it hard to explain. It's not because I don't want to be touched. It's because I do—so much—and I'm afraid I'll give away what's left of myself to feel less alone.

I already did it once.

I clear my throat, checking my watch.

"Where are you headed next?"

"We're going to visit Bea's grave. You're welcome to join us."

They dragged the lake and found her, what was left.

She wasn't that far out.

"I've got to get back." I glance at Emmy, her legs almost touching the sky. "Does she . . . ?"

Foster follows my gaze.

"It's a lot to untangle," he says. "But we're getting there."

We say good-bye shortly after that.

On my way back to the station, to the car, a current goes through my body, the feeling that I'm being watched. I come to a stop, looking up and down the street, past the sea of people heading this way and that. I press my palm against my chest, feel the fluttering of my heart, a strange pull. I turn slowly, my eyes coming to rest at the corner of Wilson Avenue and Hall Street, but there's no one there.

"Happy anniversary, newbie."

I set a cupcake I picked up at the bakery in the middle of Wesley's desk. He looks up from his computer screen, his blue eyes tired but eager. I can see the mess of Paul's Google calendar on his monitor and I don't miss it. Not even a little bit.

"How long have I been here?" he asks.

I hold up a finger. "One month."

"Feels like years."

"Paul has that effect."

"I heard that," Paul calls from the kitchen.

He and Lauren are there, talking close. The light catches her engagement ring, making it glint. I head over to my cube, right next to hers, and log into my desktop. Open up my Word document. I can vaguely make out my reflection in the screen, its title across my face.

THE PROJECT by Lo Denham

"How's it coming?" Paul asks, on his way to his office.
I look up at him.
"I just want . . . it has to be the truth, you know?"
He nods, his eyes sympathetic.
I turn back to the screen.
It has to be the truth.
I'm not the only one it's keeping alive.

2017

Today will be the last day.

Today, her life in The Project will end and tomorrow she will open her eyes to Father Michael's house, to a ketchup breakfast with Emmy, and she will begin the careful and delicate process of finally introducing mother to daughter.

The idea makes her happier than she's been in a long, long time.

She's on her way back to Chapman from Morel and is standing at the corner of Wilson Avenue and Hall Street when she sees Lo. Bea almost doesn't recognize her, but there's something about the way she pauses and looks over her shoulder before crossing the street. She stops outside of a bakery, texting on her phone. A steady stream of cars passes by and Bea steps a little forward to get a closer look, her breath caught in her throat.

She could be mistaken.

She doesn't think she is.

It's the scar that confirms it, that sharp cut down the side of Lo's face, but it looks so different on her now. When she was thirteen, it had claimed that part of Lo so wholly, was still so fresh, it was painful to look at. Now, six years have passed and it's settled in, whether Lo likes it or not. Lo is taller than Bea expected she'd get and she looks more collected than Bea ever felt at that age. The age she was when their parents died.

She wonders if Lo still wants to be a writer.

Her eyes fill with tears and she brings a hand to her mouth, pressing her fingers against it, taking this moment for all it's worth, the assurance of Lo, of a world beyond The Unity Project, no matter what Lev told her.

Your sister will *join The Project. I've seen it . . . Her faith depends on yours.*

But he is no prophet, no healer, no God, and Bea is comforted now in her faithlessness, in her beautiful little sister standing across the street, living a life Bea so badly wants to be a part of and will do everything to be a part of. Suddenly, a new vision of tomorrow plays out in front of her eyes: Father Michael's house, ketchup breakfast with Emmy, the careful and delicate process of finally introducing mother to daughter—of aunt to niece.

Why should she wait?

But she hesitates.

It terrifies her, as much as she wants it.

She closes her eyes.

It's been so long.

There's so much to say.

Where does she start?

Lo.

Bea opens her eyes, exhaling softly at the empty space where Lo just stood. She looks up and down the street for her, but Lo is nowhere to be found. She swallows hard against the bitter disappointment of it, but takes heart in the fact that today, of all days, she would look across the road and her sister would be there, like a sign, like her mother once said: a promise.

They'll see each other again.

ACKNOWLEDGMENTS

Sara Goodman's commitment to raising the bar and using every tool of her trade to ensure her authors meet it is one of her greatest skills, and gifts, as an editor; she insisted on *The Project* when I needed it the most and her persistence, guidance, enthusiasm, compassion, and attentiveness produced a story I couldn't be prouder of. There's very little we haven't been through over the course of fourteen years and seven books, but working with an editor as insightful, thoughtful, and encouraging as she is has always been a privilege and has always proven worthwhile.

My agent, Faye Bender, is one of the most unflappable people I've ever had the good fortune of working with. She has a brilliant ability to see every moving piece of the puzzle and fit them all perfectly into place. I'm grateful for her vision and savvy, steadiness, kindness, empathy, and humor. The strategy and care she has shown my career has made so much possible for me creatively and professionally. My thanks, also, to The Book Group, for being such pros.

There's a team of people behind the scenes whose tireless dedication and enthusiasm for their work made *The Project* happen. I'm grateful to all at Macmillan, St. Martin's Press, and Wednesday Books for their boundless support, energy, ingenuity, and willingness to seize and create new and exciting opportunities—and for just being so extraordinarily kind and extraordinarily cool: Jennifer Enderlin, Eileen Rothschild,

Anne Marie Tallberg, Jennie Conway, Brant Janeway, DJ DeSmyter, Alexis Neuville, Jeff Dodes, Rivka Holler. Tracey Guest, Meghan Harrington, Jessica Preeg, Mary Moates. Jennifer Edwards, Jessica Brigman, Rebecca Schmidt, Gretchen Frederickson, Taylor Armstrong, Sofrina Hinton, Mark Von Bargen. I'm grateful to Macmillan Library—Talia Sherer, Emily Day, Amanda Rountree, and Samantha Slavin—for thoughtfully and wholeheartedly advocating for my books. Thank you to the Macmillan Academic Team. I'm grateful to Macmillan Audio—particularly Matie Argiropoulos, Emily Day, and Amber Cortes—for the richness and depth they've given and the support they've shown my novels in the audio space. I'm grateful to Kerri Resnick, whose artistry and unparalleled approach to design brought *The Project* alive. Her iconic vision was perfectly complemented by Marie Bergeron's beautiful illustration. Thanks to Anna Gorovoy, who completed *The Project*'s gorgeous package with her sharp eye for interior design. Thanks to Lena Shekhter, Lauren Hougen, Chrisinda Lynch, Elizabeth Catalano, and NaNá V. Stoelzle for their painstaking attention to detail. Thanks to Tom Thompson, Britt Saghi, Lisa Shimabukuro, and Dylan Helstien for the beautiful creative work they offered *The Project*'s campaign. Thank you to all at Raincoast—particularly Fernanda Viveiros and Jamie Broadhurst—for their hard work and all they've made happen for me in Canada. Thank you to anyone I have missed. Working with this team has been a dream professionally and a joy personally.

I'm grateful to all my friends for their support and love; the bold and fearless ways they live their lives inspires me to live mine as boldly and as fearlessly. I regret I'm unable to name everyone here, but these people in particular saw me through all stages of the *The Project*'s development, and it couldn't have been completed without them. Lori Thibert has been a constant in my life and I will forever marvel over the fact I ended up having the kind of best friend I read about, and wished for, in books when I was growing up—someone smart, interesting, kind, funny, and loyal, who I'll forever admire and aspire to be as good as. The combined force of Somaiya Daud, Sarah Enni, Maurene Goo, and Veronica Roth's friendship has levelled me up as a person and I'm grateful for their wicked humor, ferocious talents and smarts, and unwavering support. Emily Hainsworth and Tiffany Schmidt have been with me since the beginning, and that I can always count on their generous hearts and brilliant minds, no matter the weather, is something I'll never take for granted. Brandy Colbert, Whitney Crispell, Laurie Devore, Meredith Galemore, Kate Hart, Kim Hutt Mayhew, Michelle Krys, Amy Lukavics, Baz Ramos, Samantha Seals, Nova Ren Suma, Kara Thomas, and Kaitlin Ward are some of the funniest, smartest, most talented and most caring people I've had the honor and privilege of knowing.

I'm grateful to the booksellers, readers, librarians, educators, and book bloggers and vloggers who have found a space for my books on their shelves. I've said this before, but it will always be true: their consistent and enthusiastic support, and willingness to follow me from book to book, is no small part of why I'm able to do what I love and why I love what I do.

Thanks to Amy Tipton and Ellen Pepus Greenway of Signature Literary Agency.

I am beyond grateful for the love and support of all of my family, near and far. I'm surrounded by incredibly intelligent and creative thinkers, the quickest of wits, master improvisers, and rule breakers and makers, and my career in writing began with their unfailing belief in me. Thank you to Susan and David Summers, Marion and Ken Lavallee, Lucy and Bob Summers, Megan, Jarrad, Bruce, Cosima and River Gunter. The impact they've made on my life cannot be quantified and so this section of acknowledgments always turns out to be the smallest in size—but make no mistake; I owe them everything.